HE SMOTHERED
HER PROTEST

The kiss was not the slightest bit sexy or romantic. With the police cruiser's engine rumbling just four yards away and the rain driving down around them like a typhoon gone wild, Caroline was in no mood to absorb any sexual overtures. But Alex's mouth was warm and he was dry inside that big coat of his, so she let it happen.

He tasted sweet, and his lips infused Caroline with a kind of liquid courage. He broke the kiss before she could open her mouth to his, and he made a pretense of nuzzling her throat.

"Make it look authentic," he muttered against her ear.

"I should bite your tongue," she murmured back.

"Why don't you try it," he said, tilting her head back and weaving one hand into her hair....

ABOUT THE AUTHOR

This is Nancy Martin's fifth Superromance, no doubt eagerly awaited by readers acquainted with her unique writing style. *Sable and Secrets*, Nancy says, turned out to be quite a different book from the one she'd originally conceived. Indeed, Nancy's imaginative powers are employed full force in this delightful story, which will surely be considered another "keeper" by fans!

Books by Nancy Martin

HARLEQUIN SUPERROMANCE
133—FLIGHT INTO SUNSHINE
170—BEYOND THE DREAM
197—AN UNEXPECTED PLEASURE
221—NIGHTCAP

Don't miss any of our special offers. Write to us at the following address for information on our newest releases.

Harlequin Reader Service
901 Fuhrmann Blvd., P.O. Box 1397, Buffalo, NY 14240
Canadian address: P.O. Box 603,
Fort Erie, Ont. L2A 5X3

Nancy Martin

SABLE AND SECRETS

Harlequin Books

TORONTO • NEW YORK • LONDON
AMSTERDAM • PARIS • SYDNEY • HAMBURG
STOCKHOLM • ATHENS • TOKYO • MILAN

Published April 1988

First printing February 1988

ISBN 0-373-70305-8

Printed in U.S.A.

CHAPTER ONE

THE MAN in the shapeless, deep-pocketed parka spotted his target when she stepped onto an escalator in St. Cloud's department store.

She was the right one, he was sure. Fresh-off-the-farm pretty, and wearing a knockout of a dress, a bold necklace and high-heeled, sling-back shoes, she had cut a tall and gutsy figure as she strode across the main floor of the elegant store. She even walked in long, sexy strides—an eyepopper of a woman in a big-shouldered minidress. Her blond hair looked like a haystack, but that was probably in style. He didn't keep up on fashion. He only knew she looked young and sexy, yet all-American wholesome.

So much for first impressions.

He stepped on the escalator and rode upward behind her, keeping a few shoppers between them, the way a suave spy might tail a beautiful double agent. Only he wasn't suave. In jeans and the ratty old rain parka, he looked like a hoodlum. With his hands thrust into his big pockets, he closed his fingers around one of the many objects he kept hidden there. It felt heavy in his hand—solid and lethal. A knife. He was glad he'd thought to carry it today. The need to use it gnawed hungrily inside him.

As she rode up the escalator, the blonde tapped her slender fingers against the handrail. Trailing along in her wake, he saw that she had bitten her nails to the quick. That was interesting. Maybe she had already sensed what kind of trouble she was in.

Since he was concentrating on his prey, he was only vaguely aware of the shoppers between himself and the blonde, but suddenly the voice of a teenage girl in front of him cut through.

"*White chiffon?* Oh, Mom, I'll *die* before I wear something like that to the dance!" The furious child swung around, folded her arms over what appeared to be a black leather corset and pouted as they rose on the escalator. She sulked a moment and then her eyes fell on him.

He said nothing to the girl, but her gaze flickered down his body and then she smiled. Coquettishly— lasciviously, even—she blinked at him in an obscene parody of adult flirtation. He stared back without expression and something in his face caused her come-on smile to freeze. Hurriedly, she turned back to her mother, who looked equally alarmed when she saw him lurking on the step below. When mother and daughter arrived on the second-floor landing, they clutched each other and scuttled off. He guessed suave spies didn't look too friendly.

The blonde stepped around the landing and got on the next escalator. He followed at a distance, observing. Despite her outwardly sexy confidence, she appeared to be on edge, all right. The sparkle of expensive jewelry on the second floor did not catch her attention, nor did the lurid display of women's night-

gowns on the third landing. She didn't even glance at
the sensuous draping of rich Oriental rugs on the next
floor or tap her toe in time to the thump of compact
discs on the floor after that. She looked preoccupied.
And she hadn't noticed she was being followed.

His quarry's name was Caroline Conover. She
probably did come from farm country—Kansas
maybe. He was struck once again by her fresh-air-and-
sunshine look—trim figure, athletic carriage, sun-
lightened hair. From what he could see, her complex-
ion was creamy gold, her nose pointed and her chin
sharp. Judging by her sleek dress and jewelry, she had
learned a thing or two about luxury, too.

She also knew about stealing. She was not a wide-
eyed country hick.

She stepped off the escalator on the top floor.
Walking smartly, she skirted the designer women's
wear department and ducked through the open French
doors of the fur salon. He had expected her to end up
there.

Voices carried to him plainly, so he lingered outside
the salon and watched the blonde from a shadow.

On the other side of the smoked glass, a younger
woman—college age with a pixie haircut and looking
both childlike and owlish behind a pair of huge pink-
framed glasses—jumped up from her seat behind a
Louis XV-style desk. "Wow, that was fast!"

"It seemed like the Spanish Inquisition to me," said
Caroline Conover. She threw her narrow clutch
handbag onto the desk and looked as if she would
have preferred to hurl it through the nearest plate-glass
window. Her jaw was tight enough to tremble, and

even the tips of her wheat-blond hair seemed to quiver. She wasn't just nervous. She was angry. "It was long, slow torture."

"Well?" breathed the saleswoman. "Were you fired, Miss Conover?"

The blonde snatched a sheaf of papers up from the desk. "Nothing that humane."

"Were you—I mean, did they—"

"Accuse me of stealing their stupid coats?" Her voice rose uncontrollably, but she checked it. "Yes. I felt like I'd been arrested for indecent exposure. Rupert got a charge out of humiliating me, too. What a skunk he can be!"

"Wow," murmured the young woman, respectfully waiting for the Conover woman to burst into tears.

But she didn't. With a visible effort, she hung on to her composure. "They think I took the coats home with me last weekend!" She flung the papers down onto the desk again and hugged herself fiercely. "As if three full-length sable coats and a pair of fox capes wouldn't be noticed going out the employee entrance!"

"But we all saw you leave the store. You didn't steal anything!"

"I won't take bets that the police believe that."

"The police! Oh, Miss Conover! You mean you're being arrested?"

"Nobody's gotten out the handcuffs so far, but it will probably lead to that." Grasping her upper arms as if to fend off a blast of arctic wind, she vowed, "I'll tell you, though, it won't be me who's dragged off to jail when this is over. I'm going to keep this job, damn it. Too much depends on that!''

"Did the police question you?"

Calming down, the Conover woman shook her head. "No rubber hoses yet. The security team is just going to keep their eyes on me. I've been warned not to leave town or they'll send the FBI after me. The store wants to avoid a full-blown police investigation at the moment—something about insurance rates, they said. It's less expensive to lose a few coats, believe it or not, than to risk higher premiums. The owners of the salon are going to investigate first."

"The owners?" repeated the salesclerk, confused. "I thought St. Cloud's owned the whole store."

Caroline put one hand to her forehead and massaged her temples tensely. "Most department stores lease space to independent vendors so they don't have to be bothered with every kind of merchandise. Shoes and major appliances, for instance. It's a common practice. The fur salon is owned by Varanov Furriers, the company that makes the coats we sell."

"So the furrier is going to find out what's been happening to the coats?"

"Right. Their insurance premiums are over a million dollars now and they're afraid the company will triple the rate or cancel completely. If possible, they want to stop the thefts without alerting any authorities. I'm supposed to cool my heels like a good little girl until their man shows up."

"Oh!" The salesclerk clapped her hand over her mouth. Her eyes nearly popping, she squeaked, "His name wouldn't be Smith, would it?"

"What?"

"There was a man here before. He said his name was Smith and he wanted to buy a coat for his wife, but—"

"If he used the name Smith," Caroline said grimly, "he wasn't buying it for his wife. Where is he now?"

That was a cue if ever he'd heard one. He pushed open the door.

The salesclerk looked around and froze. Caroline Conover also turned around as he came through the door. But she didn't look scared. She stood her ground, hands clenched at her sides.

"Oh," said the younger woman again, her eyes huge behind her pink glasses. "Uh, hello, Mr. Smith. Hello again."

She blushed and stammered, but he didn't bother to put her at ease. He slouched in the doorway and looked closely at the Conover woman, noting details. Her eyes were green, but with tinges of blue—the color of hemlock. How appropriate, he thought. There were freckles on her hands, somehow looking right—as if she'd been helping with the field work or driving the tractor without gloves. And the combination of her naked, wide-eyed face and that cosmopolitan dress made him think suddenly of a little girl dolled up in her big sister's city-slicker clothes. She looked tall and strong, but young. Not streetwise, but brave.

"Uh, this is Miss Conover," babbled the younger clerk. "She's in charge here. If you wanted—well, here she is. I—"

"You can run along, Betsy," said the Conover woman, composing herself with admirable speed.

Apparently she could act older than she looked. She said, "I'll take care of Mr. Smith."

"Okay," said Betsy. "If you're sure..."

"I'm sure. Go on."

While the clerk collected her handbag and prepared to relinquish her station, he strolled into the salon and took a good look around.

Compared to other, more trendy departments in St. Cloud's, the fur salon was an oasis of gentility. The lush, powder-blue carpet, the sedate provincial-style furniture, the pretty chintz fabrics and the polished brass appointments combined into a subtle ambience that focused attention on the coats—the luminous, rich, one-of-a-kind furs that hung on individual pedestals placed at intervals around the room so that no one garment outshone any other. Every coat was a masterpiece, decadently beautiful but inert. Each needed a special woman to put it on, luxuriate in its sensuous folds and return life to the skins from which it was made.

Though the floodlights cast just enough of a glow on them so that each individual hair shone with pinpoints of vitality, the furs still looked repulsive to him. Dead animals, they were, stitched together to give rich women pleasure.

"I'm sorry I kept you waiting," Miss Conover said, brusquely extending her hand when they were alone. "I'm Caroline Conover. You wanted to see me?"

He took her hand in his and wasn't surprised to find she had a good grip. No hothouse lily was she. Now he was sure she helped bale hay, and rode horses for fun. He could imagine her controlling a big, half-wild animal, all right. Only her clothes looked out of place. Her winter-white cashmere dress, cut in a square across her collarbones and caught snugly at her waist by a wide leather belt, pared her body into the leggy, broad-shouldered silhouette so perfect for modeling fur coats, but did not disguise her strength.

On one slim wrist was a hammered gold bracelet, and around her slender neck she wore a bold necklace of carved chunks of something heavy—jade, perhaps. She was fashionable and elegant—everything he was not. In his ratty old parka, he probably looked like a thug at a debutante ball.

She said, "Can I help you? Are you here to look at furs?"

She had a butter-won't-melt-in-my-mouth look on her face. Tamping down the heat of dislike that rose within him, he said, "Sure."

"I see. Can you give me some hints about what you have in mind in a coat?" Pointedly, she avoided looking at his parka. "What price range, for instance?"

To answer, he rummaged in his pocket and soon came up with a fistful of credit cards. An American Express platinum one was on the top of the pile. He carelessly flung the cards on her desk. Like gold sovereigns, they scattered there.

Caroline felt herself flinch inside when the man threw down his credit cards. He was ominously quiet. She told herself there was no need to be scared, but she couldn't stop the urgent messages her instincts were sending out. He had broad, angular shoulders and a sharp, austere face with heavy-lidded eyes, a blunt peasant's nose and a drooping but sensual mouth. His hair was as thick and black as Russian sable, and it crowned his forehead in a sharp widow's peak. The dent in his chin might have passed for a dimple in a gentler, more aristocratic face, but he thrust it forward with the jut of his jaw and it looked like a brawler's trophy. In his light eyes burned an unfriendly flame.

"Any price range." Gruffly, he said, "You just do your usual song and dance, Miss Conover. I'll make up my mind as we go along."

"Very well," she murmured, then glanced instinctively past the big man toward her desk. The salon was wired with several secret switches that could set off a silent alarm, sending a security team to her rescue in less than a minute. The nearest button was in the top desk drawer, and Caroline itched to get close enough to push it, should the need arise.

He gestured at one of the coats on display. "Let me see that one."

"Certainly." Figuring she wasn't going to hear the magic word from this character, Caroline obeyed.

When she went to get the coat, though, she realized her mistake. Smoothly, he stepped between her and the rescue button. Damn! Did he know it was there? Had he read her mind? Caroline swallowed and hoped her imagination was working overtime.

"This is sable," she said, taking the coat off its hanger. "A very nice choice, if you ask me."

It was an elegant garment, all right, a gift worthy of Scheherazade. Caroline was willing to bet that this guy's tastes ran more to the likes of Brunhilde, the Valkyrie. A woman probably needed a whip to keep him in line. Trying to be calm, she said, "Let me begin by saying that this coat was designed and manufactured by the Varanov family. Their ancestors were Russian furriers, servants of the czars. They made coats and clothing for generations of the royal family. Just before the revolution they immigrated to the United States and since then they have used sable from the Soviet Union to fashion what are considered to be the finest coats in the world."

Uneasily, she plunged into the details of her standard speech. Explaining that sables were raised only in Russia and were imported by just a few furriers, she brought the coat over to him so he could touch the fur and better understand her discussion of coat construction.

"Each skin is hand-selected, matched and trimmed before the furrier begins assembling a coat, so naturally no two coats are ever alike. Of course, a Varanov coat is more than a piece of workmanship. There's a mystique about owning a Varanov that surpasses—"

"Put it on," he interrupted bluntly. "Let me see what it looks like on you."

Caroline hesitated, but modeling the coats was clearly listed on her job description, so she did as she was told. She donned the coat and executed a practiced pirouette intended to give the buyer the full benefit of a sumptuous fur dramatically cloaking a slender female figure. With both hands, she held the garment against her breasts. Gracefully, she strolled back and forth to show off the coat, putting all her teenage years of ballet lessons into play. When she turned, she realized he had been looking at her legs, not the coat. He was considering them, taking his time, and after a moment she stopped sashaying and stood still, just two yards away from him. He didn't speak.

"What do you think?" she asked as the silence stretched on. "Pretty, isn't it?"

"Yeah," he said.

And then he pulled the knife from his pocket.

Caroline froze. With his thumb, he pried open the blade and it made a sharp *click* in the hushed salon. Caroline didn't speak. She couldn't. Through her mind ran all the warnings she'd ever heard, all the advice from her mother and a self-defense teacher. Like the flashing images that supposedly appeared just before the moment of death, a jumble of warnings and admonishments crowded into Caroline's brain. She felt her heart stop and then queerly start to expand in the too-small confines of her tight chest.

From his other pocket, he removed a large red apple. Slowly, he buffed the fruit on his parka, and he watched her face without blinking.

Caroline forced herself to speak. "What—what are you doing?"

He sliced into the fruit and cut a wedge. "I'm hungry." Balancing it on the blade of the knife, he extended it to her. "Like a piece?"

His pale blue eyes bored into hers. Was he serious? Teasing? Or crazy? She let out a shaky breath and couldn't seem to tear her eyes from the knife. "No," she said, almost hoarse. "No, thank you."

He shrugged. "I've been starved all day." And he ate the wedge of fruit.

He was serious. While he chewed up the piece of apple, Caroline cleared her throat. Inside she felt an awful urge to laugh. Or to cry. She couldn't decide which impulse rippled closest to reality. He had scared the daylights out of her. He was hungry, that was all. As he started to cut a second piece of the apple, she felt a high color start to burn on her cheekbones. She hugged the coat and tried to pretend the knife didn't exist. "Is—is this fur what you had in mind, Mr. Smith? If not, I have a refrigerator full of Varanov coats if you'd prefer something else."

"I don't prefer anything else," he said. He leaned against a display case, ate the second slice and used the knife to gesture at her. "I can see why you have this job, Miss Conover. You look good in that coat."

"Thank you." Still on guard, she said slowly, "However, a fur like this one makes any woman look nice."

"You look better than nice," he said. "You look expensive."

She gritted her teeth, trying to remain polite. "Thanks."

"You look like you're accustomed to owning expensive things, Miss Conover, not just selling them. Are you rich?"

"With this job?" she retorted, trying to joke.

He didn't smile. He ate a third slice of apple and said, "Did you get rich stealing coats?"

Caroline stepped backward. It was just one step, not a full-fledged escape. In a quiet, frightened voice, she asked, "Who are you?"

"A customer."

"Like hell you are," she said.

He smiled. "Do I look more like a potential accomplice?"

"What?"

"If I told you I could fence coats—as many as you could get for me—would you be interested?"

In a flash of comprehension, Caroline realized what was going on. "*Now* I know who you are."

"Who am I?" he asked.

"You're trying to trap me. You're not a fence. You're the investigator."

He tilted his head, bemused. "What makes you so sure?"

"Because you played this like amateur night," she shot back, infuriated by the smug expression on his face. "A policeman wouldn't have been nearly this clumsy. And a real accomplice wouldn't have played the sex game first."

He laughed shortly, caught by surprise. "Sex game?"

"You were trying to intimidate me."

"I plead guilty to the amateur status," he said, thoroughly amused, "but believe me, sex had nothing to do with—"

"You were practically reading the label on my panty hose. Don't insult my intelligence, Mr. Smith. And put that knife away."

Obligingly, he clicked his knife closed and slid it back into his pocket. With his half-eaten apple still in hand, he sauntered to the desk and reached for one of his credit cards. Taking a bite of the apple, he handed the card to her. "My name's not Smith. My family," he said, giving a small wave of his apple to indicate the lush salon, "owns this place. I'm Alex Varanov."

She read the name on the card just to be sure, and there it was. Alexander Varanov. She skewered him with the most hostile glare she could manage. "You could have introduced yourself properly in the first place."

"Yes," he said, meeting her glare without a qualm. "But that might not have given me enough time to size you up. I hear you're the prime suspect."

Caroline dropped the credit card back onto the desk. Tartly, she said, "There's nothing wrong with your hearing."

Her spunk apparently amused him, but his face wasn't any less threatening when he smiled. "Stealing coats doesn't seem like it would be the crime of choice for a young woman like you," he remarked.

"There's no evidence that proves I stole those coats."

"But your name turned up on a security computer printout," he pointed out, boosting himself onto the desk and getting comfortable there to finish his snack. "You were in the store after hours, unauthorized. Tell me about that."

"There's nothing to tell. I'm never here at night."

"But the computer—"

"The computer is wrong. All employees are given a passkey—it looks like a card for an automated bank teller. We use them to punch in and out of the building. The computer reads our names off the cards and records the time we enter or leave the store—"

"I know all that," he said. "The computer says last Saturday night you came into the store at 11:55 p.m. and did not leave again until 2:15."

"Well, I wasn't here. I was at home in bed."

His eyes sparkled with malice. "I suppose you can prove that."

"No," she retorted, determined not to acknowledge his innuendo. "But I was there—alone. Look, I put my passkey in my locker when I left. Somebody must have taken it that night."

"What?"

"We have an employee locker room," she insisted. "I was afraid of losing my stupid passkey—they made such a fuss about not doing that when I took this job—so I just leave the key in my locker every night— I rarely come in when the store is closed, so I can always get in the building. I punch in after I've retrieved the key from the locker."

"You're claiming someone stole your passkey?"

The derision in his voice spurred Caroline into defending herself. "I know it sounds flimsy," she said stubbornly. "Over two hundred thousand dollars worth of fur coats have disappeared, and my access code was used to get into the store. But I've only been working here a couple of weeks, Mr. Varanov. How could I have figured a way to rip off the store and still keep my job?"

"So you're blaming someone else? Another employee?"

"I'm not blaming anyone. Look, lots of expensive merchandise has been stolen lately. Two months ago, the jewelry department was hit—"

"Yes. Do you happen to know what became of the woman who worked in the jewelry department?"

Caroline willed herself not to blink or move a muscle. Quietly, she said, "Yes, I heard. She killed herself."

"She did indeed." Varanov nodded. "After Jane Wexler was accused of stealing fifty thousand dollars worth of gold, jewelry and watches from the store, she went home and ate a bottle of pills."

Still in control, Caroline said, "That doesn't necessarily mean she was guilty."

"True. She can't answer the obvious questions to clear herself, either. But you *are* here, Miss Conover. Now coats are disappearing and the clues point to you."

"Clue, Varanov," Caroline snapped. "There's only one clue pointing to me. Or do you have some real evidence?"

"No evidence. Just a theory. I think, Miss Conover, that maybe you figured out a coat-stealing scam and decided to try it."

Caroline turned away from him and began to jerk the sable coat off her shoulders. She went back to the pedestal and started to replace the coat. "You're guessing, Mr. Varanov. That's hardly a good way to start an investigation, is it?"

He didn't move from his perch and even began to swing one of his long legs languidly. "I learned how to play doctor at a young age," he said, watching her. "I figure it can't be too hard to play detective. Tell me about yourself, Miss Conover. Assure me of your innocence. Isn't that what suspects do? Before you came here to Chicago, you were working at a large department store in Philadelphia—Wanamaker's, right?"

"Obviously you read my personnel file."

"Obviously. But I noticed that you only worked at Wanamaker's for one year. Before that, you listed no other jobs for yourself. What did you do with yourself before you worked at that store, Miss Conover?"

"I was married," she said, busily arranging the coat on the pedestal. "I didn't have a job."

"That explains a lot."

She turned. "What's that supposed to mean?"

"In spite of your little-girl-from-Kansas face, you dress like a class act." He glanced down her dress again, his gaze lingering on her shapely thighs before dropping to her calves. Then he looked up into her eyes again. "You act like you've been around. Were you some kind of socialite? Is that what you did with your time?"

Coldly, Caroline said, "I wouldn't knock socialites if I were you, Mr. Varanov. Who do you suppose buys the coats your family makes?"

He let that pass, looking unperturbed. "So you don't deny it. You were a wealthy socialite. But divorce reared its ugly head and forced you into the real world."

"Yes. I got a job at Wanamaker's."

"With your good looks and good taste, you were placed in the fur salon, I suppose."

She shrugged and folded her arms across her breasts. He made her uncomfortable. "You're telling this tale, not me."

"All right, I'll go for broke. You're a penniless divorcée who's now desperate for your old life-style. You decide to try pilfering a few fur coats so you can have a little extra spending money. Maybe you have an accomplice, or maybe you're selling the goods to your old friends—rich women who always like to find bargains in furs."

"Look," Caroline snapped, "instead of making up a lot of fiction, why don't you brush up on your detecting skills? You're not collecting evidence, Mr. Varanov, you're indulging in conjecture."

He stood up slowly, uncoiling his body in one smooth motion. Standing close, almost looming over her while he looked lazily into her eyes, Varanov said quietly, "I have one advantage over a professional detective, Miss Conover."

"What's that?"

"I haven't got any professional ethics," he replied. "I can dig as deeply as I like into your background. I intend to learn everything there is to know about you, in fact. I'll follow you, keep track of everyone you meet, every phone call you make—"

"That's illegal!"

"So call the police." He gestured toward the telephone on the desk.

Caroline hesitated. It only took a split second, and she shouldn't have let it happen, but it did. In that instant, when she didn't say anything, Caroline knew she had given herself away.

Varanov laughed rudely. "Why, I think you're keeping secrets from me, Miss Conover!"

"Everyone has secrets," she shot back weakly.

Alex went on chuckling. He had caught her. She *was* holding something back. But despite the hostility that practically reverberated from her slender frame, he decided that Caroline Conover looked almost vulnerable standing there—young and a little scared once she'd let a hint of the truth slip. That was new. Until that moment, she had looked brave and tough. Her eyes still shone with anger, but her lips—the soft lower lip and the curving upper one—quivered ever so gently.

Alex stopped laughing. He pulled himself together abruptly. The last thing he could let himself feel was sympathy. Besides, he warned himself, sympathy could be exactly what she was trying to provoke. All the evidence pointed to her and it was going to take more than a pretty face to convince him she was innocent. He gathered up his credit cards and put them and the partly eaten apple back into his pocket. Suddenly he felt angry again. He wasn't going to let himself be manipulated. Alex Varanov was a loner. He liked a streamlined, uncomplicated life. Women, he had learned, generally confused clean-cut issues with matters he didn't intend to be tempted by.

"I'm not your friendly neighborhood cop, Miss Conover," he said bluntly. "I'm the son of an angry man." He eyed her sternly. "And I've got the green light from Mrs. St. Cloud herself to do anything I have to to get the job done. I can do what the police can't do—force you into the open using any means possible.''

''What do you mean?''

''I mean you could lose your job, your society friends, everything. I'll tear your life apart. Or you could talk to me first. Tell me what you know. You've worked in this department long enough to guess what's going on. I want to know what happened to those coats.''

She met his gaze and a gleam of desperation flickered in and out of her eyes. But she didn't break down—not yet. Something kept her resolve in place. She looked back at him, mustering defiance.

Lifting her chin once more, she said, ''I have nothing to tell you, Mr. Varanov. Eavesdrop all you like. Flash that knife of yours under my nose if it turns you on. There's no evidence that I'm guilty.''

''We'll see about that,'' he said.

She didn't answer. She glared at him. Under different circumstances, Alex thought fleetingly, he might have done something about the unspoken challenge reflected in her stiff posture and tight, angry face as she glanced back at him. He remembered that he had frightened her before, with the knife and his own hulking size. A sex game, she had called it. Funny choice of words.

She hadn't been afraid for her life, he realized suddenly. She had feared for her virtue. He saw it as she looked at him with something besides anger in her expression. Curiosity lurked in her eyes, too.

How might the fiery expression in those green eyes change if he really took her into his arms? Might they smolder or shoot fireworks? How might her strong, slender body react if he were to follow through with the inexplicably erotic ideas that suddenly flashed in his mind? Fight? Or give in? Wrapping one of those soft coats around her bare body and thrusting Caroline Conover down across the desk was a momentarily appealing thought.

She had glanced down his body suddenly, too. She was appraising him, taking the same quick inventory he had of her, sizing him up and evaluating her chances. Sex had occurred to her, also, he could see—a thought that had, no doubt, come out of nowhere and surprised the country girl. For an instant, it seemed they shared the same mental image of a man and a woman locked in the tumult of sexual strategy and surrender.

How did desperate women make love, he wondered? She was sunlight and volatile energy, and he was darker—more dangerous in many ways.

She looked at him—a slender, fresh-faced innocent with a trace of something else in her eyes.

Abruptly, Alex turned to go. He had seen enough. She wasn't ready to break yet and she might be the kind of female to use sex for manipulation.

Alex paused in the doorway, though, and glanced back. Coldly, he said, "You're a good-looking woman, Miss Conover. But underneath it all, I think I'm going to find you're nothing but a cheap thief. And I'm going to see that you're punished."

CHAPTER TWO

BETSY NOFSINGER liked working at St. Cloud's. She had fought her parents about going to college—two years at Parkland Junior College seemed like a fate worse than death—and when her harried father had landed her a job in Chicago after pulling some strings with an old friend, Betsy had packed her bags and left Chesterville, Illinois, within eighteen hours. She had promptly rented a room with a kitchenette and gone to work the next day. Life had finally begun!

Betsy loved the city. She loved her job. She loved having lunch with her fellow workers and had even made a few friends. Practically overnight, she had become an adult. Without her mom to help, she bought clothes and went grocery shopping and even went out with some of the women after work once in a while. Although Betsy wasn't quite twenty-one, she thought she looked a lot older. Pretty soon, men were going to start noticing her.

Of all the employees at St. Cloud's, Betsy wished one in particular would be her friend—Miss Conover, the new clerk in the fur salon. "She's so sophisticated," Betsy had written to her friend Paula, who had gone to Parkland instead of running to the big city. "She's beautiful and very smart, and I want to be just like her."

Yes, Betsy wished she had a fairy godmother who could wave a magic wand and transform her into Caroline Conover. Her blond hair always looked gorgeous. Her figure was great. Her makeup—well, Betsy had learned a lot about makeup just by looking at what little Miss Conover used. She was perfect, that was all. Miss Conover was so pretty, so clever, so calm all the time—like she was in the morning, when that awful Mr. Smith had scared them. And yet . . .

And yet there was something sad about Miss Conover. Not sad exactly, but something *underneath*. It was an air of mystery, Betsy decided after a while. Maybe that was what made men turn their heads and look at her as they passed by the salon. Maybe that was why the older women who came in to look at fur coats talked so nicely to her—like they wanted to be her mother or something. Miss Conover appealed to people. And Betsy wished she had the same quality.

She caught up with Miss Conover as they were leaving the store.

"Hi," said Betsy. "Going straight home?"

"Home?" Miss Conover repeated, looking blank as they descended the steps of the employee exit.

"Yeah, some of us were going to grab a drink somewhere—celebrate the fact that it's Saturday," Betsy said, smiling in her friendliest way. "Want to come along?"

"No," said Caroline. "I—tonight I can't. But thanks."

She hurried out the door without another word, and
Betsy faltered to a stop at the bottom of the stairs,
disappointed. For a moment she fought the impulse to
chase after the other woman. But she just shrugged.
It wasn't that important. She'd try again some day
soon. More than anything, Betsy wanted to get to
know the sophisticated Miss Conover.

Shoving out through the revolving door of St.
Cloud's employee exit at closing time, Caroline shud-
dered at the prickly sensation on the back of her neck.
"Let it be my imagination," she whispered to herself.
"He can't be tailing me already."

But she couldn't be sure. There was a crowd waiting at the bus stop on Michigan Avenue, and Caroline plunged into its midst, forgetting Betsy Nofsinger
entirely. She had to escape—to get away and think.
Nervously, she glanced around. A menacing Russian
bear like Alexander Varanov would surely stand out a
mile among the predominantly female and chatty
clerks. She didn't see him—not yet, at least. Keeping
her head down, Caroline mingled with the throng and
prayed he hadn't decided to follow through on his
threat just yet. There were too many things she had to
accomplish before Varanov or anybody else stopped
her.

The bus arrived, thank heaven, and Caroline
boarded it, pushing past other passengers to get out of
sight quickly. When everyone was aboard, the bus
lurched and sent Caroline tumbling into a back seat.
She didn't care. She was safe for the moment.

Sitting up, she tried to collect herself and think. He
was going to ruin everything! At the very least, he'd

send her to the police. At the worst—well, Caroline couldn't bring herself to think about the worst consequences. With her heart hammering, she glanced around the bus, half expecting him to materialize from behind a newspaper.

"You are under arrest," he'd say in a thick Russian accent. Except he really didn't have an accent. He didn't have a black fedora or one of those belted raincoats, either. He wasn't the KGB. Yet he *was* big and close-faced and scary looking.

So why did his appearance conjure up those dreamy Dr. Zhivago type love scenes? He was handsome and physically overwhelming, but it was that inner quality—the hardness, the confidence, the barely checked temper—that captured Caroline's imagination. He possessed a power, exuded a toughness that went beyond physical strength. But he seemed unaware of it. Apparently he didn't recognize the aura around himself. Even his clothes conveyed a certain carelessness. He was a man's man—stubborn and hostile to anything that stood in his way. Yet after ten minutes alone with him, Caroline had found herself thinking of lovemaking under layers of fur coats!

She was panicking—thinking crazy thoughts. Caroline put her face toward the window, but she didn't look beyond the glass where the first droplets of rain began to blotch and spread in pulsing veins. *Calm down, Caro. You have to think*. She knew she needed a quicker plan now that this complication had arisen.

EATING THE REST of his apple at a desk in the personnel department of St. Cloud's, Alex Varanov counted the days in his head. Seven days, that was all he had. After a week, the insurance company intended to step in. That didn't give him much time. Not much at all.

He picked up a phone and dialed Wanamaker's, the department store in Philadelphia whose manager was a college buddy of Alex's. He intended to get some hard information to back up his theory about Caroline Conover. A couple of businesslike and unfamiliar voices spoke to Alex before he heard Tommy Hollingsworth come on the line.

"Alex!" cried Tommy. "How are you, pal?"

"Dieting at the moment, Tommy," Alex growled, "and it's hell."

Tommy laughed—the same raucous howl he'd had in college. Once a rabble-rouser around the fraternity keg, Tommy didn't sound as if he'd grown up much in ten years. He was crude, but lovable in his own way. He dove into razzing Alex as if they had seen each other just a few weeks before instead of years ago. "I'll bet you aren't getting any exercise these days, are you?"

"Not enough. What about you? Still chasing women for recreation?"

"Naw," replied Wanamaker's store manager, laughing. "I'm an old married man now."

"You're kidding!" Alex found himself smiling broadly at the thought of his old friend settling down finally. "A hound like you?"

"Yep. Eloped three weeks ago. We'll be sending you an announcement as soon as they come back from the printer. Her name's Tammy."

It was better than Bambi, which was truer to Tommy's usual taste in women. Still grinning, Alex said, "I'll be damned."

"I know, I know. Will wonders never cease? I never thought it would happen, either. How's Joyce?"

"Well—" Alex stalled, genuinely sorry to throw a wet blanket on his old friend's post-wedding euphoria "—we didn't have announcements printed up, Tommy, but we're—we split up. About a year ago."

"I'm sorry, Alex," said Tommy, dropping his jolly tone of voice. "Any kids?"

"None," said Alex mildly. "That was the issue. Listen, I've got a favor to ask." There was no sense hashing over a dead marriage when there was a mystery to clear up. Alex wanted some answers.

"Sure, pal. Name it."

Alex plunged in. "I'm giving my family a hand with a problem they've got, and I need to know about a woman now employed by a store in Chicago. She claims to have worked for you up until this spring. Her name is Caroline Conover. Can you look her up in your files for me?"

A short silence greeted Alex's ear.

"Tommy?"

"I heard you." Tommy let out a short sigh followed by an expletive. "Jeez, I wish you'd said any name but that one, Alex."

Alex leaned forward, hunching over the desk and tightening his grip on the receiver. "Why? Has she given you trouble before?"

"No, nothing like that. Unless you count a few sleepless nights." With another exasperated sigh,

Tommy said, "Boy, you've put me in a tough position. I promised Caro that I would back up her story and I hate like hell going back on my word. Not to her."

"What do you mean, 'her story'?" Alex said. "Tommy, you've got to understand that I'm completely in the dark. In a nutshell, I'm investigating a theft, and all the evidence points to your Miss Conover. Now—"

"Caroline wouldn't steal anything," Tommy said at once. "She's—oh, damn, she's not the kind of lady that I like breaking promises to, so I can't tell you much, Alex. Can you just accept my word? Caroline is not in Chicago to steal anything. That's a fact."

Alex stewed. Tommy had never been a good judge of character, especially where women were concerned. Still, he wasn't the kind of man to make flat statements without being able to back them up. Alex asked, "Is she a friend of yours, Tommy?"

"An acquaintance," Tommy corrected. "No sex involved, though until my wedding I wouldn't have minded. I've seen her around town, met her at a party or two. She went to school with my youngest brother. When she approached me for a favor, I gave it to her willingly."

"Why?" Bluntly, Alex added, "Hoping to get her into the sack?"

Tommy laughed. For him, the question wasn't out of line. "I wish. No, because—well, she's got a kind of mission, Alex."

"A mission?"

Uncertain of himself and therefore speaking slowly, Tommy said, "Caroline comes from a good family. Big farm in Lancaster County, I think, an uncle who's a Main Line banker. She's top-drawer stuff, Alex. And she has something important to do in Chicago right now."

Frowning, Alex said, "But you won't tell me what?"

"I can't. Really, Alex, I promised. Ask her nicely— and I mean *nicely*—and maybe she'll tell you herself. You might even get lucky."

He should have expected his old college chum to have little more than lovemaking on his mind, Alex thought, disgusted. All he had really learned from the call was that Caroline Conover had missed her chance to bed down with the legendary Tommy Hollingsworth.

Tommy chuckled again. "What's the matter, Alex? You having trouble with the pretty Miss Conover? Or were you married so long you forget what to do with an attractive lady?"

Alex smiled grimly. "She's attractive? I hadn't noticed, Tommy."

"Bull roar. If that's true, you're blind as well as underexercised. Maybe Caro can do something about both conditions." He let out a wolfish howl. "Have you seen her in a bathing suit yet? Let me tell you, I nearly wept! I'll bet she's wild between the sheets. Imagine those luscious long legs wrapped around—"

"Listen, Tommy," said Alex, not in the mood to hear anyone else's sexual fantasies, "I appreciate your help."

"Any time," Tommy said, pulling himself together. "Hey, tell Caro that I—well, that she can call
me, too, if she wants reassurance. About you, I mean.
You haven't been acting like a SOB, have you?"

"It's working so far." Alex sat back, ready to sign
off. He stretched. "What do you want for a wedding
present, Tommy?"

"A baby carriage," Tommy promptly replied.

"Good lord!" said Alex, bursting out with a laugh.
"That explains the elopement. You've always been an
idiot, Tommy."

"But I have a hell of a lot of fun, Alex. You ought
to try it."

Alex groaned.

"C'mon, Alex! If you're dieting, pal, why not take
a bite out of the mouth-watering Miss Conover? Not
a lot of calories, but plenty satisfying."

"Tommy—"

"Hey, I'll bet you the best baby carriage on the
market that you can't bed down with Caro before the
week is out."

"Why would I want to?"

"Jeez, Alex! Are you *that* much of a lone wolf these
days? Haven't you heard about attracting bees with
honey? Be nice to her and she'll be nice back. Give it
a try. Call me when you can collect on the bet."

"I'm not a gambler."

"Like hell," said Tommy. "See you around, Alex."

With a rueful shake of his head, Alex cradled the
phone. He put his boots up on the desk, looked up at
the ceiling and began to mull things over. Only a week.
Seven days to find a thief. And his only lead was a

closemouthed blonde from Lancaster County. With green eyes and great legs.

Maybe Tommy was right. If bullying wasn't working, perhaps seduction *was* the fastest way to get the information he needed. Maybe it was time to try the Hollingsworth method. At the same time, Alex thought, he might even aim to bring to life a few of the sexual scenarios that had been playing around in his head since the moment he had laid eyes on the leggy Ms Conover. Tommy's remarks hadn't helped that situation at all. In addition to feeling hungry all the time, Alex had begun to crave a kind of satisfaction that a thousand apples couldn't provide. Another goal to accomplish before the week's end.

"It can't hurt to try," he said aloud.

As if responding to the suggestion, his stomach growled suddenly. Alex reached for the knife in his pocket, but discovered he didn't have any apples left.

"Damn," he said. Things weren't going well at all.

BY THE TIME the bus dropped her at her street, Caroline had figured she had nothing to lose. Even if it meant getting sent to the police by Alexander Varanov, she had to try the next step in her plan.

The bus thundered away from the curb, and through the spewing exhaust and dreary drizzle, Caroline set off for her temporary home, a house located midway along a block of very large, mostly run-down mansions—the kind, Caroline thought grimly, that Charles Addams liked to depict in his *New Yorker* cartoons. The neighborhood must have been glorious in its heyday, but now the buildings were crumbling and forgotten. It was perfect for Caroline's purposes, though. Urban renewal hadn't come along to bulldoze the dilapidated houses, nor had the Yuppies arrived to mend the porticos, paint the wrought iron and add window boxes, so the neighbors still kept to themselves. Litter tumbled in the still unraked leaves and people passed each other on the cracked sidewalks without speaking. It was a perfect neighborhood in which to remain anonymous.

Suddenly a platoon of unkempt little boys dashed past Caroline, jostling her elbow. She clutched for her handbag and bit back a cry. But they hadn't meant to steal anything, just to startle her, and with that accomplished they laughed recklessly and ran away.

Caroline pressed her trembling hand over the spot where her heart raced. Though she'd lived and worked in Philadelphia for three years, she was still a country girl at heart. Chicago wasn't just a windy city to her. It was a dark, rainy, dangerous place. At times, she longed to be back in sunny Pennsylvania.

"Buck up, girl," she ordered sternly. "Things are just getting started."

As if to punctuate those words, the November clouds burst open and let loose the pent-up torrents just as Caroline reached her gate. The first slashes of cold rain whipping through the air felt like angry bee stings, so she ran up the stone steps in front of her house, splashed across the puddles on the broken stones of the terrace and scrambled in her bag for the key to unlock the huge, beveled door.

She found the key and shoved it into the lock, but it promptly stuck. "Drat!"

She dropped her handbag, wrestled with the key and finally delivered an angry kick to the door. The lock clicked, but a blustery gust of wind whistled at just the wrong moment, snatching the door out of Caroline's grasp. It swung inward, squealing, and with a terrific *thunk*, it crashed back against its hinges. Caroline cried out. The whole porch shuddered with the impact, and then the door came hurtling back at her. She dove to escape the murderous rebound.

"Hold it!" ordered a voice behind her.

Caroline nearly screamed. Alexander Varanov caught the door in one hand before it inflicted any serious harm, and he steadied Caroline with an unshakable grip on her upper arm. He said, "Let me help."

He was strong enough to hold the door against the wind while she grabbed her bag and ducked inside. He followed, and released her arm as casually as if they had been dancing. He had sunglasses on—even though evening had begun to fall.

"I didn't ask you in here," she said at once, standing her ground despite the fact that she probably looked about as ferocious as a wet kitten.

Varanov closed the door and turned around, amused. "No, you didn't," he agreed. "Shall I go out again and ask permission to enter?"

He took off the sunglasses. Caroline had instinctively backed up four paces. Brushing past Alex Varanov in the doorway had given her a more tactile impression of his big frame, and his eyes, she noted with a jolt, were exactly like those of a fairy-tale wolf—clear and glittery and incredibly blue. Standing there with the rain dripping off his black hair, his

powerful hand resting on the doorknob, ready to shut
out any hope of rescue, and with his glowing eyes fixed
so determinedly on his victim, he could have scared the
hell out of Rasputin.

But it wasn't the look in his eyes that triggered her
unease, nor his size. It was something larger than those
things. A powerful life force flowed from Alexander
Varanov. If generations of stubborn peasant stock
were to distill their bloodlines for centuries, Caroline
decided, the result would be this big, autonomous
offspring. He seemed invincible, a man of deeds, a
huge cossack who did not recognize rules of deco-
rum. Any woman would see it in him. The force became a sexual thing, an aura Caroline felt as acutely
as if he'd caressed some female trigger inside of her.
Other men talked about sex. This one exuded it.

Mustering the shreds of her courage, Caroline said,
"How did you find me?"

"I'm not that much of an amateur. I read the address on your personnel file."

"Have you been lurking long?"

He pocketed the glasses and shrugged, half smiling
at her wry tone. "Long enough to have a look around
the premises. Did you know there's a brand new Volvo
locked in the carriage house out back?"

"You have *no* business—"

"Save it," he said calmly. "I've uncovered quite a
mystery, haven't I?" He glanced around the huge entry hall in which they stood. "I wonder why a young
woman takes public transportation back and forth to
a poorly paying job when she has a mint-condition

performance car and lives in—what is this place, anyway? Some kind of museum?"

Infuriated and highly suspicious of the unmistakable air of friendliness he was so obviously trying to convey, Caroline turned away and began to strip off her wet coat. "It's my home."

"I see that," he said mildly, strolling in a slow half circle to get a complete view of the foyer. "When does the butler show up?"

"I haven't got a butler," she snapped. She didn't trust his pleasant banter. "I live alone."

"All alone?" Varanov turned and raised his eyebrows. "You don't have three hundred cats in the attic, maybe? Or a few skeletons hidden in the cellar? This isn't the kind of place I imagined a woman like you would live in."

Caroline knew that things looked suspicious. The house wasn't the kind of home in which *any* woman in her right mind would live. Clearly built by a wealthy family many decades before, it was a wreck now—a good candidate for demolition. Still, signs of its former grandeur were obvious. A massive paneled staircase curved up one wall to a wide second-floor landing that had been blockaded by a carpenter's horse. A chandelier, magnificent in its day, hung overhead, broken and dusty now. Caroline fumbled at the wall switch, and half of the chandelier's bulbs flashed on. She didn't like the dark.

The light revealed a hall floor that had been laid with tiles, though many were cracked. An empty dining room lay to the left through an archway, and the wide hallway ran back toward the kitchen area where in another era a butler must certainly have presided over a small army of servants. No heirloom paintings graced the walls, however, and no rich carpets adorned the floors. It was a mighty peculiar place for a single woman, all right. She considered a lie about roommates, then decided he might have checked that, too.

"It's only temporary," she said quickly, and turned to drape her coat over the carved newel post. She pushed her damp hair back from her forehead and faced him staunchly. "Have you come for a reason? Or do you get some kind of perverted pleasure out of snooping in people's garages?"

"I came to talk," he said and put his hands in his pockets.

Caroline eyed him narrowly. "Do you have a warrant?"

"For conversation?" He smiled and shook his head. "You ought to brush up on your legal rights, Miss Conover. I don't need a warrant to ask a few questions."

Caroline hugged herself against the chill air of the unheated entry hall. "You already asked a few questions. I have nothing else to tell you."

"Maybe I've got new questions. Look, you're just going to make yourself more interesting to me if you don't, so why don't we step inside and get this over with?" He couldn't stop a quick, appraising glance down her shivering figure. "If you'll feel more comfortable, I'll take you someplace with plenty of people and central heating."

"Why the switch in tactics?"

"I don't know what you mean. Unless you think I'm playing another—sex game, didn't you call it?"

Caro lifted her nose in distaste. "You didn't care if I was comfortable before."

He shrugged. "An oversight on my part. Put it down to a jaded upbringing in the city. I'll make up for it. Shall we?" He gestured through one of the archways.

Unless she wanted to show fear, there wasn't anything to do but give in and lead him under the arch and onto the bare parquet floor of the parlor. Caroline made no secret of her suspicion of Alexander Varanov as she stalked across the echoing room to the only piece of furniture—a pretty quilted and flowered sofa that, together with a simple brass floor lamp, was a recent purchase from St. Cloud's furniture department. She turned the light on quickly, nervous in the semidarkness and hoping he didn't notice. He'd learn too much about her just by the state of her temporary home. There were no magazines on the floor, no photographs on the mantel and no paintings on the walls. The only sign of habitation was a telephone and an answering machine, both on the mantel.

In the stillness of the empty room, one single sign of life blinked as obviously as a harbor beacon on a foggy night. On the answering machine, the little red message light flashed frantically. Caroline saw that Varanov noted it at once. She held her breath. But he ignored the light for the moment and scanned the rest of the room, no doubt looking for clues of her larcenous personality, Caroline thought grimly.

"Quite a place," he remarked.

Caroline couldn't help glancing at the message light a second time, but she didn't dare find out what calls had come in while she was away. Nor would it do to stand in front of the machine to try to block his view of it. Composedly, Caroline walked past him and sat down smack in the middle of the sofa. She crossed her legs with ladylike precision—quite a trick considering the shortness of her fashionable skirt. She saw that Alexander Varanov had momentarily forgotten about the rest of the room and was watching her intently.

"I'm glad you like it," she said tartly.

He snapped out of his brief trance. "The house? I wouldn't say I like it, exactly. It must be great fun at Halloween."

"I wasn't referring to the house." Caroline laid her hands on her knees and went on without missing a beat. "Since I'm new in town and haven't had time to find a suitable apartment, I took this place." Blithely, she lied, "It was cheap and convenient for work. No mystery."

He decided to accept that—temporarily, at least—and allowed his gaze to wander around the rest of the room. With his hands clasped loosely behind his back he strolled to the large bay window that overlooked a side lawn. Weeds had long ago taken over there, and the new spring growth already looked like a jungle. He regarded the tangle passively. "You rent the whole house?"

"Yes."

"The carriage house, too?"

"It came with the rest."

"So the car is yours?"

There was no use lying. "Yes," said Caroline.

"Part of the divorce settlement?"

She smiled coldly, having been given a logical story on a platter. "Yes."

He looked at the ceiling. "How many bedrooms are there?"

"Several," she said, bracing herself for the innuendo that was sure to follow. "But I don't use the second floor."

He turned and blinked at her. "Where do you sleep?"

"There's a room off the kitchen—maid's quarters at one time, I imagine. I have a bed and a dresser. Would you like to see them? Take an inventory of my panties, perhaps?"

He sighed. "Look—"

"I'm sure you're hoping to find out all kinds of fascinating things about me. What brand of toothpaste I use, maybe? Or have you already dug through my trash can to find that out?"

He shook his head and stayed planted at the spot by the window. "I've already found a couple of interesting things, Miss Conover. But not in your garbage."

"Oh?" she asked archly, staring straight at him. "Have you hired the neighborhood children to keep an eye on me around the clock?"

Explosively, Varanov sighed again and he swore under his breath. "You're a damned irritating woman," he said. "Sitting there, you look about as approachable as an ice sculpture."

"I don't care to be approached."

"Damn you," he said. "I'm trying to apologize."

Caroline couldn't summon an answer. That he was acting so nicely now puzzled her. He'd been nothing short of a mean-spirited skunk before.

Before she had much time to wonder about the change, Varanov spoke. "After I looked at your file in the store," he said swiftly, starting to pace, "I made a phone call—to Wanamaker's."

That startled Caro. So he *had* started to investigate her. Caroline hoped she wasn't trembling visibly. "Well? Did they confirm the information on my résumé?"

"No. As a matter of fact, your phony background was blown wide open."

Caroline began to protest, but he cut her off.

Raising one hand, Varanov said, "Before we go any further, Miss Conover, I should tell you now that I'm an acquaintance of Tommy Hollingsworth, the manager. We knew each other at school, long before he went to Wanamaker's."

All the air seemed to have evaporated from her lungs. Caroline whispered, "Oh."

"Yes," said Varanov, watching her face. "I called Tommy. He says you never worked in his store. He says you're a friend and you asked him for a favor— to allow you to claim you'd been a clerk in his store."

"And?"

"And," Varanov continued, "he says I should believe everything you say because you're—how did he put it exactly? He says you've got a mission. That was his word. A mission."

Caroline stood up and walked away so he couldn't see her expression. She went to the bay window and leaned both hands against the sill. He was going to discover everything if she wasn't careful. And Caro wasn't sure she could talk about the whole terrible ordeal yet.

"Tommy refused to tell me what you're up to. He said he didn't dare break a promise he'd made to you." When Caroline didn't respond, Varanov gathered in a breath and said, "So I suppose I owe you an apology for this afternoon. The—my cheap-thief crack was out of line. Judging by Tommy's opinion of you, I should—"

"Apology accepted," Caroline said shortly.

Behind her, Varanov said, "Just who the hell are you, Caroline Conover?"

She tried to cut past him, to get away. She had things to do and he was only going to complicate matters. Or make her talk, which was infinitely worse. Caroline bolted.

But he blocked her escape, stepping into her path. He would have caught her arm to stop her, but Caroline veered aside and halted before him. Suddenly the niceness was gone. The danger was back. Alex Varanov was tall and scruffy and menacing again, and his voice sent a shiver along each of her nerve endings. He said, "You're not leaving until you tell me."

CHAPTER THREE

FOR AN INSTANT Alex thought she might answer his question. Staring down at her, he saw that she was trembling. Her short-nailed but slender hands quivered, and even the slightly golden flesh of her forearms seemed alive with tension. Gone was the tough glint in her eye. Oddly, an acute expression of guilt crossed her face. She seemed ready to crack, all right.

But the telephone rang.

They both jumped at the sound. Alex realized they must have remained frozen for nearly half a minute—both mesmerized by something in the other. He knew that *his* brain had already leaped a synapse or two away from the original question and was certainly mulling over the prospect of touching her. Putting his hands on the woman's slim shoulders to steady her—to comfort her, even—was an impulse so natural that for an instant Alex was afraid he'd actually done it. But the phone rang again and the spell was broken.

Caroline spun around and looked at the jangling instrument as if it had betrayed her.

"Phone's ringing," said Alex, striving to sound bland.

She didn't budge. He had guessed right. Whoever was calling might give her away.

He shrugged amiably. "Okay, I'll get it."

But she beat him to the receiver. On the third ring, she snatched it up. "Hello?" she said, breathless and staring at Alex as if he were a baying hound in hot pursuit. To her caller, she said, "Yes."

While listening to the voice on the other end of the line, she went on staring at Alex with those vibrant green eyes of hers—clearly wishing he had the good manners to leave her alone. But Alex didn't move an inch. He recognized a good opportunity when it bit him. He stayed put and prepared to listen.

Consequently, Caroline simply picked up the telephone and carried it through the swinging door to the next room. She closed the door after her without apology and began to speak to her caller.

Alex was no fool. That sort of behavior went under the heading of suspicious. He knew that following her into the next room, however, could jeopardize his plan to befriend and bedazzle the fair Ms Conover, so he refrained from tagging along. While he pondered his remaining alternatives, he found himself frowning at the blinking answering machine.

Temptations, Alex decided, were wasted on men who didn't take advantage of them. He crossed to the machine and flicked on the messages button. The machine whirred, rewinding, then clicked, and a recorded voice echoed in the room.

"Miss Conover," came the first message, "this is Judy at the office. The Lowell litigation starts on Wednesday, and if Harry is going to take over for you, he needs a consult. Can you call on Monday morn-

ing? He's working on your caseload, so he'll be in
early. Thanks. Bye.''

"My God," said Alex. Transfixed, he let the machine keep going.

"Caroline," said a smooth male voice this time,
"this is Rupert. I'd like to talk to you." He paused.
"And apologize, I guess." Another pause, suggestive
this time. "For a couple of things. Can we—" he inquired gently. Then he chickened out. "I mean—well,
listen, I'll call you later."

"Rupert?" Alex murmured aloud. What kind of a
guy had a name like Rupert? And where had he heard
the name before?

Caroline came back through the swinging door just
in time to hear the start of the third message. It said,
"Miss Conover, it's Judy again. Sorry to bother you,
but I've got some papers for you to sign. Shall I send
them or—"

Alex shut off the machine.

But she'd seen exactly what he'd done. Instantly
boiling mad, Caroline slammed the receiver down
onto the telephone and shouted, "You had no right to
do that!"

Alex said, "You're a lawyer."

She stalked toward him, eyes flashing murder-
ously. "You son of a bitch, you can't come in
here—"

"You're a lawyer!"

"*You're* a skunk!" She threw the phone onto the
sofa and whirled to face him. "A low-down, sneaky
skunk!"

"Who are you representing?" he demanded, catching her wrist just as she raised her hand to strike him. Suddenly he was angry, too. She'd tricked him, that was clear. She'd been hiding plenty. "Are you with the insurance people?"

"I'm nobody," she retorted. "Nobody but myself!"

"What does that mean? Tell me, damn you." Without thinking, Alex shook her. "What are you doing here?"

She writhed in his grip like a wildcat. "Stop it! Let go!"

He remembered himself and released her. Maybe he'd been rougher than he'd realized. She spun away, rubbing her wrist and still spitting mad.

"It's none of your business!"

"It's a quarter of a million dollars worth of my business!" He followed her to the doorway. "You're a lawyer who's come all the way from Philadelphia to play a very complicated charade that includes my family's expensive merchandise. I'd like to know what—"

"It's not a charade," she said, turning to face him. "At least, it didn't start out that way." She flattened her back against the doorway, pressing as far away from him as she could. The force of his presence was more than she could stand. "I took the job and—"

"Why?" he interrupted. "Why become a salesclerk when you could be making big bucks?"

"It's not bucks that I care about!"

He found her wrist again and squeezed it. The bones beneath her flesh felt delicate, but he increased the pressure as if to wrench the answer he wanted from her body. "What's important to you? If not money, what is it you're looking for, Caroline?"

"Don't call me that!"

"It's your name, isn't it? Or is that part of your scheme, too?"

"It's not a scheme. That's my name, but—"

"But what?" he demanded sarcastically. "You don't think we've known each other long enough?"

"I don't want you calling me that," she said, nearly choking on the words. He could see her struggling to gain control again—to be the sophisticated woman in charge, but she couldn't manage. She was pale and clutching the remnants of dignity with all her strength. Her voice quavered suddenly. "I just—I don't want your interference."

He had a feeling she didn't want any interference at all, but his was especially galling to her. Something existed between them already, something he couldn't put his finger on. Even the warmth of her skin under his grip held him like a magnet.

But only a moron could go on muscling a woman who looked so distraught. Alex felt the fight drain out of her and he released his grip. "I'm not interfering," he said, almost coaxing her. "I could be helping."

She pulled out of his loosened grip and if he hadn't moved she might have escaped. Alex blocked her instinctively. She braced her free hand against his chest, and Alex didn't move. He stood still and let her feel his determination. In turn, he felt her trembling. Quietly, he asked, "What's so important? Why are you doing all this?"

She dropped her hand as if the heat of his body had burned her. When she looked away, her fine, fair hair fell across her forehead, obscuring her eyes for an instant. "For my sister," she said softly.

"What?"

Her head came up, but she refused to look at him. "My sister!"

"Who's your sister?" Alex asked, still mystified.

"Jane Wexler," she said. "The woman who killed herself was my sister."

It was obvious that Caroline was telling the truth. Her face was naked again—bare and defenseless. So startled by the information, Alex couldn't find any words, and Caroline stormed to the farthest end of the room and stayed there, breathing in great gulps of air to compose herself.

Alex stayed back, thinking. Jane Wexler and Caroline Conover. Nothing had prepared him for that new development, though he knew he shouldn't be all that surprised. In these modern times surnames got changed, dropped or hyphenated with ease. His own family was a good example of how marriages, divorces and adoptions could make a once well-unified group sound like a bunch of names pulled at random from a phone book. Numbly, he looked across the room at Caroline. Against the backdrop of the garden window, she looked willowy and fragile—not a tough-talking woman from the wide-open spaces anymore. Her long legs curved beautifully upward into her lovely hips, but they didn't look strong. Even her posture lacked conviction. Still shaking, Caroline Conover looked to be on the verge of tears.

And a part of Alex wanted to gather her up and hold her.

He brushed aside that foolish thought at once. "Let me warn you," he said as mildly as he could manage, "I don't cope well with weeping women."

She glared at him furiously, and even though her eyes were brimming, she said, "I am not crying."

"Good," he replied, sauntering to the middle of the room. He took care not to show how surprised he was by her revelation. "Then you can finish the story. If Jane was your sister, what the hell are you doing working for her former employer? Trying to prove her innocence?" When she didn't respond, he figured he might as well be a total bastard. "It's a little late," he remarked, "now that she's dead, don't you think?"

Furious, Caroline cried, "You wouldn't understand!"

"Try me. We've got plenty of time."

"No," she said, rapidly wiping her eyes with her hands. Her mascara ran in blotches, heightening his first impression of youth disguised in polished packaging. She hated being weak, he could see.

"What do you mean, no?"

"I mean we haven't got time," she muttered, stiffly. "*I* haven't got time. I have to leave."

"Where are you going?"

"It's none of your—"

"It certainly is my business," Alex cut in, though gently this time. The new information had changed his attitude enough that he couldn't be threatening anymore. "Tell me where you're going, blast it. Tell me what you're doing."

She lifted her head and glared at him, her teeth clenched so tightly that her jaw trembled. "I came because I have to know why she died. You don't have to understand, but I have to learn the whole story."

"So do I," said Alex. "I want to know what's going on, too. For different reasons, maybe. Both my father and Mrs. St. Cloud want some answers and I'm here to find out everything." Her gaze flickered, but remained steadily on him, so he went on. "As I see it, your sister got into trouble and died for it. Now you're in her shoes. If she was framed, you could be on your way to the same fate."

"That's the way I want it," said Caroline.

Alex stared. *"What?"*

"I want to be a decoy."

"A—"

"It's the best way, I'm sure," she said. "The police don't care what happened to Jane, and the store is just interested in finding their precious merchandise. But her death must be connected! Now I'm in a position to find out—as long as I can stand to be around all those poor—all those animal skins. Animals that *your* family—"

Alex cut her off before she digressed into a lecture about the wrongness of fashioning coats out of pelts in an age when excellent synthetics should surely please even the most discerning and style-conscious consumer. He said, "You hope to be approached by her accomplice?"

"Or her boss, yes."

Alex considered her words. "That kind of plan could get dangerous."

"I can take care of myself."

Alex hesitated. That refrain sounded like famous last words to him, but he decided against pointing that out to her. For a moment, he was at a loss. She was looking at him like a woman with a mission, all right.

Finally, he said, "I ought to talk you out of this."

"You couldn't," she replied, obviously hoping she sounded tough.

But to Alex she seemed as nervous as a high-strung colt. She held a lot of things against him, he could see. That he was a member of the Varanov family obviously meant he killed defenseless creatures to make a buck. But now wasn't the time to point out that his long-standing feud with his family had started with his objection to the whole idea of slaughtering animals for luxury. Alex meant to make peace some day—and that day had grown closer as his father's health had begun to fail—but he wasn't as blindly committed to that plan as Caroline seemed to be to the idea of learning everything about her sister's passing.

Alex hoped she didn't plan on finding out *everything*. To make life easier—both for himself and for her—he had a few facts he intended to keep secret from the fetching Miss Conover.

"Look," he said, trying to talk some sense into her. "I'd hate to see you suffer the same way your sister must have. It's— You're shivering at this very minute, you know." He would have had to be legally blind to miss the way her nipples stood out under the soft cashmere of her dress. Willing himself not to linger on that tempting sight, however, he said, "At the very least you must need help."

"Forget it." With that, she began to walk past him toward the door.

Alex stepped into her path again. When she faltered to a stop, he said, "I may not approve of your methods, but I share your goal."

"What do you mean by that?"

"It's obvious. Let me help."

Her green eyes widened. "You've got to be kidding!"

"I'm not. Let's join forces."

"With the Russian bear and his electric knife?" She laughed abruptly. "I'd have to be crazy!"

"You're half-crazy now. You're scared and that could lead to recklessness."

"I don't *trust* you, Varanov. I don't *know* you."

"My name's Alex," he said simply.

She stared at him a while longer. Then she shook her head, her blond hair rippling. "I have to do this alone."

"No," said Alex. Summing up his argument, he said firmly, "Either you do it with my help or you don't do it at all."

She blinked. "What?"

"I have enough evidence against you to make the police very interested." Counting on his fingers to make each point, he said, "One: your passkey was used the night of the last theft. Two: you work in the fur salon where the coats were stolen. Three: you pretend to live a life of poverty, but you've got a spanking new, fairly expensive car hidden out back. That's enough information to keep you in police custody for a day or so—"

"That's blackmail!"

"You could call it that. And when the police finally learn that you're a lawyer, they're going to wonder why you're fooling around outside the law. Isn't that the kind of behavior that gets lawyers disbarred?"

"You're a skunk," she said softly. "Either I let you tag along or you'll turn me in to the police?"

He smiled pleasantly. "I thought lawyers were more complicated with their language. You summed up the situation very neatly."

Caroline was silent.

"Where are you going tonight?" Alex asked.

She licked her lower lip, thinking. With great reluctance, she finally said, "Back to the store."

He waited for more.

"That was Rupert—St. Cloud's store manager—on the telephone," she said slowly, not wanting to divulge a single iota of information more than was necessary. "He wants to meet me at the store tonight."

"Why?"

She shook her head. "I don't know for sure. He's been making overtures, though."

"Overtures?"

"Yes, overtures. You know what that means?" she questioned sarcastically.

"I know what it means," he responded mildly. "What kind of overtures?"

With a sideways look at Alex, she said, "Ones that I encouraged."

"Why, Miss Conover, I didn't think you were the type."

She glared. "I did it on purpose. He's been very interested in the fur inventory since the day I started working at St. Cloud's. I even discovered him in the vault one morning before the theft took place. There's no need for the store manager to go snooping into every nook and cranny, is there?"

"Maybe he's just the conscientious type."

"And maybe not. I decided to learn more about him."

"Hence the overtures?"

Her look was withering. "I thought he was acting suspiciously, so I tried to be friendly. I won't find out anything unless I go meet him tonight."

"What are you hoping to find out? You think he's going to confess? Do you plan on torturing him with glimpses of your pretty legs, Miss Conover?"

"You're a skunk. I don't know what to expect. I'm making up this plan as I go along."

There was something to be said for that, all right. Alex's careful plans hadn't worked out so far, he had to admit.

He considered the situation. "So maybe Rupert is some kind of ringleader, hmm? The man who's behind the thefts?"

"Maybe."

"Or maybe he's just hoping to make friends," Alex said, watching her face. Somewhere inside himself, he felt the dull beginnings of a new emotion: not anger; not need, exactly. Something akin to possessiveness. With a twinge of hostility, he said, "Has your buddy Rupert expressed much interest in expanding your boss-employee relationship?"

"I've been friendly," she said calmly. "Until tonight, he hadn't responded. But he called and asked me to meet him, and I think that's a good sign."

"The overtures are finished," said Alex. "The main event is about to begin."

"He hasn't made a pass," she retorted calmly, "and he may never."

"Then he can't be a very smart ringleader," Alex replied. "All right, grab your coat. Let's go."

"What? Wait!" she cried. She reached out to hold his arm, then broke the contact as if she'd been scorched. She said, "I can't meet Rupert with you tagging along like a trained Russian bear on a leash."

"Then we'd better hurry." Alex found her hand and slipped his comfortably over hers. They fit together perfectly, and he found himself smiling at the sensation. The Russian city slicker and the Pennsylvania farm woman. Their differences were almost poetic. Tommy's suggestion of a seduction seemed funny, and yet somehow inevitable, too. They were opposites, but opposites could definitely attract.

It wouldn't hurt to try, Alex thought.

She looked into his face with suspicion written all over hers. "What do you mean?" she asked.

"I want to keep my presence a secret. Until we find our crook, only you and Mrs. St. Cloud are going to know I'm here." He smiled. "Tonight you're going to smuggle me into the store before you meet your boyfriend."

"He is *not* my boyfriend!" Caroline objected at once.

Alex grinned. She looked beautifully outraged, precariously off balance. Even if Tommy hadn't suggested the plan, he wouldn't have been able to stop himself, he thought fleetingly. He bent and brushed his mouth across the soft curve of Caroline Conover's lips. They tasted warm and provocatively sweet. The contact he made had the same effect as an electric current—acting to pop her green eyes wide open with surprise. Her expression showed that she'd been completely taken aback by his impulse. So had Alex. The quick kiss had happened before he could think, but suddenly he wanted her whole body in his arms. He wanted to feel all of her, to see if the attraction was as strong as he thought it was.

He held back, though, and said, "He's not your boyfriend? That's very good to hear, partner."

The shock evaporated from Caroline's eyes as quickly as it had come. In its place in the next unguarded moment, Alex read something new. Interest. Curiosity. And the sparks of mutual attraction. Little girls learned a lot of things down on the farm, he knew. Like biology; earthy stuff with animals and birds and bees. Alex wondered how much she had learned during her sojourn in the fields and barns. She was an interesting combination of innocence and sophistication.

She was studying him, too, measuring and wondering things that put a speculative expression in her eyes. "Partner?" she repeated, trying the word out on her own tongue.

"That'll do for now," said Alex. "Come on. We've got things to do, Caroline."

CHAPTER FOUR

SITTING BESIDE HIM on the front seat of a rented Ford Taurus with the wipers swishing from side to side and the rain pulsing down the windows, Caroline willed herself not to panic. She didn't *want* a partner. She had been doing just fine without one! And Alexander Varanov was more of a distraction than anything else. He was even aggressive in the way he drove—passing cars and speeding through yellow lights unmindful of the rain. Like a New York cabbie, he was pushing the car to its limit, treating it roughly. In the eerie half light of the dashboard, he looked tough and preoccupied. His profile was hard as he watched the dark street ahead of them. He'd be at home in darkness, Caroline decided, sneaking a look at him. At night he was in his element.

No, he was not the kind of man she'd choose for a business partner.

As a lover, though, he'd be electric.

That thought startled Caroline. Where had it come from? Just watching him maneuver a car in and out of traffic? Speeding recklessly one minute and then reaching forward to turn on the heat when he noticed Caroline hugging her raincoat close to her body? Women of the eighties weren't supposed to fall for worldly, macho chauvinists with knives in their pockets and chips on their shoulders. She brought herself up short. Was she falling for him?

Suddenly Caroline wanted nothing more than for the drive to be over. She didn't want to answer that question. Sitting so close to the man gave her the jitters.

Finally Alex whipped the car into a downtown parking garage directly across a side street from St. Cloud's. When he'd plucked the ticket from the turnstile and rolled the car window up, he said, "Tell me what you know about store security."

Caroline jumped, having become accustomed to his silence. It was easier being with him when he didn't talk. Now he was demanding her participation, and she wanted to prove she could be as cool as he was. "Well, I told you about the passkey system."

"Right. What about forms of detection outside the store? Cameras, for instance?"

"They're around," Caroline said cautiously, putting a hand on the dashboard to steady her balance while he drove up into the parking area. "I haven't noticed specific locations exactly."

"Near the night watchman's station at the employee entrance?"

Caroline frowned, thinking. "No, there's no camera there. Not on the outside of the building, anyway." She stole a look at him. "This is starting to sound suspicious. How are you planning to get into the store?"

"We're not going to present our invitations at the door, that's for sure."

Her heart thudded. "You mean we're *breaking* in?"

He pulled into a parking space and glanced at her. "I thought you were the one willing to risk everything?"

"I am, but— Well, breaking and entering is so—"

"Crude? Not your style?" he taunted. "Relax, we're not going to be using a crowbar and sledgehammer." He put the car into park and shut off the engine. "You have your passkey with you tonight?"

"I— Yes, I do."

"Learned your lesson about keeping it in the locker, huh?"

Caroline thought she caught a flash of a grin, but Alex popped open his door and climbed out of the car before she could be sure. He slammed the door shut, and Caroline did not wait for him to come around and let her out of her side—which was a good thing. When she stepped out of the car and closed her own door, Varanov was already on his way across the floor of the garage to the stairwell.

He didn't even pretend to be a gentleman, she mused. Somehow, that was comforting. She preferred his bluntness. It made him easier to deal with, somehow. Caroline caught up with him on the landing, her high heels clicking on the concrete.

He plunged down the steps without waiting for her to catch up. He had taken charge of the plan, she realized. Clearly, Alex couldn't be just a partner: he intended to be the boss.

"Exactly what crime am I going to commit?" she asked, hustling down the steps after him. "Am I allowed to know that much?"

"Sure. When you use the passkey to open the door, I'm going to slip past the guards. No one will know I'm in the store."

"How do you expect to *slip* past two armed guards? You're not exactly the size of Tinkerbell."

"That," said Alex, "is where you come in."

"I was afraid you were going to say that."

He grinned and stopped at the door at the bottom of the stairwell. He held it for her this time. "We're going to use a technique called a diversion."

Caroline stopped in the doorway. "A diversion? That's covered in Chapter Three of the *Gumshoe's Manual*, I suppose."

"You have a nasty sarcastic streak, Miss Conover."

She brushed past him into the rain. "Just tell me what I'm supposed to do. I hate being impulsive."

"That attitude must make life boring."

"It makes life safe, which is the way I like it. What's my role in this diversion of yours?"

"Smile." He caught up and took her elbow. "Look like you belong with me."

"*That* will be a trick! You're not exactly every woman's dream, you know."

With one hand, he turned up the collar of his parka, and glanced up and down the street. It was empty on the drizzly night, so he escorted her—no, propelled was a better word—across the road. He didn't want to give her time to think things over and quit on him. "Just act happy to see me. Pretend I'm Alan Alda."

"This is not turning out to be an equal partnership, Varanov. You're giving all the orders. And not very politely, I might add. Alan Alda you ain't."

"You'll get your share of the action," he shot back, "you thrill seeker, you."

Under her breath, Caroline grumbled, "If a policeman comes along, ten to one I'm supposed to show him my legs."

He laughed rudely. "Don't do that. We don't want a traffic jam."

Caroline attempted to remove her arm from his grasp, but Alex held on tightly and they reached the curb.

"Take it easy," he said, steering her down the wet sidewalk. "That was a compliment. Here we go. We'll walk past the employee entrance first to make sure about cameras."

"Couldn't we have cased the joint from *inside* the car? It's raining!"

"We're a couple of star-crossed lovers too distracted by each other to notice the weather. For the benefit of the guards, how about looking mildly cheerful at least?"

Caroline took a deep breath and matched steps with him. The store's employee entrance loomed just half a block away. A blazing street lamp cast a glaring light onto the rain-soaked sidewalk directly in front of the security door. It made Caroline think automatically of prison searchlights. Quaking suddenly, she said, "I can't look cheerful."

"Think about something nice," he advised, his voice low.

She drew a blank, of course.

Out of the blue, Alex asked, "What are we having for dinner?"

"What?"

"Dinner," he repeated, scanning the side of the building for surveillance cameras. "I haven't eaten yet. I want to know what we're having tonight."

"How in heaven should I— All right, all right," she muttered. "Dinner. Let's see...."

They drew closer to the entrance where the security guards stood in a bulletproof glass cage. Alex's grip tightened on her arm. No cars traveled the shining street, and no other pedestrians were in sight. No doubt every sane person was inside out of the rain. In another two paces, they were within hearing range of the security booth. Rainwater streamed down the window, but Caroline could see two uniformed guards inside the cagelike enclosure. One was hunkered over a newspaper he'd spread out on the desk. The second man was reclining lazily in a swivel chair, viewing a set of five flickering video monitors while eating a Hostess fruit pie directly out of its wrapper. When Caroline and Alex came into view, the first guard glanced up from his paper. He used his forefinger to push his policeman-style cap off his forehead so he could get a better look at them.

Like a nervous understudy suddenly thrust onstage for the first time, Alex said, "What *would* you like for dinner tonight, uh, darling?"

Caroline clenched her teeth. "I'd like to get out of this rain before we drown, *dear*."

"A little water never hurt anyone, *sugarplum*."

"You could have at least brought an umbrella, *snookums*."

He pinched her arm harder. "Why don't we just grab some hamburgers and go back to your place, *hot stuff*. We can take turns licking catsup off each other."

"Not on your life," Caroline snapped. "You skunk!"

They ducked around the side of the building and instinctively flattened themselves there. Furious, Caroline burst out, "You idiot! What was *that* conversation supposed to prove?"

"Shut up," he commanded, wiping water off his forehead with his palm. "See the window down that way?" He pointed. "The last display window. I'm going down there and you'll stay here to—"

"You're *leaving* me here?"

"Watch for police cars," he ordered, all business once they were past the guard station. "Or anybody else who comes along. Only nitwits would be out in this rain, but you never know."

"Nitwits, hmm?"

He sent her a withering look and pulled a small, round-nosed hammer out of his pocket. Showing it to her surreptitiously, he explained, "I'm going to tap a little hole in the window—"

She couldn't stop the whimpering noise that escaped her throat, but Alex ignored it and kept on, saying, "I'll just make a hole big enough to set off the alarm, that's all. With luck, both guards will go looking for the trouble and leave the security booth. When the coast is clear, you can open the door with the passkey and I'll—"

"You'll show up in your own sweet time, right?"

He grinned suddenly and his eyes twinkled as he met her gaze. "Right. I'll teach you to call me names."

Caroline hunched her shoulders against a fresh blast of rain. "Tell me one thing before we go through with this."

"What?"

"Have you got a gun along with everything else in those magic pockets of yours?"

Amused, Alex shook his head. "Nope. Guns are out of my league, dear heart."

"Then you're truly an amateur at this stuff?"

He was going to answer, but a set of headlights swung around the corner and impaled them against the side of the store building. Sure enough, a police car nosed its way onto the otherwise deserted street and maneuvered toward them. Alex grabbed Caroline by both arms. "Don't move," he said tightly. "Kiss me."

"What?"

He didn't answer and pulled her closer. Caroline instinctively jammed her hands between them on his chest, but then she realized that one false move could land them both in jail. The police car slowed and eased closer to the curb. Panic swelled up inside Caroline. Against her palms she could feel Alex's heart beating, too, and its tearing rhythm nearly matched her own. She looked up into his face, wondering if it was because he was as scared as she was, or if he liked the excitement.

"What d'you think you're doing?"

"Trust me," he said. "It'll work." He delved one hand inside her coat and snaked his arm around her

back. Swiftly, he pulled Caroline against him so
firmly, she could feel the heat of his tall, dark body.
Every contour, too, in fact. His braced legs were
sturdy, his chest and belly taut and solid. He felt
strong, every inch a man and poised for danger—in
command and master of both their fates.

"Please—" she began.

He smothered her protest with his mouth.

For a first kiss, it was not the slightest bit sexy or
romantic. With the police cruiser's engine rumbling
just four yards away and the rain driving down around
them like a typhoon gone wild, Caroline was in no
mood to absorb any sexual overtures. But Alex's
mouth was warm, his arms were snug, and he was dry
inside that big coat of his, so she held on and let it
happen. He tasted sweet and faintly aromatic, and his
lips infused Caroline with a kind of liquid courage. He
broke the kiss before she could open her mouth to his,
though, and he made a pretense of nuzzling her throat.

"Make it look authentic," he muttered against her
ear, "can you?"

"I should bite your tongue," she murmured back.

"Try it," he said, and tilted her head back with one
hand weaving into her hair.

The second kiss made her forget the police car.
Alex's mouth grazed hers, then brushed her hairline,
her ear and the curve of her throat. Then he seized her
hair, and their embrace tightened convulsively. He
tilted her head so their gazes met and burned in-
tensely. Then he kissed her lips, and the contact stirred
her blood deep down. His left hand sank lower on her
back and dallied there, pressing Caroline more com-

pletely into his frame. He swiped his tongue across her lower lip and barely held back a laugh when she made a small sound. He *did* like the excitement! And, damn him, he was making *her* forget the danger they were in, too. When she caught his tongue in her teeth teasingly, he made a funny moan in the back of his throat, and Caroline choked on a laugh.

Then they were both laughing—laughing and kissing at the same time. Swiftly, he bent her backward, and Caroline gripped his shoulders tightly to keep from falling onto the sidewalk. For some reason she couldn't tear her mouth from his, though the voice of common sense was shrieking in the back of her mind. She was playacting, that was all—a wanton woman kissing her lover in a downpour.

The car was long gone, Caroline was sure, but he didn't stop and neither did she. She even wound her arms around his neck and pressed close to him. Alex went on kissing her until she couldn't stand it anymore. She felt a torrent of hot pinpricks surge through her body, the heat turning her inside out.

That response wasn't playacting. It was real. Too real.

Her mental faculties returned. What a fool she was! Kissing a strange man in the middle of all her troubles! Caroline finally wrenched free and pulled out of his grasp. She teetered slightly, catching her balance by reaching instinctively for his shoulders. He caught her, smiling arrogantly.

She glared at him through the rain. "That was the oldest movie ploy in the world, you know."

"Have you ever seen it fail?" he asked, letting go and looking positively triumphant in spite of the raindrops streaming off his nose.

"It might have, Varanov!"

"I think you can call me Alex now," he said easily. "You want to reconsider that crack about my amateur status?"

"I retract the comment," she said, unconsciously touching the back of her hand to her tender mouth. The police car had disappeared, and the kiss seemed to have fulfilled its purpose. Still, she fumed that he'd taken what he'd obviously wanted for some time. Caro didn't like being used. And then there was the matter of what he'd done to her. In just seconds, Caroline's common sense had been stormed by a mindless hormonal hurricane.

Smiling despite the rain at her sulky expression, Alex said, "Ready now?"

"Let's get this show over with!"

He saluted and set off walking along the side of the store. Feeling deserted, Caroline suddenly longed to dash after him or at least call him back. She was scared—petrified—and not just from being left to stand on a semidark street by herself. When he reached the last window Alex turned and looked back at her. Caroline checked for oncoming traffic, saw none, and nodded vigorously at him. Alex directed his attention to the window, swung the hammer smartly, and Caroline heard the sharp tinkle of breaking glass.

Immediately, a horrible alarm bell sounded.

Caroline clapped both hands over her mouth to stifle her scream. She hadn't expected the alarm to be so loud. It clanged like a firebell.

"Go!" Alex shouted.

She obeyed. Dashing around the edge of the building, Caroline didn't even notice if the guards were looking until it was too late. Fortunately, both men were in the act of bolting out of their booth and into the store. Caroline skidded to a stop in front of the door and waited a few seconds before she inserted the passkey. It stuck. She jiggled it, biting back a frustrated cry.

In the next second, Alex was behind her. He jammed the passkey to the left and heaved her through the doorway. Alex yanked the passkey out again, then crossed into the security booth. Caroline followed. A series of department keys hung on a pegboard, and she pointed. "There. The key to the salon."

He grabbed the key off its peg and turned to her.

"Which way?" he asked, panting.

Without pausing to think, Caroline led him up a wide set of stairs to the store. They entered the first floor at the Estée Lauder counter. It was dark, except for the emergency lighting. In the far corner near "Better Handbags," both security men were talking at once, shining flashlights to and fro. Caroline couldn't make out their words above the clang of the alarm system. Alex pushed her down, and they hid behind the counter.

From somewhere above them, Caroline suddenly heard barking.

"Dogs," she said, seizing Alex's sleeve. "I forgot about the dogs!"

Alex swiped a test-sized bottle of perfume off the counter, and then he pointed and pushed. Together, they sneaked along the counter, making their way toward the escalator. The barking came closer, and Caroline realized that the guard dogs had heard the alarm or had been summoned by dog whistles away from their usual patrol through the empty store. Barking madly, they were hurling themselves down the motionless escalators. Alex yanked the top off the bottle of perfume and sent a long stream of it splashing across the floor at the bottom of the escalator. Then he pulled Caroline back behind the cosmetics counter and they huddled there together, dripping rainwater and holding their breath.

The dogs—two Dobermans and a German shepherd—came flying down the escalator in a frenzy of angry noise. When they leaped off the escalator, they landed in the middle of a fog of Joy. Growling, the dogs milled around and began to sneeze and snort ferociously. Caroline squeezed her eyes shut and choked back a sob of genuine terror. She could hear the click of their teeth as they snapped at the pungent air.

But the dogs didn't see or smell her, thank heaven. The guards called to them, and they tore off past the cosmetics department, heading for their masters.

"Come on," whispered Alex. "Now's our chance."

He disengaged her hand, and Caroline realized she had been gripping his shirt with all her strength. Collecting her wits, she hustled after him, doubled over to avoid being spotted. Together, they dashed up the escalator.

On the second floor he paused and reached for her hand. "You okay?"

She grabbed for his support unashamedly. Her voice was shaky. "In a minute."

"Can you keep going? Okay, come on. They'll be busy downstairs for a while. Once we get up to the fur salon, is there a place we can hide where the dogs won't find us?"

Her heels kept getting caught in the grooves of the escalator steps, but she kept moving, holding on to Alex for help. She said, "The vault."

"Is it locked?"

"Yes, but the key's in my desk. I leave it there every night."

He nodded and drew her up the next flight of escalators. "Let's move."

"The dogs—" she said.

"It's okay," he murmured, still holding her hand as they hurried upward. "They won't catch us. The perfume ought to mess them up for a little while, at least."

"Listen, Alex," she panted, "I—I'm really afraid of dogs."

"What? I thought you lived on a farm."

"Alfalfa," she said. "We grew alfalfa and oats. Dogs terrify me."

"Wise woman," he said.

Pulling her up the escalator like that was when Alex decided he truly liked Caroline Conover. For all her prickly edges, she was rather nice underneath—and vulnerable. She gritted her teeth, fighting back her fear, and followed him without stopping.

They reached the top floor in a matter of a minute or two. Rain was pounding on the skylight and sounded like a waterfall in the empty store. Only the emergency lights lit their way, but they were enough. Alex handed the key to the salon to Caroline so she could do the honors. She was shaken up, and he figured a task might help her calm down again. Her hands trembled so badly it took three attempts before she got the door unlocked and open.

"That wasn't so tough," said Alex, closing the door behind them and sauntering into the salon. "Was it?"

"Are we— Can we hide in the vault now?" she asked in a very small voice. "Before the dogs come?"

One look at her, and all Alex wanted to do was take her into his arms again. She was a bedraggled version of the cool, crisp woman he'd met that morning—no longer the defiant tigress who had argued with him in the parlor of a crumbling old mansion. She looked so fragile with her wet blond hair hanging in waiflike tendrils around her pale face, he thought.

Without thinking, Alex used one finger to ease an especially wet lock of her hair away from her cheekbone. Her skin felt as soft as porcelain, but not nearly as cold. She smelled of exotic perfume—so did he, for that matter—but the scent of wet hair smelled even nicer, somehow. Yes, he wanted to take her shivering body into his arms there and then, but he knew what her reaction would be. He had seen the fire of outrage in her eyes after he'd kissed her. Fear had been reflected there at first, then passion—just a flicker of it—and then anger. The pretty Miss Conover wasn't as completely in control of herself as she liked to believe.

But she'd had enough for one night. A little jocularity was in order. Alex dropped his hand and said, "Sure, we can hide in the vault. I should have brought along some marshmallows to toast while we wait, but I wasn't thinking. When's your date with Rupert?"

She regarded him, fighting down all sorts of natural urges. But good girls didn't throw hysterics. Mustering some of her old pluck, she said, "At ten."

"Rupert may remember me. We met briefly a few months ago, and I've got to stay out of sight or he'll suspect something's up." Alex consulted his watch. "We've got an hour and a half to kill until then, but chances are the guards will take a walk around the store once they've got the window situation under control. I suggest we don't tarry. The vault keys are in the desk, you say?"

In a drawer, Caroline found the key that opened the refrigerated storage room where most of the fur inventory was kept. The vault opened easily and she slid the key into her pocket.

"It'll be dark in here," she warned. "Oh, here's a flashlight. I forgot—"

"Don't flash that damn thing in my eyes!"

"I wasn't! Just—"

"Turn it off," he ordered. "It'll give me a headache. Can't you see well enough in the dark?"

"I don't like the dark," she said, sounding very young all of a sudden.

"Afraid of the dark? Do you sleep with a night-light, Miss Conover?"

"It's none of your business what I sleep with," she said. "I should have remembered that skunks are nocturnal animals. Here."

She led him into the vault. Although he'd spent a great many hours in the workshops of Varanov Furriers, Alex had never gotten used to the cold-storage closets where the skins and coats had to be stored. The cold, in fact, was probably another thing that had driven him away from his family and their multimillion dollar enterprise. Alex liked things to be nice and warm. When the refrigerated air hit him in the face, he said, "It's freezing in here."

"It's forty-five degrees constantly. The best temperature for preserving the coats. You're the night owl. Don't you like cool places?"

"Dark places can be warm, too, you know. Body heat is better than sunlight, in my book."

Caroline ignored that. The vault was a room no more than fifteen feet long and half that wide. "There's a shipping crate over here," she said. "A place to sit, at least."

Alex laid one hand on the crate. "If you sit on that you're liable to freeze solid—you're soaked to the skin."

"It was raining outside," she said, eyeing him testily. "Or didn't you notice?"

"One kiss from you, and I lost my powers of perception. Take off the coat. We'll warm you up."

"That's an adolescent ploy, Mr. Varanov. Just because I'm a little wet doesn't mean I'll take my clothes off for you." Infuriated, she added, "This whole thing was a dumb idea. I don't need you tagging along while I talk to Rupert. You're jeopardizing everything I've done so far."

"*That's* a fine thing to say. Who do you suppose will come to the fair maiden's rescue when Rupert tries to jump your bones?"

"Jump my— For crying out loud! *You're* the one I ought to be leery of. Just what were you trying to get away with down on the street?"

"I didn't get anything you didn't want, too," he retorted. "You've been wondering about me since we met. I just satisfied your curiosity."

"Look, Varanov," Caroline began sternly, "you'd better get one thing straight. I'm here because I want to find out what happened to my sister. Nothing's going to get in my way. If you've got sex on your brain, you had better put a lid on it. I've got more important issues on my mind."

"Relax," he said. "I haven't got time for fun and games, either. I've got to find our culprit in one week or the whole deal gets turned over to the police. You're my only lead at the moment, and if this Rupert angle doesn't turn into something worthwhile, you can bet I'll go looking elsewhere."

Still miffed and not completely satisfied, Caroline said, "Fine. Just so we understand each other."

"Just so *you* understand something," Alex replied with force, underscoring his own determination to keep emotion and purpose far apart. "I don't intend to waste time while you pussyfoot around Rupert. If he wants to play slap and tickle, you'd better cooperate. String him along if you must, but get him to tell us something useful."

"Are you suggesting—"

"You were the one who said nothing would stop you," he snapped. "I presume you meant flirting with Rupert. I was just warming you up downstairs, that's all. That's what partnerships are for. I just hope you put a little more enthusiasm into your act when you're with him than you showed in my arms."

"You are," said Caroline, "the worst skunk I have ever met."

She was blushing, he was sure. She began to snatch off her soaked raincoat, but her fit of pique seemed to have made her clumsy. The sopping fabric stuck to her arm, and Alex had to help her out of the jacket.

"Get your paws off me," she snapped.

"My pleasure," he replied. He took down one of the coats hanging nearby. It was sable, if he was any judge of fur by touch. "Here, put this on."

"I'm wet," she said stubbornly, hugging herself against another onslaught of the shivers. "I'll ruin it."

"It's a coat, for Pete's sake. What good is it if you can't get it wet?"

Her back was up, though. She obviously didn't intend to accept any kindness from him. "It's worth a fortune and it doesn't belong to me!"

"It belongs to *me*, as a matter of fact—or my family, if you want to get technical."

"I don't *like* fur coats! I'm only working here until—"

"I know, I know. I have moral objections to killing animals for their skins myself, but this is an extenuat-

ing circumstance. Put the damn thing on! Your teeth
are chattering. Someone's going to hear."

With a curious glance at him, she turned and allowed him to help her into the enormous coat. He had
surprised her with his confession of moral objections.
She put on the garment and cuddled the collar pro-
tectively around her chin. Looking up at him, she
muttered, "There. Satisfied?"

No, he wasn't satisfied. His hands lingered on the
coat, feeling the contour of her shoulders beneath.
Alex remembered how she'd moved against him when
he'd kissed her. He felt a tug in his vitals at the thought
of what she must look like without any stupid coat
cloaking her body. He wanted to find out more about
the woman, to see her and touch her to satisfy himself.

But Alex stopped himself. As she had said, there
were more important matters to consider. His deadline was getting closer by the hour, and Alex was reminded that a lot of unfinished business between
himself and his father depended upon the success of
his mission. Alex decided he wanted to draw Caroline
out on a few points—without giving away the fact that
he knew more about Jane Wexler than he'd admitted
so far. He released her. "We've got time to kill, I
think," he said smoothly. "This is a good opportunity to hear your side of the story. I want to hear about
your sister. And you. What started this mission of
yours?"

She sighed, irritated at being put on the spot. But
there wasn't anything else they could do with their
time alone—short of continuing what they had started

on the sidewalk—so she began with a shrug. "I need some answers, that's all, and so do my parents. I want my sister's name cleared legally, and I want to know why she—why Jane did what she did." When Alex sat on the crate and patted the spot next to him, she added, "I meant what I said. Nothing's going to interfere with learning what happened to Jane. So don't get your hopes up, Varanov."

"My hopes couldn't be lower," he shot back. "I'm stuck in a refrigerator with a woman whose body temperature is probably below freezing anyway. Hell, we could turn off the air conditioner and let *you* keep the damn coats cold!"

She smiled, pleased that she'd managed to exasperate him. "Do you expect me to be friendly? After the way you treated me earlier today?"

"I thought you were a criminal," he objected, remembering he ought to be nice to her. "Anyway, I apologized. I'll do it again if you like. I'm sorry. We are on the same side now, you know. Sit down. I won't bite."

She had stood still during his outburst and remained standing for a moment afterward. Then she regally sat down on the shipping crate and arranged herself there, tucking the collar of the coat up around her chin with the air of a satisfied princess. She said, "All right, partner, suppose you tell me exactly what your connection to all this is. Information goes two ways. If you're not a professional investigator for your family, what are you, exactly? In the fur business somehow?"

"Heaven forbid. No, I have no ties to the family business. My father and uncle and brother are the Varanov Furriers. I left the family fold a long time ago, thank heaven. I have my own business."

"Which is?"

"Importing," he replied evasively. Why was *he* doing the talking, anyway?

"Fur importing?" she pressed.

"No, liquor. Vodka, to be exact."

He thought she was smiling. "That makes sense," she said. "But how did you get mixed up in this trouble?"

He shrugged. Uncomfortable telling his life's story to anyone, let alone this particular woman, he decided to be evasive. She didn't need to know about his motivation in coming to Chicago. "My father asked me to look into the matter," he said simply. "I was— I had some free time, so I agreed to help."

"Some free time?" she repeated, slanting a shrewd look up at him.

"You're no dummy, are you? All right," he admitted, "my business wasn't going too well. When my father asked for help, I had nothing better to do."

"That's all?" she asked. "No personal connection to the goings-on?"

He looked into her face. Had she inferred something by his tone of voice? Could she have seen there was something more to it than a simple request from his father? Alex had become a loner in recent years, and he hated to think he had given away family secrets in so short a time.

In the half darkness, it was hard to judge her expression, but Alex made a good guess. "What's the matter, Caroline? Don't you trust me?"

"I don't trust anyone," she said.

"Words to live by," Alex replied, then he paused, listening. "Did you hear that?"

Caroline stiffened. "What?"

"I think," said Alex, "that the dogs have found our trail. Don't say a word, all right?"

"Oh, God," she whispered, sliding instinctively closer to him.

"That's two words," said Alex, slipping one arm across her shoulders. "Now shut up."

CHAPTER FIVE

THE DOGS CAME BACK, all right. In the darkness of the cold vault, Caroline couldn't see their progress, but she could hear them with eerie clarity. As she pressed herself against the only person with her—one she wouldn't have chosen as a protector had she had a choice—Caroline heard the clamorous barking as the dogs came closer and closer to the fur salon.

"They're following our scent up the escalator," Alex said in her ear. "Damn, I thought they'd be busy downstairs a while longer."

"What can we do?"

"Do the guards have keys to this vault?"

"I don't know for sure. But probably. Oh, God, we're trapped!"

"Steady," he murmured.

The dogs stopped outside the salon doors. Enraged, they barked like mad and flung themselves at the glass. Each time, Caroline thought the impact of their bodies might shatter the doors. From farther away, she heard the shouts of one of the guards.

"Think fast," Alex ordered in her ear. "If they checked the computer, they know you're in the store. Brazen it out. You were supposed to meet Rupert. Just play it cool and pretend I'm not here."

Caroline turned toward him. "Alex—"

"Don't give me away," he said, pushing her to a standing position.

"I'm afraid!"

"Of the guards?"

"No, the dogs!"

"Think Walt Disney," he coached. He helped her off with the sable and thrust Caroline's coat into her hands. "Remember Pongo and Tramp and Old Yeller. Now, go. The guards are probably on their way."

Caroline tottered out of the vault just in time. She could see the furiously barking dogs as they danced on the other side of the salon doors, and beyond them, the bobbing beam of a high-powered flashlight. The store's emergency lights provided just enough illumination for her to make out the silhouette of the man who approached.

Steeling herself, Caroline went as far as the salon doors. The dogs spotted her right away and flew into a frenzy of barking. Streaks of saliva splotched the doors.

Caroline raised her hand to the man with the flashlight.

"Hello?" she called through the glass.

The flashlight caught her straight across the eyes and she flinched from it. The guard's belligerent voice demanded, "Who are you?"

"I'm Caroline Conover. I work up here," she said. "Rupert Watkins, the store manager, asked me to meet him here tonight."

"Conover? Ain't you the lady we're supposed to be on the lookout for?"

"Well, I—"

The flashlight didn't waver from her eyes, nor did the guard command the dogs to be quiet. To Caroline, he said, "You got any ID?"

She'd left her handbag on the desk. Shaking, Caroline retrieved it and found her passkey, complete with its tiny photograph in the top right-hand corner. She returned to the door and held it up for the guard to examine. "I'm sorry I caused a fuss. I'm supposed to meet Mr. Watkins. I wouldn't be stealing anything if I was going to meet him, would I?"

He trained the flashlight on the passkey, then let the light trail down Caroline's body. He studied her legs, then brought the light back up.

Finally, he switched it off. "Zack, quiet! Spinks, Lobo, down!"

He was the guard who'd been eating the Hostess fruit pie, Caroline realized, and she thanked her lucky stars. The other one might have recognized her from her walk past the station. When the dogs settled down, she unlocked the door and cracked it open. The German shepherd named Lobo sniffed her knees suspiciously. He wasn't as appreciative of her legs as his master, apparently.

Caroline gave a nervous smile—one she didn't have to fake. "They're pretty scary, aren't they?"

"Tonight they're fired up, all right," drawled Hostess Fruit Pie, snapping short leashes on two of the three dogs. "Somebody broke a window downstairs. A lot of activity. You're here to see Mr. Watkins, you say?"

"Yes, we were supposed to have a meeting. Nobody stopped me at the employee entrance, so I came up here to wait. The dogs—I'm truly sorry if I caused a problem."

"Oh, no problem, ma'am. They like the exercise. Come downstairs, though. You can wait in our booth."

"All right," said Caroline. "Let me get my coat."

She returned to the desk for the garment and had sense enough to leave the salon key right where Alex would be sure to find it. He'd never get out, otherwise.

With her wet coat over her arm, Caroline accompanied the guard and the three dogs downstairs. On the way, she found a pair of bobby pins in her handbag, and she used them to alter her hairstyle—pulling the hair up, twisting it sharply and anchoring the whole wet mess at the crown of her head. Nothing chic, but it was just enough of a change, she hoped, to confuse the other guard. With a little luck and bad lighting, he might not associate her with the woman who had walked by the employee entrance just half an hour before.

Caroline spent a brief moment hoping Alex Varanov could take care of himself. She had her own skin to worry about.

Fortunately, the second guard was too busy resetting various alarms and other such things to be much interested in Caroline. She sat outside the booth on a folding chair with Zack and Lobo and Spinks lying alertly at her feet and Hostess Fruit Pie ogling her legs and making conversation. The best topic seemed to be guard dogs.

"Oh, yes," he said, rubbing Lobo's ears with affection, "these boys could rip a man's arm off if they wanted to. Why, back in my home town in Kentucky, I saw dogs that could kill a full-grown man in less than a minute."

"You don't say," Caroline murmured.

"Sure! And there's no telling what might happen if these boys got hold of a man's throat!"

Fortunately, Rupert showed up in less than half an hour.

Rupert Watkins, St. Cloud's manager, was a svelte, poised man with an amazingly good tan for a Chicago resident, slender, manicured hands and prematurely salt-and-pepper hair. Caroline suspected he cashed in on his vague resemblance to Ralph Lauren by wearing stone-washed denims during his off-hours, but during working hours, he could be seen in suits by Alexander Julian or Armani. He wasn't a fool, though. He had sharp eyes that foretold a quick brain. He took one look at Caroline's drenched clothing and immediately asked questions.

When he'd heard the guards' story, Caroline gathered herself together for a performance. "Rupert," she said, mustering heartfelt contrition, "I'm so sorry I caused such a fuss."

"It wasn't all her fault," Hostess Fruit Pie interrupted generously. "Somebody outside the building broke the window. She was an innocent bystander, that's all."

Rupert shot a fish-eye look at the guard that told him to shut up. Then he clasped Caroline's hands and devoted his full attention to her. For all his cosmopolitan manners, Rupert had one quality that seemed to be in glaring contradiction to the sophisticated image he projected. He still talked like a boy from the Bronx. In fact, he still talked like a boy from the Bronx whose father was a gangster.

"Caroline," he said when he'd heard everything, "I shoulda warned you about the dogs in the store. I blame myself. I coulda had the boys take you to my office and spare you this unhappy ordeal."

"It wasn't really an ordeal," Caroline said. "I just waited in the salon until this very kind gentleman arrived to call off the dogs." She gestured to indicate Hostess Fruit Pie, who was lingering close by.

"I'm Bob," he said, blushing.

"Bob, then." Caroline beamed affectionately at the endearing young man from Kentucky. "These fellows really do their job, Rupert. The men *and* the dogs. I was so impressed."

"Yeah," said Rupert, eyeing Bob while Bob ogled Caroline's legs some more. "The boy's are okay." He let go of Caroline and gave Bob four hard pats across his cheek to punctuate his words. "They're—definitely—o—kay."

Bob blinked. He touched his cheek and tested his jaw to see if it was still working.

Caroline said, "I can't imagine how any thief could get past them to steal fur coats."

"Let's don't talk about that business tonight." Rupert turned his back on Bob and slipped his arm through Caroline's again. He pulled her away a few steps, smiling with oodles of charm. "We need a break from all that unpleasantness, am I right? After today, I thought to myself, let's me and Caroline have a nice quiet tête-à-tête and get to know each other better. But I oughta check the damage to the store first." He patted her hand. "Then we'll go out for a drink, okay?"

"Fine," Caroline replied, relieved that she would still be meeting with him. "But I'll stay in the booth while you look around, all right? Spinks is a sweetie, but Lobo and Zack make me nervous."

Smiling, Rupert patted her hand some more. Then he turned, grabbed Bob by his tie and set off to assess the damage caused by the broken window. The other guard and the dogs trotted after them.

When she was alone, Caroline hurried into the guard's station to the swivel chair in front of the video monitors. Each screen showed a different location in the store. On the top row, Caroline recognized the jewelry counters and the housewares and electronics departments. She sat down, scanning the screens.

"Alex," she murmured, "where are you?"

Whether Alex realized it or not, he was trapped. Once Caroline and Rupert left the store, another chance to escape might not come up until the store opened again on Monday morning. Unless another diversion drew the guards and the dogs away from their posts, Alex was stuck. Frantically, Caroline tried to concoct an idea.

"Fire alarms?" she asked herself. "That's too risky. The place will be crawling with firemen all night."

Risks? Alex liked those, apparently. Before Caroline could figure out a way to divert the security team's attention, she noticed a movement on one of the video monitors. Taking a closer look, she immediately saw Alex—plain as day—sneaking out of the fur salon. As she watched, Alex pocketed her key and headed toward the escalator.

"Hurry up, you maniac," she muttered.

He started down, and went out of camera range. Caroline quickly searched the other monitors for a glimpse of his progress, but he didn't appear again. Straining, Caroline listened and watched.

Caroline calculated that it would take him two minutes at the most to make the trip down the escalators. But then she heard voices, and suddenly she knew Alex wasn't going to make it. The guards and Rupert were returning to the security booth.

How was Alex going to get out of the store undetected?

There was only one answer.

Like a bullet, Caroline shot out of the security booth to intercept Rupert and cause another diversion. The three men and the three dogs were just passing the cosmetics department when Caroline showed up.

"Rupert!"

"Caroline, what's wrong?"

"I got frightened," she said, automatically veering away from Lobo's inquisitive nose as he strained on his leash to get a good sniff of her knees. She blundered into Bob's arms, but the poor man reacted as though she were a hot potato. Caroline headed for

Rupert, and his hands closed firmly on her shoulders. Breathlessly, she said, "It's so strange being in the store at this time of night, and with all the excitement, I just— I couldn't—"

"Take it easy."

Hugging Rupert, Caroline looked over his shoulder and spotted Alex. Quick as a cat burglar, he ducked as he came off the escalator and made a beeline for the perfumes again. Nobody else saw him. But Lobo turned, his ears pricking at the sound of Alex's nearly noiseless footsteps.

Suddenly Caroline let out a strangled moan and put her hand to her forehead, trying for all the world to swoon like Miss Pittypat did whenever Scarlett O'Hara committed an indiscretion.

"What the— Caroline!" Rupert shot forward to save her from falling.

But he didn't make it in time, and Caroline discovered that faking a faint could be a painful experience. She clonked her head on the marble floor, and knew immediately that the bump was going to be a beauty. But the effect was worth it. Both the guards and Rupert quickly rushed to her aid, and the dogs began to bark and whine with excitement.

In all the turmoil, Caroline couldn't tell if Alex got out of the store or not.

ON THE STREET, Alex ducked around an idling newspaper truck and arrived in the parking garage panting as if he'd run a marathon. He bounded up to the second floor in hopes of watching the store entrance from that vantage point. He cut between cars, plastered himself up against a pillar and peered around it, over the low wall to the sidewalk below. With a cloud of perfume wafting around him, he waited and watched.

In a few minutes, Caroline came out of the store on the arm of Rupert Watkins. From where he was hiding, Alex thought she looked unsteady—like a woman who had just awakened from a dead faint. She seemed to be hanging on to Rupert pretty tightly, and Rupert was responding by wrapping his arm around her body. Caroline looked grateful for the support.

Alex found himself muttering. ''I hope that's an act.''

Rupert helped her into the passenger seat of the Mercedes he'd left parked at the curb. A moment later, they drove off together.

Standing in the parking garage, Alex said aloud, ''Now what?''

He hadn't figured on getting left out of the action.

So he drove the rental car to his hotel, went up to his room and phoned Caroline Conover's house. Her answering machine picked up the call.

''Hello,'' said Caroline's husky voice. ''You have just reached—''

Alex hung up. She hadn't gotten home yet, of course. The other possibility was that Rupert *had* taken her to the house, but for some reason she wasn't answering the phone. Alex decided he liked that alternative the least. Even from a distance, Rupert Watkins looked like the kind of guy pictured on the cover of *Gentleman's Quarterly*. No, that wasn't it. He was like the character in the perfume ads—crouching near a campfire wearing exquisitely clean jeans, the kind of ultracivilized man women swooned over.

To ease his hunger pangs as well as his disgruntlement, Alex called room service.

"I'm sorry, sir," said the voice from the hotel kitchen. "We don't offer room service after eleven o'clock."

So he walked down the hall to the vending machines and bought three cellophane bags of pretzels and a root beer. To hell with his diet. Before heading back to his room, Alex added a Snickers bar to his cache of food. Sitting on the edge of his bed and dialing Caroline's number over and over again, he devoured the feast. She didn't answer.

Finally, Alex dozed off. He dreamed, too. He dreamed Caroline was swimming in root beer and calling for him. He couldn't get to her because somebody was holding his leg. And when he looked down to see who it was, he saw himself. It was a weird sensation. He was holding himself back.

Alex awoke, startled, when the silence of his room was split by the sound of his telephone ringing. Groggily, he picked it up and collapsed back onto the bed, the receiver at his ear.

"Varanov, you skunk," said Caroline plain as daylight in his ear, "the least you could have done was tell me which hotel you were staying in."

Eyes still closed, Alex asked, "What time is it?"

"Three-thirty," she said. "I've been calling every hotel in town trying to find you."

"So you found me." Her voice didn't rouse him. Listening to her, in fact, made him relax even more. If he closed his eyes, he could imagine her lying there beside him.

"I was worried," she said finally. "I wasn't sure you'd gotten out of the store safely."

She was worried. For some reason, that sounded good, too. Alex slid one arm under his head and stretched, grinning to himself. Then he remembered what he'd seen from the parking garage—Caroline smiling gratefully into the handsome puss of Rupert Watkins. Alex pulled himself up short. "Well? What happened with the boss man?"

"A few things," Caroline said. "Alex, I think we're getting somewhere."

Alex sat up. "He told you something?"

"Just hints, mostly. But I think Rupert's a good starting place. Mostly, I just listened tonight. He talked a lot—trying to impress me, coming on a little. We went to a *very* expensive restaurant. With dancing. I think he's got a plan up his sleeve."

"I'll bet he does," said Alex, letting the implication hang between them.

"Not sex," she objected. Then Caroline laughed ruefully. "Well, I guess it *was* sex. We had wine and sat at a candlelit table in a corner making eyes at each other. But I think he's got more on his mind than that."

"Making eyes? Stick to the pertinent facts, will you? How can you tell he's got more on his mind?"

"What's the matter, Alex?" she asked coolly. "You sound grumpier than usual. Did I interrupt a particularly skunky dream?"

"What the hell does a skunk dream about?" he grumbled.

"*I'm* asking *you*," she replied liltingly.

"Girl skunks," he snapped. "I'd describe the good parts, but you'd probably hang up."

"You might be surprised," she said, amused.

"Why? Did Rupert turn you on, Miss Conover? Now you're calling me for a little satisfaction?"

That got her. "I just called because I thought you'd like to hear what happened," she said, "but it sounds like you want to get back to your fantasy, so—"

"I want to hear everything. Just leave out the wine and candles, will you? Start talking."

"Forget it," she said airily. "I'm going to bed. From the sound of things, I would advise you to get some sleep, too."

"I *was* sleeping," he growled. "Now I'm probably awake for the rest of the night." He didn't want to end the conversation. Aggravating as she was, Caroline had kindled a very pleasant warm spot deep down in Alex's chest. Better to apologize and keep her talking. "I'm sorry I was a grouch, Caroline," he said contritely. "Just talk and I'll listen like a good boy."

"It's too late. Bye, Alex."

"Meet me in the morning," he said hurriedly, clutching the receiver as if that might keep her on the line. "Here at the hotel—neutral ground. I'll buy you breakfast—"

"Make it brunch," she said. "I want to sleep late. I have a few fantasies of my own."

Alex groaned. He heard her laughing as she hung up.

He tried to sleep, but after an hour, he knew he couldn't. His head had begun to hurt. Alex recognized the aura of twinkling lights behind his eyes, and knew he'd somehow triggered one of his headaches. His diet had been miserable lately, and he hadn't been sleeping well. But stress was probably the trigger—he'd certainly experienced more than his usual allotment of that in recent days.

He got out of bed unsteadily. The headache was out of control already, and it promised to be a skull splitter. He took his last pill and knew within a few minutes it wasn't going to be enough.

In pain, Alex got up and took a shower to wash off the lingering scent of Joy, but that didn't help, either. By the time dawn began to break, he hadn't slept. And his head pounded.

BETSY NOFSINGER WAS SURPRISED and delighted by the phone call that woke her early Sunday morning. An invitation to brunch! It sounded so sophisticated.

She changed her outfit three times before deciding on a sexy red dress she'd bought with the last of the money she'd made working at the ice-cream stand in Chesterville. Looking at herself in the mirror, Betsy tried to imagine what Miss Conover might wear to a brunch date. She was so sophisticated. She'd probably wear a dress, wouldn't she? Not a suit or something sporty. Betsy made her mind up. Yes, the red dress would be Miss Conover's choice, too.

Lately, Betsy had done a lot of imagining what Miss Conover would do in certain circumstances. Betsy wanted to be just like her. She had even made an appointment to have her hair cut the way Miss Conover wore hers. Miss Conover had everything—great hair, great figure . . . great everything.

Except for one thing. She didn't have a date for brunch, Betsy was willing to bet. Not with the manager of the whole store.

Mr. Watkins had said he could do things for her, and Betsy intended to take him up on the offer. She wanted to be a head clerk like Miss Conover, and Mr. Watkins could undoubtedly promote her soon.

"He practically promised," Betsy said to her reflection.

She was prepared to do anything he wanted. Maybe if she had Mr. Watkins as a boyfriend, people like Miss Conover would want to be her friend.

Betsy grabbed her purse and headed out.

CAROLINE SLEPT LATE on Sunday morning and awoke gradually, fuzzy, rather pleasant dreams playing around in her head. Sunlight played through the curtains and Caroline reluctantly roused herself to greet the day. Deliberately, she decided not to think about her evening with Rupert Watkins. That could wait. For the moment, she wanted to enjoy the morning. It was her favorite time of day, and she didn't want to darken it with the memory of Rupert Watkins's face across the table from her.

She showered quickly, shampooed and blew her hair dry until it was very full, then dressed in a long, full skirt and boots to make up for yesterday's minidress. As she drove into town, she realized she was feeling happier than she'd felt in a long time.

What was the cause? She wasn't sure. It wasn't her meeting with Rupert. That had been education, not pleasure. No doubt it was knowing she'd made *some* progress on Jane's case that had provoked the first rays of happiness Caroline had experienced in a long while.

She picked up a courtesy phone in the Hilton's cavernous lobby. "Alex Varanov's room, please."

The hotel's phone system clicked and the call rang through to Alex's room. Except he didn't pick up the phone. The phone rang and rang, but there was no answer.

Caroline hung up and went looking for him. She checked the restaurant and the lobby. She asked around, then called his room again. But Alex had disappeared.

"Where could he have gotten to?" She stood in the lobby, tapping her foot and wondering.

"Miss Conover!" called a voice.

But it was a woman's voice. Caroline turned and saw Betsy, her assistant clerk from St. Cloud's. The young woman hurried down the curving stairs and across the carpeted expanse of the lobby's main floor. Sans glasses, she looked quite different to Caroline. Her eyes were lavishly made up and her lipstick was a vivid red.

"What a surprise! Miss Conover, what are you doing here?"

"Um, I'm meeting a friend." Startled by having encountered a co-worker in an unexpected place, Caroline couldn't think up a lie in time.

Betsy smiled coquettishly. "A boyfriend?"

"No, I—just a friend. What about you? You look marvelous this morning!"

Betsy laughed and preened. Her dress was slinky and red, more of a Saturday night seduction getup than Sunday morning attire, Caroline thought. Betsy spun in a circle, causing the dress to float around her legs. "Do you like it? I've got a date. Brunch and whatever comes next." She giggled. "We may end up in a room of our own!"

"I see," Caroline said faintly.

"Pretty classy hotel, huh? This is where you come with older men, I guess."

"It's a nice hotel, yes."

"Well, I've got to run. Can't be late!" She wrinkled up her nose like a cute rabbit and waved her fingertips. "See you at work!"

Caroline waved halfheartedly. "Bye, Betsy."

What a sweet girl, she thought. She never would have expected the young woman to have such a sophisticated sex life. Then Caroline scolded herself. Not everybody was a prude like her. She watched Betsy swish toward the restaurant.

Suddenly, a man stepped out to meet her. Caroline nearly choked. Hastily, she stepped under the curve of the stairs so as not to be seen, then couldn't resist peeping once more to be sure. It was Rupert Watkins! He extended his arm. Betsy giggled and accepted it, and together they sashayed into the restaurant.

Caroline was floored. She gave up looking for Alex. Too stunned by what she'd seen, she pushed through the revolving door of the hotel to escape.

Pushing his way *into* the hotel, however, was Alex. They looked at each other through the glass, and she saw his face clearly. "Alex!"

He saw her, too. Alex went around again and came out onto the sidewalk to join her. Looking very tall and vaguely satanic in a black leather jacket, he was a far cry from Rupert Watkins's style of handsome. Alex was larger than life, and his impressive presence jolted Caroline. Overnight, she had forgotten what an impact his appearance had on her.

The sunlight was bright on the sidewalk. Alex winced like a vampire confronting daylight, and he quickly put his dark-lensed sunglasses back on again.

Caroline realized he was white. And he seemed preoccupied—distant and perturbed. "Alex, what's— you look terrible!"

"Thanks," he said sourly. "You, on the other hand, don't look any worse for last night's wear."

"I mean it, Alex! What's wrong?"

Alex figured he looked pale and shaky. People didn't expect big, tough guys like him to get sick, and Caroline was clearly surprised by his appearance. She grasped his arm, and Alex reeled a little.

"Alex!"

"It's just a headache," he said quickly. "I get them now and then. I just got some tablets, so it'll go away in a few minutes."

It had already let up somewhat. He had gulped down a couple of prescription pills right in the pharmacy. It was his own fault for traveling without his usual full supply. He'd let last night's headache get out of control. A poor diet and lousy sleep, not to mention the sexual tension that arose in the company of a particular sassy blonde, all added up to a headache of epic proportions. He should have known better.

The headaches had plagued Alex since he was thirteen, but it wasn't until his college days that he was able to describe exactly what the pain was like. It felt like a wild fraternity party was being thrown inside his skull—one with plenty of loud music and strobe lights. Even the sour taste of stale beer seemed to linger in his mouth. The inside of his eyelids felt as if they had a rash on them from too much cigarette smoke. And sometimes the clamor in his head was so loud and terrible that his vision was affected. He saw double images regularly and even triple images when the agony was at its height. The headaches were a large part of the reason he couldn't make a go of his business. There were days upon days when he simply couldn't concentrate. He willed his mind away from the pain and looked at Caroline.

Seeing triple images of her wasn't such a bad thing, he decided as he looked her up and down. She had dressed in a bright, multicolored skirt that clung to her hips with the help of a sashed scarf, and a loose, sky-blue blouse that somehow called more attention to her curving breasts than a skin-tight swimsuit might have. A delicate silver filigree necklace teased the smooth skin at her neck. Her hair, obviously freshly brushed, looked soft and tempting. The sunlight cast a brightness into her blue-green eyes that rendered them nearly impossible to look away from. She looked radiant, there on the sidewalk. Bright and alert and lovely. He felt a queer tug in his chest.

Just gazing at her seemed to ease the pain in Alex's head. Maybe he wouldn't need to go relax in the soothing darkness of his hotel room. Maybe a couple of hours of looking at her would cure him this time.

"Are you sure you'll be all right?" she asked.

"Yeah," he said manfully. "I'm just hungry."

"The restaurant still has our reservation. But I think you'd better—"

"No restaurants," he said, catching her arm as she started to walk past him toward the hotel door. The momentum swung her around so that they bumped gently, thigh to thigh. It felt good, that small contact. It made Alex think of their time together last night— when he'd kissed her...when he'd held her tightly against him.

"I don't feel like sitting inside," he said, impulsively deciding to brave the bright sunlight. "It's warm enough. Let's take a walk and see what we find."

"You're sure?"

"Yes," he said. Suddenly he wanted to explore a lot of things with Caroline Conover. He'd had enough of darkness for a while. It might feel good to look around the world in daylight.

CHAPTER SIX

AT A BANQUETTE in the restaurant, Betsy tried very hard to remember all her manners. She'd been brought up pretty strictly by most standards, but suddenly she was glad her mother had been so fussy about behaving right at the table. She wanted to impress Mr. Watkins. With her napkin in her lap, her elbows off the table and her feet flat on the floor, she accepted the glass of wine Mr. Watkins poured for her and took a sip.

"Oh," she said, swallowing the stuff bravely, "it's really good."

"Kinda on the sweet side," Mr. Watkins replied after he had sampled the vintage. "But it'll do. Now." He leaned forward and looked carefully into Betsy's face. "Let's talk about you."

"Me?" Betsy giggled and tried to stop herself. *Keep it dignified,* she thought, rearranging her expression. "What about me?"

"Have you thought over what I suggested the other night?"

Betsy gulped then, not sure how to answer. "You mean—"

"About the coats. Do you want to help me this time?"

"I—well—"

"I could do so much better if I had a helper. And you need the money, right? For those new clothes you wanted? And a car?"

Having worked in the department store for a while, Betsy was acutely aware of her youth. She needed so many things before she could be treated like an adult. A real apartment, for example, would be so much nicer than a room with a kitchenette. And lately she had taken to strolling past an automobile showroom just to look at the sporty little convertible they had in the window. Men like Mr. Watkins were sure to notice her more if she drove a fancy car. And it would be so neat having Mr. Watkins for a boyfriend!

Betsy nodded. "I could use some extra money."

"Good," said Rupert Watkins. "Then it's settled."

"But—" Betsy fought with her feelings, and finally said, "I just—I'm worried, that's all."

"Worried?" he repeated, sounding surprised. His graying eyebrows rose gracefully, like a movie star's. "Worried about what?"

"What if we get caught?"

"We won't get caught. I know a man on the security team, and he'll take care of us." He swirled the wine in his glass and sniffed it appreciatively. "It's only a matter of slippin' in and slippin' out."

"But," she began cautiously, "don't you think it's—well, wrong?"

"Wrong? What's wrong? To lift a few things from the store?" Mr. Watkins set down his glass and scoffed, "Honey, you must be a raw beginner. Nobody thinks twice about taking a few things home from a big store like St. Cloud's."

"Well—"

"C'mon," said Mr. Watkins. "Didn't you ever take a pencil from the teacher's desk? A towel from a hotel? An ashtray from a bar? It's natural!"

"Natural?"

"Sure. Businesses count on having a few things lifted. They build it into the operating expenses. A coupla coats won't be missed."

"They're worth a lot of money, though," Betsy offered carefully.

"Not as much as you think. I know a guy who'll take 'em off our hands, but his price won't come near what some society dame would shell out. The price of coats is inflated. The store won't miss 'em for long. And the store expects the employees to take a little something home now and then. It's part of the game."

"It is?" She was doubtful.

"Sure! Someone like you gets paid slave wages, right? So you oughta be allowed an occasional take-home present, I always say. It'll be fine. And easy."

"How easy?"

Mr. Watkins leaned closer and patted Betsy's hand. "Easy as pie, honey. Easy as pie."

Betsy looked at him without speaking. He was so good-looking for an older guy—and so sophisticated. The kind of guy Miss Conover would date. He knew all about wines and food and the price of luxury merchandise. He was pretty neat, Betsy decided. And the look in his eye was very complimentary.

"Besides," he added, dropping his voice to a murmur, "it'll give us a chance to spend a night together."

"A night?"

"Sure." His touch on her hand became a caress. "A whole night."

CAROLINE AND ALEX set off down the sidewalk together. Alex looked better and better with each passing minute, and finally Caro was reminded of what she'd witnessed in the hotel. "The strangest thing just happened," she said. "I saw Betsy, the woman I work with at the store, in the lobby."

"What's so strange about that?"

"You won't believe it. She was meeting Rupert."

"Aha. So Betsy's involved with the boss."

"Yes, and—she hinted she was joining him for more than a meal."

"Did she now?"

"It's—well, I think she—it's—"

"What's wrong?"

"It's upsetting, that's all."

"Upsetting?" The word amused Alex. "Why?"

"Seeing her go off like that—I don't know. She looked like a lamb headed for slaughter. She's so young."

"Young or old, the urges are the same." Alex shrugged and kept walking. "The way I see it, Rupert has chosen to work on her instead of you. That puts a crimp in our plans, if you ask me. I thought the seduction went well last night."

Trust Alex to miss the point, Caroline thought, sighing. "You're such a skunk," she said.

"I know." He sounded unaffected by the criticism, and because of the sunglasses, she couldn't see if he was dismayed in the least. He seemed out of sorts, but not miffed at her remark. All business, he asked, "What happened last night? I didn't get a full report out of you on the phone. Fill in the empty spaces for me."

Caroline nodded, acknowledging to herself that she and Alex were partners, nothing more. He wasn't bothered by Betsy's situation any more than he was bothered by the idea that Caroline had spent an evening with a totally unpleasant man just for the purpose of extracting information. Caroline, on the other hand, felt decidedly unclean. She had put off thinking about her rendezvous with Rupert. Suddenly she wanted to keep on putting it off. But Alex was right. They had a job to do. She ought to be more tough-minded, she told herself. She needed a thicker skin.

She walked quickly beside him, as if the brisk pace might get the interview over more swiftly. "All right," she said. "When Rupert and I left the store, we went to DelFabo's. It's a restaurant and night spot overlooking the lake—"

"Skip the color commentary," he suggested. "It wrecks my concentration."

She sighed, annoyed that he couldn't be civil, at least. "We went to the restaurant, ordered drinks and chatted for a while. Nothing earth-shattering. Rupert did most of the talking. He assumed I was upset about having fainted in the store—"

"That was good thinking, by the way—faking the faint."

Caroline glanced up at him. "How did you know I was faking?"

"You may not be the silver spoon type," said Alex, "but you aren't a sissy, either."

"Thanks," she said tartly, hoping she could continue to live up to that reputation. "I *did* save your neck, in case you hadn't noticed."

"Did you?"

Caroline sighed again. Grouchy didn't even describe his mood. He was a bear this morning. "Anyway, at the restaurant I let Rupert talk. He asked about me after a while, and I was evasive—but friendly. Pretty soon he started asking me if I moonlighted."

"What did he mean by that?"

"If I had another job or not. He said a lot of the women who work at St. Cloud's also have part-time employment on the side."

"Is that true?"

"Not that I've heard. Being a clerk is not as easy as I thought. It's a physically wearing job. I can't imagine having enough energy to go somewhere else to work after a full day. Go ahead. Tease me about being a weakling."

Alex didn't bother. He continued to walk, stepping off the curb and going across the intersection. In his black leather and sunglasses, he made a pretty intimidating picture, Caroline thought. He looked like a Mafia prince. He appeared to be frowning. "So Rupert asked about moonlighting," he said slowly.

"Right. He said if I was interested in other work, he might be able to help me find another job. I said I was very interested."

"Good."

"I made up a story about lots of bills and wanting some furniture. He thinks I'm anxious to get rich. He said he'd ask around to see if there were any openings for me and get in touch in a couple of days." She hesitated. "Actually, he said he'd call me today, but I don't think that was in reference to the job idea."

"What was it in reference to?"

"Friendship," Caroline replied steadily.

He glanced down. "You want to be friends with a criminal?"

"We don't *know* if he's a criminal," she retorted. "Rupert just might be a conscientious manager who looks out for his employees. You said that yourself."

"That was before I knew he invited women for brunch and bedroom games on Sundays or suggested they meet him at ten o'clock at night in the empty store."

"Last night was nothing. He only wanted to talk."

Alex snorted. "Don't kid yourself."

"For heaven's sake—"

"C'mon," he said, irritated. "If he only wanted to talk, he'd have set up the meeting at a time when there were other people in the store. Or he could have met you someplace public—a restaurant, for instance. The guy's a crook. The whole setup smells."

Smoothly, Caro said, "Maybe your nose is just out of joint."

Alex missed a stride and tilted his sunglasses to look down at her. "What?"

Sure she was right, Caroline said blithely, "You wanted to get all the action last night, that's all. I got to play detective instead of you, so you're reacting like a jealous little brother."

"I am not jealous," Alex said with as much dignity as he could manage. The fact that his whole scheme for last night had backfired *was* grating on him—not to mention how his imagination had played with the scenario of Caroline and Rupert alone together. His tone was frosty when he spoke again. "What do you think Rupert is up to, Miss Marple? You don't think he's our man?"

"Yes, I do," she said reluctantly. "If I was the kind of woman to make guesses, I'd say that Rupert Watkins is recruiting."

"Oho," said Alex.

She glanced up, her face polite. "Oho?"

"That's detective talk. You'll get the hang of it. So Rupert recruits from St. Cloud's employment lists."

"I think so."

"First he feeds 'em, beds 'em and then he uses them to help steal merchandise."

"I don't *know* that—"

"But it's probably true. Even you, Miss Sweetness and Light, have to admit that's what it looks like."

"It's so disgusting!" Caroline said, throwing her head back to look up at the sky and draw a clean breath of air.

Alex shrugged. "It happens. It's a pretty sweet setup if he can pull it off. If I were you, though, I'd be offended."

"Offended? Why?"

Alex grinned. "He didn't invite *you* to the Hilton, did he? He must have figured you were an easy target. I mean, why pay a hundred bucks for a hotel room when you've got a perfectly good setting for romance in the workplace?"

"Exactly what are you babbling about?"

He shoved his hands into his pockets. "A woman Betsy's age needs a seduction like she's seen in the movies—wine and violins and tapestry on the walls. You're a different case."

"What's *that* supposed to mean?"

"It means Rupert probably figured he could get your engines running without an expensive setting. Remember last night? Those fur coats, the soft lights—and you in a sopping wet dress. I'll tell you, Miss Caro, those things had *me* thinking about taking off my clothes."

"Alex," she said, enunciating carefully, "you're a throwback in evolution. It's amazing you don't carry a club."

She stalked away and sat down on a concrete bench—the picture of affronted femininity. Head high, she refused to look him in the face. Alex stood in front of her for a few moments, then sat down beside her and stretched out his legs. Next to her stiff figure, he looked rumpled, but felt relaxed. She was as tight as piano wire.

"Okay," he said, sticking to the problem at hand. "Let's agree that Rupert is probably some kind of kingpin: the mastermind behind the disappearing coats and stolen jewelry. He'd need help, wouldn't he? Inside help. The most obvious choice would be his employees. They're already on the payroll, and he's got some clout with them. He used Jane first to get the jewelry. When she died, he had to move in on somebody else. Betsy works in the fur salon."

"You think *she* helped steal the coats?"

"Makes sense, doesn't it? She's young and easily impressed, easily duped. And if they pulled off the theft together, he would have had to keep her quiet afterward. He picked an expensive hotel and they hit the sheets—"

"Alex," she warned. "Your loincloth is showing."

He grinned. "Probably the best way to manipulate a woman like Betsy is to get her to fall in love."

Her glance was withering. "Is this the voice of experience talking?"

"It's logical, that's all. But affairs with young women can get messy. If I was thinking like your old pal Rupert, I'd be working on a backup. Betsy might get emotional. I'd want somebody waiting in the wings."

"You're talking about me now, aren't you?" Caroline kept her profile stiffly averted. "You think Rupert is approaching me to replace Betsy."

"Sure." Alex leaned back to get more comfortable. "Obviously, he knows quality when he sees it. You're worth getting messy over, Miss Caroline."

Maybe he was leering too much. Tommy Hollings-worth would have played it with more subtlety, but Alex was out of practice. Caroline got up hurriedly and began to walk again. Alex stayed on the bench a little longer, watching her long-legged stride. Nice swing. Clearly miffed, she had shoved balled-up fists into her skirt pockets. Her back was ramrod straight, but her hips had a natural sway, the kind that prompted wolf whistles on the street. From a passing car came just such a whistle. Alex stood up and gave the whistler—a young punk in a shabby Camaro—a look that caused the kid to roll up his window and speed away.

Caroline didn't hear a thing. Though her heels clicked ominously fast on the pavement, Alex caught up with her easily.

"It's only a theory," he said.

She was clenching her jaw so tightly that it trem-bled. "You think you can say anything you please hiding behind those dark glasses."

"I'm just thinking out loud," he retorted. "That's what detectives are supposed to do."

"Then you think Jane was having an affair with Rupert?"

"I think so, yes."

Stiff and angry, Caroline said, "She might have killed herself over a man, you know. Jane was like that."

"What was she like?"

"Not—not very sensible." Caroline's breathing was funny. She was pretty upset, Alex could see, though he was unable to guess exactly how much. What amazed him was that it wasn't her own virtue she was distressed about; it was her sister's. She inhaled deeply and seemed to collect herself. "Jane's job was important to her, but it was her love life that really—that was the kind of emotional upset that used to put her over the edge a lot when we were growing up. I knew there had to be a man involved." Her voice rose, tightening. "I just knew it! Rupert makes me sick!"

Trying to sound light, Alex said, "Jane wasn't as careful as her little sister, is that it?"

"Jane was high-strung," Caroline said. "She was the emotional one."

"And you're the repressed one."

"*You'd* like to think that," she said bitterly. "Repression and control are not the same thing!"

Alex laughed. "And what happens when you lose control, Miss Caroline?"

She glared up at him, her green eyes full of fire. "I haul off and slap the nearest target. So watch yourself, Mr. Varanov."

She looked as if she meant it, too. Abruptly, she stepped off the curb to cross the street and was narrowly missed by a thundering taxicab. She kept walking, deaf to the cabbie's shouts. Alex cut around the cab and caught up with her.

She said, "Leave me alone."

Alex said nothing. He could feel his headache still— the party hadn't broken up yet. "Cripes," he muttered.

"I beg your pardon?"

"Nothing," he said shortly. "I was just lamenting why your good looks were combined with such a bitchy personality."

"Bitchy!"

"You heard me."

She choked but didn't break her rapid stride. "Listen, buster, I haven't come to Chicago to win a congeniality title. I'm here for a purpose, and I won't let you get in my way."

"Get in your *way*? I like that! Who saved your neck from a pack of dogs last night?"

"I see no reason to keep score. A partnership is supposed to be equal. That was your idea, by the way. If you want to dissolve our alliance and go our separate ways, I'll be delighted."

"No way. If Rupert is our man, you're the best way to get to him. Believe me, if there was another way to break this case, I'd be working on it."

"Try Betsy," she retorted. "Maybe she's not as bitchy as I am."

"That's a good idea," Alex said. "I think I might."

Caroline stopped dead on the sidewalk and swung on him. "Like hell you will!"

"What?"

She jammed one finger into his chest. "You keep your hands and your—your stupid knife off of Betsy, do you hear me? Stay away from her!"

"Hey, I've got a purpose," he mimicked, taunting her, "and nothing's going to stand in my—"

"Shut up," she snapped.

"Shut *up*?" he repeated, feigning shock. "Ladies don't talk like that!"

"You're too strong," Caroline said trembling with fury. "You'll overwhelm Betsy. Rupert's bad enough, but not you! I won't let you do it. We've got to have some scruples or we're no better than they are." Suddenly she was shaking. "Do you understand me? I'm willing to risk a lot—my own career and—and my family life, but—"

She caught herself, realizing she'd lost her temper, and clamped down.

In a moment, Alex said, "You find me overwhelming, do you, Caroline?"

She seethed, glaring up at him. "I won't be rotten. I won't start hurting innocent people to get what I want."

"Betsy may not be so innocent."

"You don't understand!" she burst out, her voice splintering. "Jane wasn't a bad person in the beginning, either! She was nice and kind and—and Betsy's just—she's young and—"

"Hey," said Alex, touching her arm.

"Don't!"

But she burst into tears. She lost it there on the city sidewalk and might have crumpled to the pavement if he hadn't caught her. Without a word, Alex took Caroline into his arms and drew her back against the nearest building. Caroline clung to him, not thinking, and his body absorbed her tremors. She melted into him, glad of some support, and was clearly beyond caring who it came from. Alex smoothed one hand up her slender back and gently eased her head onto his shoulder. She cried and shuddered, letting all the pain out in one gushing torrent.

"It's all right," he murmured. What a heel he could be. What a lousy investigator, too. So far that morning he'd gotten a headache and made a nice woman cry. He was worse than a heel. He was a skunk.

Her body was wracked by several more terrible sobs before she began to come around. Alex didn't speak anymore and let her cry herself out. She had a lot more emotion invested in the investigation, he reasoned. From the start, her motivation had been her love for her sister. Caroline had been walking a kind of tightrope; it was only natural that she'd slip if he jiggled the wire. He had miscalculated, pure and simple—she wasn't as tough as she pretended to be. Her fear of the dogs should have tipped him off, he realized. Caroline was a gentle young woman who had loved her sister. It had taken guts to come to Chicago and find out about the suicide, but Caro wasn't cold-bloodedly looking for answers: she was working on instinct, motivated by love.

True to form, however, she managed to get herself under control single-handedly. After a full minute, she pushed her hands against his chest. "Let me go."

He didn't quite. With one arm still holding her against him, he fished into his trousers pocket for a handkerchief. She accepted it obediently and wouldn't look up at him. A shy lamb, that was what she was, he mused. Alex felt his throat swell queerly.

Some people walked by: an elderly black gentleman in a checked suit, his wife, who wore a hat with a tall flower stuck in its brim, and two granddaughters, both with cornrows and hair ribbons. The gentleman steered his family around Caroline and Alex, took one look at Caroline's tear-streaked face and gave Alex a stern look. Alex discovered that he and Caroline had stopped in front of a pizzeria next to a Baptist church. The time must have been close to noon, he realized, because the church was emptying out quickly and a great many parishioners were entering the pizzeria for lunch—including the family who looked dubiously at the way Alex was holding Caroline. And while Caroline looked like a princess in her blue ensemble, Alex figured he looked like some kind of a mugger in his black leather jacket. He tried to smile disarmingly.

The church-going family disappeared into the pizzeria, but not without a few more suspicious stares. Dabbing her eyes, Caroline said, "We're making a public display."

"I'm from New York," Alex said. "A public display involves murder, nudity or politicians—preferably all three. But those folks looked like they were going to call the police. Unless you want me arrested, I think we'd better move along."

She sniffled and didn't speak. At that moment, Alex was completely absorbed in the job of holding her. She felt slim but womanly in his arms, and her hair smelled of sunlight. Her cheek was wet with tears he suddenly wanted to kiss away. Maybe Tommy Hollingsworth could be cool with women—make bets where their bodies were concerned—but Alex felt quite differently. Suddenly he wished he'd been kind to her from the start.

She seemed to have read his thoughts. She pressed gently out of his embrace.

"Look, I'm sorry." He took off his sunglasses. "I've been making your life miserable for the last twenty-four hours and I—I'm really not as bad as I seem."

She didn't answer. What did he expect? She certainly wasn't going to argue the point. Alex took her arm and turned her toward the sidewalk again. She didn't resist.

He didn't have the faintest idea where they were going to go, and he didn't care. Caroline looked beautiful and miserable and he didn't mind the prospect of spending the whole day wandering around the city with her, especially if he could cheer her into smiling once again.

"Let's go get something to eat," he said. "You're probably hungry, and I'm starved."

She gave him a quick glance. In a small voice, she said, "You're always starved."

He almost muttered, "Not just for food," but instead he pulled her away from the pizzeria. "The lynch mob is gathering. Come on. Can you walk a little farther?"

She could and did. She was very quiet, though. Alex was afraid he'd pushed too far. But miraculously, in just another three blocks they came upon some kind of neighborhood street fair. Caroline seemed to perk up. The avenue had been blocked off, banners festooned the streetlights, and the sidewalk was crowded with booths and people. Music swelled in the air, mingling with the laughter and chatter of the throng, and the smells that wafted around Alex's head were heavenly. On one side of the street a bunch of Girl

Scouts was grilling hot dogs. Across from them, the
Rotary Club was cooking hot-sausage sandwiches and
piroshki. A Vietnamese restaurant had set up temporary shop on the corner and appeared to be doing a
brisk business in assorted delicacies. Everywhere,
families seemed to be enjoying the sunshine and the
conviviality of the day. A pair of teenage boys whizzed
by on skateboards. A matronly woman strolled along
with a grizzled wolfhound on a leash. Two families—
with at least a dozen kids between them—greeted each
other in the middle of the street, exchanging hugs and
jokes.

Caroline blinked at the sight. "What's this?"

"Heaven," said Alex, gazing hungrily at slices of
pumpkin pie that the Ladies Garden Club had on display. "Let's eat."

CHAPTER SEVEN

HE BOUGHT HER a paper cup of cider and stood with her as they listened to a fife and bugle corps perform in an adjacent schoolyard. Afterward he led her past a throng of skittish children lining up for pony rides and they meandered down the street through a crush of folding tables, makeshift booths, cardboard signs and happy people.

Caroline felt strangely disembodied—as if she had walked off the Chicago streets into another world. Everyone seemed happy; everywhere she looked there was gaiety. After crying out her grief and frustration, she felt tired and light-headed, unable to concentrate or make decisions. To wander among laughing strangers at a festive street fair felt unreal.

As if sensing her bewilderment, Alex took her hand in his. Caro let him take charge.

He was solicitous and catered to her as if she was a bereaved widow. After the tart cider, he bought her tidbits of fish on a skewer and coaxed her to eat all of it. Then came honey-sweet triangles of baklava, and he helped wipe the dribbles on her palms afterward. His attention made her feel shy.

He shielded her from buffeting teenagers and steered her around overly rambunctious toddlers. He stayed far away from the lady with the Irish wolfhound, and Caro was touched. She didn't speak, though. Suddenly she wanted to absorb, to stay silent and allow the world to revolve around her. Alex was a tall, careful, guardian presence beside her.

A conspicuous presence, too. As they strolled along together, Caroline couldn't help noticing the glances Alex drew. His size alone rendered him a daunting sight, but that dark, unnameable force, that certain air of omnipotence she had recognized within moments of their meeting, was clearly evident to other people as well. Men unconsciously stepped out of his way. When he laughed suddenly at some remark made by the baklava seller, half a dozen women turned to look and smile. And more than once, Caroline caught a particular young woman eyeing Alex's backside with nothing short of lascivious pleasure written on her face. She followed them a while, then drifted off into the crowd, disappointed.

Alex *was* handsome, Caroline had to admit—and not just his backside. His dark hair—exactly the color of his black leather jacket—ruffled in the autumn breeze. The outdoor air and sunshine had brought a ruddy glow to his sharply cut cheeks, and his eyes, blue as ice water, packed the power of infrared beams when Caroline caught his glance. She looked away at once, of course, afraid he'd seen exactly what she'd been thinking.

"Try these," he said, passing a paper napkin full of candied nuts into her hands. "They're terrific."

Caroline nibbled and let herself be swept along, hoping the sights and sounds would heal her and that the afternoon would never end.

But it did, of course. The sky began to cloud over and rain looked imminent.

"Come on," said Alex, when a huge thundercloud obscured the sun at last. "We'd better get back."

Caroline resisted, the first voluntary action in two hours, at least. "But Alex," she said. "I think you actually missed three food booths."

He contemplated the dilemma with obvious regret. "Well, there's nothing to be done, I guess." Then he snapped his fingers as an idea hit him. "Wait! We could take stuff back to your place for a picnic. Perfect! It'll— I mean, that is if you don't . . ."

Caroline's heart jerked at the thought of being alone with Alex once more. But he looked so unthreatening just then—like an overgrown boy longing for a treat. Smiling a little, she said, "I wouldn't want to deny you the firemen's fried chicken."

"Have I told you yet," Alex asked, smiling back, "what a wonderful woman you are?"

"Last I heard, you thought I was bitchy."

"Forgive me," he said with all evidence of sincerity. "That was before you pointed out the funnel cake down the alley. Oh, my God!"

Caroline jumped. "What's wrong?"

"The hospital auxiliary booth. They've got Russian tea cakes," he said prayerfully. "Oh, and salmon! Look at this stuff! It's everything my mother makes on Thanksgiving."

"Somehow," Caroline replied, "I can't imagine you having a mother."

"Of course I do. She's a nice little old immigrant who still makes her own sauerkraut and— Caroline, you've got to try some of this. They've got real Russian delicacies here. We'll buy a little of everything for a picnic. All we need is vodka."

"I think I've got a bottle," she said without thinking.

"Not Polish stuff. It's got to be—"

"It's Russian, I'm sure."

He bent and kissed her swiftly and exuberantly on the forehead. "You're a *wonderful* woman."

It happened so fast there wasn't time to react. While he bought the food, Caroline considered the sensations that his sudden, impulsive kiss had induced. It had been a natural response for him—not calculated . . . not sneaky and sexy like the kiss in the rain. This one had been spontaneous, an affirmation of their partnership—and more. Inside, Caroline felt a glow of pleasure. It felt dangerous, too. She shouldn't trust him, she thought frantically, shouldn't be thinking this way about him.

But when Alex took her hand again, she let her fingers entwine with his.

They took a cab back to the Hilton and picked up Caroline's car. Feeling strong enough, she drove home while Alex sat in the passenger seat happily taking inventory of the parcels he'd bought. Alone in an enclosed space with him again, Caroline hardly heard a word he said. She was too busy worrying that she was about to make a huge mistake. The mystical, disembodied feeling she'd experienced at the fair had begun to wear off. Alex was real.

She parked the Volvo in the carriage house, and they dashed through the backyard just as the first raindrops began to fall. She unlocked the back door and they tumbled breathlessly into the kitchen. Caroline flicked on the lights and in the almost surgical glare she watched nervously as Alex spread his packages out on the counter.

"We need plates and glasses," he said, already digging into a drawer for cutlery. "Napkins, too, unless you lick your fingers, which I doubt. Let's see, what else?"

Things were going too fast. Caroline made an effort to sound normal, to get herself firmly in control again. "Slow down, Varanov," she said. "At least take the time to hang up your coat. You can stave off the hunger pangs for five more minutes, can't you?"

"Maybe not," he said, pulling off his leather jacket and waggling his eyebrows at her. "Did I hear you say you had some vodka?"

"Yes, but—"

"In the freezer?"

"No, I'm sorry. It's in the cupboard."

"Get a wine bucket then, and fill it with ice. The stuff has got to be as cold as we can get it."

"Anything else, lord and master?"

He acknowledged her tart tone with an undaunted grin. "Since you know your way around this kitchen, I'll trust you to prepare the food. I'll take care of the atmosphere."

"Atmosphere?"

He didn't stop to explain, but pushed out through the swinging door to the living room. Uneasily, Caroline got busy, collecting dishes and utensils and arranging them on a tray. Two plain white plates and a pair of solid, not fancy glasses. There was no sense making an occasion out of the afternoon.

She wasn't keeping tabs on Alex, she only knew he was thumping around her home as if he'd moved in. He had even gone snooping into her bedroom—the former maid's quarters adjacent to the kitchen.

Within a few minutes, he came out with a blanket under one arm and two pillows under the other. He made straight for the living room, and when Caroline followed, balancing a tray of fragrant food and the ice bucket of vodka, he was spreading out the blanket, picnic style, on the floor in front of the fireplace. Then he proceeded to rip the plush pillows off the sofa and throw them haphazardly onto the blanket. Caroline stopped uncertainly in the doorway, but the door swung shut and whapped her into the room.

The place had been transformed. Using the gas jet, Alex had managed to set the logs in the fireplace to burning, so a cozy fire crackled cheerily and cast a flickering light on the polished wood floor. The shabbiness of the empty room wasn't apparent now—just the graciousness of former glory. With the rain pelting against the windows and darkness rapidly falling outside, the shadowy room looked like a picture from a storybook. The warm half circle of firelight encompassed the pillows and blanket so that it resembled a private niche in the seraglio of Scheherazade. Even a stubby candle had been lit, and Alex lifted it from the mantel, then crouched and set it on the blanket.

It was his milieu, that half darkness. Alex usually seemed all darkness, Caroline thought, but now and then she saw flickers of light, of niceness.

Seemingly unaware that he had managed to create an enchanting setting, Alex sat back on his heels to survey his work. He nodded once, as if pronouncing it perfect.

Then he grinned up at Caroline. "All we need is an anthill."

Only then did Caroline move forward. She jolted herself out of her trance and said, "I'm sure you'll be pesky enough by the end of the evening."

Alex took the bottle off the tray, clasping it by its neck. "If you have an itch, I'll be happy to scratch it, Miss Caroline."

He relaxed on the floor, stretching out his long legs and making himself comfortable in the welter of pillows. He set about opening the bottle with great ceremony. "This is my competitor's brand, but it'll do in a pinch." He cocked his head to look up at her. It took a long time, because he let his gaze travel up the length of her legs and the curve of her hips before meeting her eye. "Going to join me?"

"Is it safe?"

He sighed and shook his head. "There's that word again. You must have a pretty boring time of things if you go through life asking that question. Don't you like adventure once in a while?"

"Adventure?" Caroline mused. She knelt cautiously on the edge of the blanket, putting down the tray to tuck her skirt around her knees. "Do you mean things like breaking into department stores late at night? Being chased by the Baskerville hounds? Things like that?"

"Exactly," said Alex. He poured vodka into the glasses and passed one to Caroline. "Now," he commanded, "go ahead and tell me that you didn't enjoy last night's exploits just a little bit."

"Enjoy them!"

"I saw the gleam in your eye today. I think detecting agrees with you, partner."

Deliberately calm, she said, "That's silly."

"Is it? I'm serious. Didn't you get a charge out of all the excitement?"

Caroline considered his question seriously. "Well, maybe I—all right, I admit I do feel better today. It wasn't the excitement, though. It's because I'm making progress, that's all. Since Jane died, it's been hard to—well, no one in my family has been very happy."

He lifted his glass. "To progress, then."

Caroline hesitated, glancing into her glass and the clear liquid that refracted the firelight into a rainbow of color. No doubt the vodka had the power to create rainbows in a woman's head, too.

"Come on," he coached, amused by her cautious air. "It's not going to taste like champagne, but it's got a charm of its own. Watch. Flick your wrist, tilt your head and knock it back." Alex demonstrated how to drink the vodka. He executed the gesture with panache and swallowed every drop in a single, smooth swallow—then lifted the empty glass in a kind of triumph and winked at Caroline with the devilish air of a conquering cossack. "See? It's excellent. Now you try."

There wasn't any use in objecting, she knew. He'd goad and pester until she did what he commanded. Caroline shut her eyes, took a swig from her glass and nearly choked when the liquor hit the back of her throat. It burned like dry ice, then turned vaporous and hot as it seethed down her throat. She braced herself for the moment of impact, but the vodka seemed to evaporate somewhere in her chest. Just a tingly warm sensation remained, and it slowly dissipated, traveling out to her limbs until the feeling reached her fingertips and glowed.

Alex smiled, having watched her face as she experienced the process. "Not bad. But you forgot the eye contact."

"I beg your pardon?"

He leaned forward on one elbow and refilled her glass. "That's one of the most important points. You've got to look at me when you swallow."

"Really, Alex, it's too strong to be gulping like this—"

"We're having a traditional picnic," he said. "You've got to follow all the traditions. Try again. Here, I'll do it with you." Pouring more vodka into his glass, he said, "What shall we drink to? Your turn to come up with something."

Caroline picked up her glass determinedly. "All right," she said. "Let's drink to self-control. After all this booze, we're going to need it."

He sighed. "To self-control, then. We'll see how long it lasts. Now—eye contact. Bottoms up."

Caroline drank her vodka and held Alex's gaze until the tingle in her fingertips receded, leaving each and every nerve ending in her body alive and ready. In his eyes, Caroline could see amusement... appreciation, too, which was flattering, but also something darker, something knowing. She felt her hormones respond to it before her brain could put a name to the expression he sent her. The look that passed between them communicated sex, the spark of almost electrical proportions that could flash between the right man and woman. There was longing in the look, excitement and hunger. Alex had never kept his sexual interest a secret. But looking at him, Caroline realized with a start that she was probably returning the same message.

Caroline broke the eye contact immediately. And naturally, she blushed.

"More?" Alex asked mildly, reaching for the bottle and pretending not a thing had happened.

"Not in this lifetime," Caro retorted. "I'm not a drinker."

"Once in a while, circumstances call for the right libation. My grandmother used to say that. Food, now, please, or we'll both be drunk. Ah, try this."

He passed her a plate and proceeded to serve her one delicacy at a time. He was right. The food was delicious. There were spicy vegetables and smoked fish, rich breads and salty tidbits that Caroline couldn't identify, but loved as they melted on her tongue. The strong flavors did, in fact, require an occasional sip of vodka to maintain a balance. Caroline poured more drinks herself, and Alex did not protest when she refilled his glass. He began to talk, then, and Caro was faintly surprised by his animated tone.

He told her about his mother's kitchen. "It smelled just like this bread," he said. "All the time. And there was always somebody sitting at the table eating a piece. My mother was always good for a handout. Still is."

For some reason, Caroline still couldn't imagine Alex with a mother. He seemed more like the mythical characters who sprung fully formed from the heads of gods than any human she knew.

"We lived on the Lower East Side then," he told Caroline, not aware of her awakening interest in this new side to his character. "Before it started getting fashionable. A tiny shotgun apartment over my dad's first shop, and we had seven people in the family. I've got three brothers and a sister, and we went through more food than any family on the block. My mother spent her whole day in the kitchen—baked her own bread and all kinds of treats. No wonder I fight a running battle with my waistline. I'm better off living alone." He served Caro another curl of salmon balanced on the edge of a knife. "When we were kids, my mother canned cabbage once every six months. What a stink she made! The whole building smelled of that stuff for weeks after she finished. But it was terrific cabbage, let me tell you. Like nothing I've ever eaten. Better than caviar."

She didn't know whether it was the vodka or the lulling crackle of the fire or even the melodic quality in Alex's warm voice that caused it, but Caroline began to relax as the picnic progressed. She even stretched out on the pillows, propping herself on one elbow and reaching for one of the tiny rolls of smoked salmon with her left hand when he passed them. As she listened to Alex she wondered why she'd ever despised him. He could be thoroughly charming when he chose to be.

"You sound as if you miss living with your family."

"Miss it?" he repeated. "Hell, no. There were arguments all the time. We are not the kind who sulk when we get angry. No, I don't miss it a bit. I have fewer worries and fewer responsibilities. I like having my own place."

"What's it like?"

"My apartment? Not too big. Efficient. Close to the places I like to go."

"It's dark, I'll bet."

"Oh, sure. I hate those places where the furniture is white and the walls are white and the floor is bleached. They're too sterile. Like living in an art gallery."

Caro figured Alex would hate art galleries, all right. Not just the light and the brightness, but the number of people. Alex, she decided, was a loner.

"You come from a big family?" he asked finally.

Caroline shook her head. "No. Just me and my— well, just me now."

He popped a marinated mushroom into his mouth. "I thought all farmers had lots of kids."

Perhaps it was time to clear up a lot of misconceptions. Caroline said, "My father's more of a gentleman farmer than the kind who goes off to the barn every morning. He's the president of a small-town bank, as a matter of fact, and has some fields he tends on weekends. He used to work in Philadelphia, but when he married, he vowed he would raise his family out in the country. He bought a small farm in Lancaster. That was before the county turned into some kind of sideshow for tourists. Now it's overrun with billboards, and the Amish—well, I feel sorry for them. They're exploited. I'm glad I don't live there now."

"You regret not being raised in a city?"

"Not at all," she said at once. "Oh, sometimes I wish I had a different kind of savvy, I suppose."

He smiled. "Yes, your wide-eyed and innocent look gives the real you away now and then."

She didn't get outraged. Instead, Caroline said, "Maybe I am naive at times. I don't have much sophistication. But I have a—well, a kind of common sense about things that many of my college friends didn't seem to have. I can drive a nail straight and change a tire without calling the auto club. I learned a lot on the farm. Now, of course, I live in Philadelphia."

"Practicing law."

"Not the way you might think." Caroline smiled a little. "I'm not trying cases in criminal court—I work for a political lobby."

"A do-gooder," Alex guessed wryly.

Again, she didn't take offense. "I hope so. I'm part of a lobby group for environmental issues."

His brows shot up. "Is that why you have mixed feelings about working in a fur salon?"

"You bet I have mixed feelings about killing innocent animals. I may start my own lobby when this is
over."

"Are you based in Washington?"

She shook her head. "The rent's too high there. We
work out of Philadelphia and travel to Washington
when we have to. Mostly, though, we help prepare
cases for lawyers around the country who are dealing
with issues we'd like to change."

"Like what?"

"Strip-mine laws seem to be my specialty lately. It's
not very glamorous, I'm afraid. But I've never looked
for glamour."

"Or money," said Alex. "I don't suppose being a
high-minded lobbyist pays very well."

She shrugged. "Well enough. I have a small apartment. I don't take extravagant vacations. Until now,
my wardrobe wasn't anything *Vogue* might want to
come take pictures of."

"Until now?" he asked.

Caroline sighed. They had managed to avoid the
topic of her reason for coming to Chicago, but there
was no pretending it didn't exist. She stretched her
boots toward the fire, suddenly feeling the need for
some warmth. She said, "I figured I'd better dress the
part if I intended to get a job in a luxury store like St.
Cloud's. I bought some clothes before I came. Jane
always—she always looked very up-to-date. I live
pretty quietly, but Jane, she was a swinger."

Alex laughed at the word. "A swinger?"

Caroline flushed again. "You know what I mean. Parties, drinking, lots of friends. She was flamboyant. She lived here, you know."

That startled Alex. He glanced around the room, as if he could see the entire mansion in a single glance. "Here? In this house?"

Caroline nodded. "It belonged to some relatives of my mother's. When Jane moved out here, she got the family to rent her this place. I think she planned to have costume balls here or something. But she—I guess she never scraped up enough money to make it very livable."

"For all its color," said Alex, "this place is a dump. I can't believe you're living here for a short term, in fact. It's not your style, at all."

"What do you think *is* my style?"

He grinned. "A pristine castle in the clouds."

She made a face. "I don't need anything that fancy. This house isn't going to collapse around my ears, so I don't mind it. I wanted to be near Jane's things. I thought I might be able to find out about her."

"What did you find?"

Caroline wrinkled her nose. "A mess. Jane was— she must have been very depressed before she died. There was garbage piling up in the kitchen, liquor bottles all over the place. It's her vodka we're drinking, not mine. She didn't have any furniture to speak of. I sent what was left to the Salvation Army."

"What was left?" Alex repeated.

"Yes. I had a feeling she must have had more. Maybe she sold some of her things."

"Any idea why?"

Caroline shook her head. "I can't imagine. I don't understand what happened to Jane at all, as a matter of fact. We were never very much alike, but what she did was—it's something I'd never consider doing."

"You've got alternatives in life," Alex said. "Maybe Jane didn't think she had many choices."

His face was somber, his blue eyes unwavering. Suddenly Caroline felt uncomfortable. They had become too intimate too fast. She sat up and rearranged the folds of her skirt with nervous hands. "Alex, I—"

He waited, but she couldn't find the words to finish her thought. In a moment, the thought seemed to have evaporated, too. Her mind was a muddle. First there was Jane, and now there was Alex. They were separate entities, but somehow they'd become stirred in together. Her mission had changed when Alex had arrived. Suddenly things didn't seem as painful, as immediate as they once had. And yet Alex also represented a whole set of difficulties she hadn't expected to face.

"Yes?" he asked, the snap and hiss of the fire the only sounds between them.

Caroline shook herself. "Never mind. I feel uneasy with you sometimes, and talking like this—I don't know. We don't know each other very well. I shouldn't—I'm happier when we argue, I guess. I can think straighter when we fight."

He didn't budge from his relaxed position. "We're supposed to be on the same side."

"I know, but—it's easier, that's all."

"I'm sorry," he said out of the blue. "About this afternoon. I pushed too hard. I like arguing, too. It's—it's stimulating, I suppose."

Caroline swallowed hard.

"Very stimulating," Alex said. "But I went too far. I'm sorry."

"You don't have to apologize," she said hurriedly, toying with the hem of her skirt, afraid to see his expression. "I deserved it. I can take it, too. I just—something cracked, that's all. I'd prefer it if we could keep things nice and hostile, as a matter of fact. I'm—This is silly, but I'm a little afraid of you when you're nice."

She dared to look at him then and discovered that he was smiling.

"You like me better when I'm a skunk?"

"I didn't say that. I just meant that you're easier to be around when you're—"

"A skunk."

"Well, yes."

Alex put his glass down on the blanket. "Is it me you're afraid of, Caroline? Or maybe part of yourself?"

"I don't know what you mean."

He said, "You look like a Victorian lady sitting there with your knees tucked up and your hands folded. The Victorians were well-known for their straitlaced attitudes about sex and how men and women ought to behave when they're together."

"See here," she began, fearing that she'd lost control of things once more.

"Well, I'm not a Victorian. I like sex and the way I feel when I'm—"

"Please," she said desperately. "Stop."

"I think you're afraid of what might happen if you loosen those laces, Miss Caroline," Alex went on. "You're not afraid of me. You're afraid of yourself and what you might do if I stick around."

"That's nonsense."

"Is it?" He leaned closer, over the bottle and the plates and the food. "I might kiss you again tonight. I might be tempted to unbutton that pretty shirt of yours. And with a little more vodka, I might carry you into the next room and do my worst. What would you say to that?"

She tried to smile. In control, that's what she wanted to be. "The caveman approach has never appealed to me."

"Until now," Alex said.

He gathered her up swiftly, but as carefully as if she'd been made of the finest china. Slipping one arm around her back, he used the other hand to catch up the tumble of her hair and held Caroline fast, molding her softness to his own harder frame. Caroline didn't gasp. There wasn't enough air in her lungs to manage it. Alex hovered for an instant, giving her time to fight, to protest. But Caroline suddenly couldn't move. She didn't want to. She was mesmerized by the firelight in his eyes.

He searched her gaze for a signal of rejection. It didn't appear, so Alex dipped his head and warmly touched her lips with his.

Caroline trembled once, but his kiss tasted like sun-warmed liquor on her mouth—sweet, delicious and tempting. Without thinking, she deepened the coupling until their mouths parted and ground together so sensually that Caro's mind went blank. A surge of bubbling-hot sensation came washing up through her, starting deep inside her body and gradually eddying higher and higher until her breasts ached. Unconsciously, she pressed against Alex's hard chest, longing to feel his strength more fully. She slipped her arms around his neck and she heard Alex make a quiet sound. His mouth was smiling against hers, and soon Caro heard herself laugh—quietly, but with joy. It felt good—wonderful, in fact.

Alex tightened his hold on her hair and tilted her head, moving it gently until he had plundered every surface of her mouth. Next, he began a wicked exploration with his tongue. He arched her body, and before Caroline knew what he was up to, he had expertly found her breast with his hand and was cupping it and playing with her already aching nipple while continuing with his savory kiss. Caroline's composure dissolved completely. She couldn't breathe! Nor could she laugh or make light of what was happening anymore.

Alex tore his mouth from hers, his breath ragged, too, and he pressed more kisses down the column of her throat. In another instant, he'd want to open her blouse and finish the job his teasing fingers had begun.

If he kissed her breast, Caroline thought fuzzily, she would implode with pleasure. Lurking inside her like

the devil's own temptation was the exasperating urge
to yield, to let Alex press her down into the pillows and
loosen her clothes. A simple movement of acquies-
cence might prompt him to fulfill both their darkest
wishes.

Mustering what few wits she had left, Caro pressed
her hand against Alex's chest and held him off. He
didn't fight it, but loosened his embrace only slightly.
His hand slipped from her breast, and he brushed a
small, final kiss on the corner of her lips.

Caro couldn't look at his face. "That was close,"
she said before she could think.

He laughed softly. "Was it?"

She averted her head for fear he'd see how near
she'd gotten to giving in, to having it all. "Alex,
please."

His whisper was as quiet as hers had been—un-
bearably intimate. "Please what?"

"Stop. I can't." In spite of herself, Caro began to
smile. "I don't want to get carried away."

"You?" His most roguish smile flashed in the firelight. "I doubt that's possible."

"Don't tease me. I just—I don't like being forced."

He petted her hair, running his fingers tantalizingly
through the strands. Almost whispering, he asked,
"Am I forcing?"

"N-no," she said. "Just don't make me do something I'll regret later."

Alex blew a soft sigh into her hair. "Nothing that
feels this good could possibly be bad."

It did feel good in his arms, and Caroline didn't
have the wherewithal to push her way out. She al-

lowed him to go on holding her, caressing her back, nuzzling her hair, and realized that she was unconsciously reciprocating. Her fingertips traced the curve of his shoulders, the back of his neck and the soft, short hairs on the back of his head. She couldn't stop.

But she said, "I've been unattached most of my life. I don't— I've never given myself to anyone without—without a great deal of thought and—and a kind of commitment. I'm not interested in quick sex, Alex.''

"Me, neither,'' he murmured. "Long sex is much better.''

She laughed. "That's not what I meant, and you know it! This is—it's very nice, but it's fleeting. Like an ice-cream sundae. I love to eat them, but I always feel terrible afterward. As though I've been weak, and I'll be punished when I get on the scales in the morning. Alex, please—''

"You want me to stop?''

"Yes— I— Yes and no.'' When he touched her breast again, she whispered, "I can't think straight.''

Smiling, he kissed her mouth and her nose and went on caressing her breast, making gentle, wonderful circles. "Neither can I. I only know I've got a week to finish my business here, and then I go back to my real life.''

"You're not a part of my real life. And I'm not a part of yours.''

"Yes, exactly.'' Alex used his forefinger to tip her chin so that they looked deeply into each other's eyes. "Caroline, finding you was a fantasy trip. You're an unknown woman: a sexy, beautiful woman and I want you. Do you feel how much I want you?'' With her palm pressed firmly to his chest, Caroline could indeed feel his heart beating as if he'd been running. And his eyes were vibrant, too. Excited and dancing with light. "A week," he said. "We could have a week of doing whatever we want."

"A week in bed?"

"Wherever you like," he murmured, lips to hers, coaxing. "In bed, on the floor, anywhere. As wild and crazy as you like. For a week."

"And then we go back to our old lives? No strings attached, is that it?"

He laughed softly. "It's tempting you. I can hear it in your voice."

"Of course it tempts me." Caroline pressed out of his arms, however, and Alex sat back to listen. She said, "But this isn't fantasy. If I sleep with you, I'll still have to get up in the morning and look at myself in the mirror. Great sex isn't my goal in life, Alex. It's icing on the cake once in a while, but I'm not like you. I can't be cold-blooded."

"It could be good, Caroline. Not cold in the least. We'd be terrific together."

"Maybe so, but—"

Alex squeezed her hand to silence her. "I thought I was beyond this kind of reaction to a woman. The sight of you, the smell of your hair—everything about you makes me take a mental dive into bed. I can't help it. Tell me you haven't felt the same way."

"I can't deny that I'm attracted to you. But there are certain things I don't do. I don't go jumping into bed with strangers. Not when I—when I'm trying to find out what happened to my sister."

Alex released her hand at that. Caroline sat stiffly, letting the words sink in. He sat back at last and reached for the vodka bottle.

"Are you angry?" she asked, watching his bent head as he poured another glass for himself. The firelight played on his hair, on the tight planes of his face.

"Yes, but I'll live." He raised the glass and looked over its shining rim at her. The look in his eye was complimentary, not reproachful. He even smiled a little. "You're a lady of virtue."

He didn't say it with mockery in his voice. Caro nearly asked him then and there for another kiss. Perhaps there *were* times for propriety and times for seizing the moment.

But Caro didn't get a chance. From the foyer of the house came a pounding, as if someone had begun to beat his fist against the massive front door demanding entrance to their evening in Eden.

Startled, Caroline leaped to her knees.

"Did you plan this?" Alex asked, moving easily to his feet. "A convenient interruption?"

"No," she replied, and accepted the hand he extended to help her up. "I'm not expecting anyone. Alex—"

"Rupert, perhaps?"

"I don't know."

Already they were moving toward the foyer. Alex said, "Answer it yourself. I'll wait around the corner. If you need me, I'll hear."

Caroline nodded. She left him at the archway and continued to the door herself. The light switch in the hall didn't work very well, but one switch did command a single bulb to flicker on. Caroline unlatched the door and pulled it wide. Outside, evening was beginning to fall.

"Yes?"

A grimy figure stood there, a wiry, unshaven young man in a hooded sweatshirt and filthy jeans, both glistening with raindrops. His age could have been anywhere from eighteen to twenty-five. He had a knit cap on his head, a weasel-thin face and darting eyes. They scooted down Caroline's figure and back up again. He kept his hands in the front pocket of his wet sweatshirt and bounced slightly on the balls of his feet as he stood under the portico.

"You Jane Wexler?" he asked.

"No," Caroline said. "I'm— Why do you ask?"

He looked like an outcast from the underworld, all right. A suspicious-character label practically swung from his earlobe along with the diamond stud he wore there. He squinted at Caroline. "You sure you're not her?"

"I'm not, but if you've got something—if there's anything I can do to—"

"Janey owes us some dough. I came to collect."

"She— Jane owes money? To you?"

He jerked his head in a nod. "Yeah, to me. An' a few others. She around?"

"No, she's not. I—"

"Listen, lady," said the young man, stepping over the threshold and lowering his voice as if to speak confidentially. "I need the dough pretty bad. If Janey doesn't come up with it soon, she'll be in deep trouble. What d'you say me and you talk a little business?" He grabbed Caroline's elbow and twisted it.

Caroline didn't have to answer or react. Alex stepped around the corner at that moment. The young man in the knit cap spotted him and registered consternation at once. He began to step back, finding himself at least six inches shorter than Alex and significantly lighter in weight.

"Listen," he said, spreading his hands innocently, "I didn't do nothin' to the lady. I'm a businessman, that's all. Nothin' bad, man. Nothin' bad."

Alex caught him by his collar. "Close the door," he said to Caroline.

Effortlessly, he pulled the young man back into the foyer. Caroline noted that the newcomer's feet barely touched the floor as they made the trip. Once inside, Alex spun him and slammed his body against the wall, pinning him there about six inches off the floor.

"Alex," she began, tugging at his steel-like arm. "Please, let's not have any trouble."

"Let me work off my aggressions," he said over his shoulder. "It'll be easier on your virtue this way. Okay, punk, tell me what business you've got with Jane Wexler."

"Nothing, man. Nothing!"

Alex shook him the way a grizzly bear might handle a flopping salmon. "You caught me at a bad time, friend. I'm down to my last ounce of patience. Jane owed you money? What for?"

"My boss took some bets for her, that's all. Just—"

"Gambling? How much did she owe?"

"Not much, man. Not much!" He struggled, trying to pry Alex's immovable hands from his shirt. It became obvious at once that he wasn't going to escape. One look into Alex's taut face made the young man spill the rest. "Twenty-five hundred," he said. "That's it. It's her friend that owes the big bucks. I only came to shake her up a little before we put this squeeze on the other guy."

"What other guy?"

"Rupert something," said the young man. "An uptown guy. He owes plenty more than she does."

"Oho," said Caroline.

CHAPTER EIGHT

"IF RUPERT WATKINS has a gambling problem," Alex said when he returned from the portico and closed the front door against the rain, "he'd have a motive for stealing merchandise from his own store."

"But we need proof he's the thief," Caroline agreed, folding her arms over her chest and unconsciously taking the posture of a woman making a stand. "I think it's time to call the police, Alex."

"With what evidence? The word of a bookie's errand boy?" He snorted. "Believe me, that won't interest the cops very much."

Caroline regarded him shrewdly. "Besides," she said, "going to the police will make your insurance company sit up and take notice, won't it?"

He looked sharply into her face.

"Alex, please, I'm a lawyer, an officer of the court. I can't go on playing detective like this when I know the police would do a better job. What if we make a mistake and Rupert goes free? The police could—"

"I promised my father I'd try to settle matters without involving any authorities."

"Your father?" Caro repeated stupidly.

Alex looked annoyed. He didn't like talking about his family, and the thought of revealing any further information made him testy. He said, "If the police get involved, it'll cost him a fortune, not to mention the aggravation of an insurance investigation if the insurance company finds out what's been happening. I promised I'd do what I could. It's only a week. I'll give up if I haven't closed the matter by then. But if I *can* find the thief—or even better, locate the stolen coats—my family will be spared a great deal of pain."

"Mostly you'll be saving them some money," Caroline remarked, challenging him.

Alex sighed. He paused, clearly wrestling with some additional information he hadn't intended to reveal. "My dad's sick," he said shortly. "I don't want to stir up any trouble that's going to make him worse."

"Alex, I—"

But he cut her off rudely, annoyed that he'd been forced to tell her about his father's illness. "You can understand that, surely? Aren't you trying to smooth things over in your family, too?"

Torn, Caroline hesitated. She hadn't expected Alex to be motivated by affection. It was easier to believe he had money on his mind. Alex liked things nice and clean, she had decided, not muddied up with emotion.

"Just a few more days," Alex said. He touched the underside of her arm, his fingertips caressing, but he didn't meet her eye. "If we haven't found any solid evidence against Rupert, I'll take you to the police station myself."

"In the meantime, we've got to go on playing Sherlock and Watson."

He smiled then, and his blue eyes sparkled. "How about Nick and Nora Charles? I like those two better. They took some time out for recreation."

He leaned closer, bent on kissing her, Caroline knew. She stopped him by pressing two fingers against his lips. "Nick and Nora were married," she reminded him. "And they drank plenty of bathtub gin to keep their inhibitions down. I'm a nice girl from Pennsylvania who's had a little too much vodka at the moment, that's all. I'm not ready for recreation, as you call it."

He clasped her hand in his, turned her palm up and kissed it. His mouth was warm, but the message in his face was warmer still. A week of fun sex? The idea sounded recklessly delightful, especially when backed up by the gleam of good humor in Alex's eyes.

Caroline wouldn't have minded a real kiss from him just then—if she thought Alex might have settled for that alone. But his scuffle with the errand boy had only heightened his energy; she could see that in his eyes along with the fun, and Caroline wasn't sure she would be able to stop Alex if he really wanted to make love to her. His darker side still made her nervous. He had slammed their visitor against the wall so hard she had seen veinlike cracks in the plaster near his shoulder. But his lips on her palm were tantalizingly gentle.

Carefully, Caroline disengaged her hand and tucked it behind her back. It was better to end things now, before they got out of hand. "Good night, Alex."

She had an appealing, winsome quality, he thought, looking down at her upturned face. With dewy green eyes softened by firelight and vodka and perhaps a changing opinion of him as well, Alex suddenly began to hope, she looked as fresh as a girl. Her beauty was cool and her touch-me-not air had a maddening allure. But she reacted to every nuance of his seduction with little intakes of breath, a quickening of her pulse and a tremble in her hands. Her inexperience was tantalizing to a man like himself—tantalizing and therefore dangerous. Caro was open to sensation and responded naturally, with curiosity and pleasure, when she allowed herself. Making love to her would be exquisite, he knew. And that kind of pleasure often made idiots out of strong men.

If he pushed tonight, he thought, she might give in. He was almost willing to risk it. But he had already pushed too hard for one day, and he didn't want to face a weeping Caroline Conover in the morning. No. He wanted to wake up with her laughing and tussling in the sheets. No tears and no strings. That was the way he wanted her.

With a grin, he said, "This isn't how traditional picnics are supposed to end, you know."

"We'll start a new tradition."

"I'll help with the dishes. Should I take out the trash?" He caressed her cheek lightly, putting every ounce of his personal magnetism into coaxing a few more minutes out of her. He dropped his voice to a seductive murmur. "Don't you think I should put out the fire before I leave?"

"I think," she said, cocking a determined look up at him, "that we'll let the fire burn itself out."

The woman was made of steel.

She called him a taxi, and Alex was forced to say good-night. At the last second, standing in the door-way with the embers of the fire glowing inside and a cold rain falling outside, and Caroline looking as delectable as the sweetest pastry on earth, he almost snatched her up and kissed the stuffing out of her. But he refrained. The voice of reason prevailed.

In the cab on the way back to his hotel, Alex brooded for a while and finally startled himself and his driver by speaking aloud. Out of the blue, he said, "I should have told her in the beginning."

The driver looked back over the seat. "What's that, Mac?"

"Nothing," Alex said, running his hand through his hair in exasperation. "I just— I wasn't honest with a woman."

"Tsk, tsk," said the driver, a bald-headed, pink-cheeked chap with a cigar in his teeth. "You gotta be up front with dames. Take it from me, buddy. If you start with the lies, you'll end up catchin' a fast train out of town. Take it from me. What didn't you tell her about? Your wife or something?"

"No," said Alex. "Her sister."

"Uh-oh," said the driver, looking reproachfully at Alex in the rearview mirror. "You're foolin' around with her sister, huh?"

"Not anymore," Alex replied. He stared out the cab window at the dismal rainy night. "But I used to."

The driver wagged his head mournfully. "Tsk, tsk. You're gonna be in big trouble someday, pal. Mark my words."

Alex sighed. "Don't I know it."

He went back to his hotel room and tried to sleep. But more than unfulfilled desire kept him awake. Alex began to wonder if he hadn't made a whole lot of mistakes where the virtuous Miss Conover was concerned.

WHEN MONDAY DAWNED, Caroline almost expected to find Alex Varanov's head on the other pillow. She rolled out of bed, cursing herself for having such a fertile imagination. What a dream she'd had! A whole week of sensual pleasures, naked games and a hot-blooded Russian taunting her into letting down her inhibitions. How could her subconscious allow her to fantasize so graphically about the man? Making love on a hard wooden floor was not Caro's idea of pleasure at all—Alex had planted that idea in her brain! All his suggestive talk had driven her sleeping mind beyond the limits of propriety.

The vodka hadn't helped. Her head ached enough to send her staggering for the aspirin. She wasn't at all used to strong liquor.

He wasn't her type, she decided in the shower as the aspirin began to work. He liked short-term relationships based on sex and nothing more. She'd known him for two days, and he'd already made that perfectly clear. He wanted to save his family some money and get her into bed as a bonus. No, Alex wasn't her type. If they had longer than a week together, she might consider getting to know him, but it just wasn't possible. She had a deadline now. One week to close the mystery. One week to learn Jane's secrets and find a way to explain them at home.

So she had better stop dreaming about Alex Varanov pronto, she ordered herself. Other matters required her concentration. She put on a winter-white dress and went to work.

The employee entrance was crowded with arriving clerks when she got there. Caroline bumped into Betsy, and they headed up the stairs together.

For an instant, Caro got the impression that the younger woman was frightened of her. Betsy ducked her head, seemingly wanting to avoid Caroline, but Caroline caught up, and Betsy's face turned red.

Several more clerks brushed past them, hurrying to get to their posts.

Trying to put an obviously nervous Betsy at ease, Caroline said, "What's the rush this morning? Everybody seems in such a hurry."

"It's the Veteran's Day sale," Betsy answered shortly. Then, realizing she must have sounded brusque, she said, "It runs all week, but customers really crowd into the store today. And on Friday, too, because everybody figures we'll mark down the merchandise even further, just to get rid of it. The whole store will be mobbed."

"Except for the fur salon," Caroline guessed. "Fur coats don't go on sale."

"Not this time of year, that's for sure. Listen, I'm going to be floating through other departments today so clerks can take breaks. Can you handle the salon alone? I'll relieve you for lunch, of course."

"No problem." Caroline noted the look of relief on Betsy's face and wondered if the younger woman was glad to have avoided spending time with her. Trying to be friendly once more, she said, "Say, Betsy, how was your date on Sunday?"

Betsy laughed tightly, nervous all over again. "Oh, it was dreamy. Lots of fun."

"Oh," said Caro. "Good."

"You think so? I mean, he's so much older and I—well, I'm not looking to get married, you know?" Betsy shrugged, suddenly blasé. "He wants a few quickies with me, that's all."

Caroline started to speak, but Betsy rattled on hastily, "I don't mind a bit. He's got sophistication, you know?"

Caroline nodded weakly, and another clerk called to Betsy and engaged her in a conversation. Caroline headed for the escalator alone, rode upward and got out her key to unlock the fur salon. As she approached the salon, however, she saw that the lights were on and the door was open.

She entered hurriedly, and found Rupert conferring with Bob, the young man from the security team. Bob spotted her first, and he flushed with pleasure.

Rupert turned and saw her also. "Caroline!"

"Good morning, Rupert. Hi, Bob. What's all this about?"

Bob began, "Oh, we're—"

But Rupert cut him off importantly. "Nothing to be upset about," he said soothingly, taking her arm. "A new store policy suggested by Mrs. St. Cloud. She wants an inventory taken in the vault every morning."

"An inventory? To see if anything's been stolen, you mean?"

"Exactly. Bob is going to take care of it for Mrs. St. Cloud. You won't have any extra duties."

Caroline shot a suspicious look at him. "Primarily because I'm still the one suspected of taking coats before, right?"

"Now, honey, there's no sense getting sarcastic." He drew her out of Bob's earshot and said, "You look great this morning. Prettier than ever."

Caroline didn't feel pretty, thanks to Alex and his vodka. But she managed a smile. To get close to Rupert she was going to have to send her sensibilities on vacation. "Thanks, Rupert. You look wonderful, as usual. I love your tie. Pink looks good on you."

He admired the tie, too. "Yeah, nice, huh? Say, Caroline, I came up here to soften another blow for you."

"I beg your pardon?"

Rupert spread his hands. "I know it seems silly, but I have to station a security man up here."

"What? What for?"

"I met with the store's security team to prepare for today's sale. They have to deal with increased customer traffic, but they haven't forgotten this assignment where you're concerned—"

"Then I'm still Public Enemy Number One?"

"I'm sorry. You and I both know you're innocent, but *somebody* stole those coats, and until we find out who, you're still the only suspect. The head of store security says you shouldn't be left alone in the salon anymore."

"I see." *That* policy was certainly going to put a crimp in her detecting.

"It's a temporary situation, I'm sure," Rupert assured her. "Until it's over, there'll be a man assigned to you."

"Bob?"

"Uh—yes."

Caroline looked longingly into Rupert's face. Steeling herself, she said, "I wish it could be you."

He smiled, not surprised. "So do I."

Bravely, she said, "Why don't we have lunch together? I had such a pleasant evening with you on Saturday, I'd kind of like to try again. To see if we're as compatible as I think we might be."

Caroline nearly winced at the line, and she figured Rupert would see right through her act. But he responded as if the praise were his due. "I like the idea," he said, smiling. "We could go out for lunch—avoid the cafeteria."

"Can you get away from the store? There's the sale today. I know you're busy—"

He waved that off. "This store is a well-oiled machine, thanks to me. It'll survive if I step out for an hour. Let's do it. I'll come get you at one."

"Wonderful." Caroline wrinkled her nose the way she'd seen Betsy do it, and waved her fingertips. "See you then."

Rupert left, looking pleased.

Caroline led Bob into the fur salon and closed the door. "Sleaze," she muttered.

"Excuse me?" said Bob, looking bright and alert. A lock of brown hair hung over his forehead, giving him the appearance of a perky Shetland pony.

"Nothing, my friend." Caroline turned and smiled at him. "Well, since you're here, how about if you help me with some spring cleaning?"

"It's November."

"The concept's the same. Didn't your mother ever make you help with the cleaning?"

"Oh, yes, ma'am," said Bob. "All the kids in my family helped out. I know all about cleaning and such. You got any aprons up here?"

"No," said Caro. "But we'll make do."

She and Bob worked well together. He was an earnest young man, a hard worker and pleasant company. Since the Veteran's Day sale was raging in the rest of the store, only one customer appeared in the fur salon all morning.

Betsy arrived at one to relieve Caroline. After one look at her, Caroline thought poor Bob was going to swallow his teeth. He looked as if he'd been instantly smitten. Betsy, on the other hand, treated him as if he were invisible.

Rupert arrived a few minutes later. He obviously hadn't counted on Betsy being the clerk who would be standing in for Caroline during her lunch hour. Seeing Betsy sitting at the desk sent Rupert into a sputtering bluster.

"This is a business lunch," he explained to Betsy as Caroline gathered up her handbag. "I want to discuss future plans for the salon with Miss Conover."

Betsy looked suspicious. "Sure," she said, unconvinced by Rupert's flimsy story.

Caroline figured her best bet was to play dumb. She left Betsy in Bob's care and waved to both of them, saying, "See you in an hour."

On the escalator going down, Caroline gathered that Rupert was obviously uncomfortable at having been found out by his current girlfriend. He talked rapidly to Caroline, saying, "Betsy's a good girl. A good employee. I'm sure she'll go far in the organization. She's young, of course. But she's got potential. Yes, I'm sure she'll go far. I should take her under my wing, I suppose, but—well, you know how that sort of thing can be misinterpreted by other people."

"Yes," Caroline agreed. "It must be difficult balancing your relationships with the employees."

Rupert nodded vigorously. "Very difficult."

"Discretion must be important."

"*Highly* important," said Rupert.

"Showing any favoritism could be disastrous for everyone involved, couldn't it?"

"Absolutely," he said. "I could help a great many careers if people would just remember that I can't be *viewed* as helping anyone in particular."

Caroline giggled. "You can be biased as long as you don't *look* biased."

"Exactly." With a shade of bitterness, he said, "If Betsy would just keep her mouth shut, I could do her some good."

Caroline sighed in sympathy. "It's a shame more people don't see what a fine line you must walk."

He smiled at her. "Caroline, you have an uncanny insight into the problems I face." He took her arm like a courtly gentleman and patted her hand. "You're an understanding woman."

"It's nice of you to think so, Rupert. Where can I take you for lunch?"

"Oh, let me be the host. I'll take you to my club."

"No, no, I insist. I invited you, remember. You've been so kind to me in my job, I'd like to repay you in this small way." She paused, and bit her lip gently. "And I—well, I was hoping we could finish the conversation we started Saturday night."

"What conversation was that?"

"About my moonlighting. I thought things over and I—a little extra income sounds very tempting."

He smiled benevolently. "Having trouble paying your bills?"

"A little."

"I was looking at your personnel file the other day," he said suddenly, still oozing kindness. "I couldn't help noticing that your address is the same house where another employee of mine used to live."

"Oh?" said Caroline.

"Jane Wexler was her name," he said. "Have I mentioned her before? She's no longer with us. I see you're living at her old address. It was an expensive place, if I remember what she used to say. Funny how you ended up at the same address."

"Yes." Hastily, Caroline said, "I asked about apartments when I applied for this job. Someone in the personnel department—I forget who—suggested I check that house. I was lucky. The place hadn't been rented. But I'd like to buy some furniture." Trying to steer the conversation back where she wanted it,

Caroline said, "I could use some added income right now."

Rupert was still smiling. Caroline hoped he'd swallowed her lie. He patted her hand again. "Let's talk about it over lunch," he said. "I have a few ideas."

Unfortunately, he didn't have much of a chance to discuss them. At the Indian restaurant where they ended up for lunch, Rupert was accosted by a man who introduced himself as a business associate and soon pulled up a chair and monopolized the conversation. He wanted to talk large-screen televisions.

"I know where you can get a sweetheart of a deal, Rupe," he said. "A couple hundred sets for St. Cloud's inventory."

Caroline tuned out their dialogue and fumed that she wasn't going to get to pump Rupert for the information she wanted. She checked her watch a few too many times, and Rupert finally noticed. "It's getting late, isn't it? I'm sorry, Larry, but we've got to get back to the store. Call me. We'll set up a lunch and talk figures."

All smiles, Larry stood up and shook hands.

"I'm sorry," Rupert said as they walked back to the store. "We didn't get to have our conversation, did we?"

Caroline smiled. "I'm sure we'll get another chance. How about dinner tonight?"

"Wonderful. After work, I'll meet you."

"Good. I'll just remember the key word."

"What's that?"

"Discretion."

"Yes, discretion," Rupert agreed. "Absolutely. You're a clever young woman, Caroline. You know the rules, don't you?"

"I hope so."

She didn't see Rupert again at all that day. He was busy in his office or floating through the store supervising the sale, so she stayed at her post and made the most of Bob's company.

"Who do you think is stealing from the store?" she asked him curiously.

He was relaxing on the powder-blue settee, looking faintly stunned by his good fortune—spending the day with Caroline and seeing glimpses of pretty Betsy had sent him to seventh heaven. But he considered her question seriously. "Everybody," he said.

"Everybody?"

"Sure. It's the biggest problem stores like this have. Shoplifting is minor compared to employee theft. Some clerks borrow a pencil and forget to leave it at their register. A hosiery girl needs a pair of stockings for a date, so she 'borrows' them."

"But that's small stuff," Caro objected. "What about coats and jewelry? That's not petty theft."

"I don't know," Bob admitted. "But it's somebody smart, that's for sure—somebody who can get in and out without raising suspicions."

"Like who? Who comes into the store after hours, Bob?"

He lifted his shoulders. "I can't tell. I'm usually on the day shift. I was just filling in Saturday night. Mostly, I stay down in the basement near the vault."

Confused, Caro said, "There's another fur vault downstairs?"

"Not a fur vault. A money vault. St. Cloud's doesn't take money to the bank every night the way smaller stores do. We keep cash in a vault—until Thursdays, when an armored car comes. Mostly I keep an eye on the vault."

"So you don't know who comes in at night?"

"No, but I could get a copy of the printout, I suppose."

"Maybe you should," Caroline suggested, "since we're not selling many coats today. While we're stuck up here, you and I could spend the time trying to solve the mystery."

Bob smiled. "I'd like doing something with you, Miss Conover. Do you think Miss Nofsinger might help, too?"

Caroline patted the young man's shoulder. "I think Betsy's got something else on her mind right now."

So until the store closed, Bob and Caroline discussed the possibilities. Bob wasn't very imaginative, though, and mostly shot holes in Caroline's theories. At closing time, Caroline was almost glad to have a date with Rupert to look forward to.

Bob escorted her down to the employee exit. Caro left her passkey in her locker, figuring if she was going to be a decoy, she had better go on giving the real crooks all the chances she could. Then Caro saw Rupert and waved. He waved back, but pressed out through the revolving door to the sidewalk.

Caroline hurried to catch up. Rupert stood on the curb, hand up to flag a cab.

Caroline tugged his sleeve. "Rupert, are you ready for our dinner date?"

He turned and laughed. "You're persistent, aren't you, Caroline?"

She smiled. "Sure—when I find something I really want." She dusted an imaginary fleck off of his tie. "And I really want to spend some time with you, Rupert . . . to get to know you."

He removed her hand, gently but firmly, and his eyes flickered around the area to see if anyone had witnessed the small familiarity. "I'd like to get to know you, too, Caroline. But not tonight. Sorry. I've got an appointment I can't miss. It just came up."

She managed a disappointed expression. "All right. But some day soon, I hope? I really want to talk with you, Rupert. My pocketbook is awfully empty. Maybe tomorrow?"

He pinched her chin lightly, smiling. "It's a date. I'll check with you during your shift."

She winked. "Thanks."

He caught his taxi then, and she melted back into the crowd, worrying. Maybe she had overdone it. Why was he so anxious to avoid her all of a sudden?

A horn tooted in the street. Automatically, Caroline turned her head to look, and there—to her profound surprise—was her very own Volvo sedan swinging toward the curb with Alex at the wheel. She marched over and yanked open the door.

"What the hell are you doing with my car?"

"Get in," he ordered. "Before somebody sees us together."

Caroline climbed into the car and slammed the door. "I asked you a question. You've stolen my car! You probably broke into my garage and hot-wired—"

"I needed wheels today. I returned my rental and taxis are too expensive. I saw you with Watkins just now."

"What?"

"I saw you gazing adoringly at Rupert Watkins. I take it your relationship is warming up?"

"Of course it is. That's the whole point, isn't it? Look, you can't go around helping yourself to my property, Varanov. I'm not insured for other people driving my car." The Volvo lurched into traffic, tires squealing, and Caroline grabbed for support. "Alex! Pull over and let me drive. You're—"

"What the hell were you saying to him, anyway?"

"I was wheedling a date with him, if you must know. I may have overdone it, as a matter of fact. Slow down, will you?"

"You weren't wheedling, you were drooling. And petting him! The guy wears a pink tie, for God's sake!"

"I wasn't drooling or wheedling. I was being nice."

"You were coming on like a hooker," Alex snapped. "Making cow eyes at him like—"

"*Cow* eyes?" Caroline repeated, laughing suddenly.

"How far do you plan on going with him?"

"What?"

"You heard me. Are you going to sleep with that guy?"

Caroline couldn't come up with an answer. Alex was in a fine, high temper, and looked rougher than usual in a dark, rumpled shirt, his black jacket, jeans and his sunglasses, which didn't mask his foul mood. The sunset, vividly bright through the windshield, glared down through the city's buildings and caused Alex to furrow his brow like Dracula in daylight. Caroline tore her gaze from him and glanced to the street. At once, she grabbed for the dashboard. "Alex! Watch the road!"

He jerked the car back into his own lane of traffic just in time to miss an oncoming city bus. A horn blasted to let Alex know he'd nearly caused an accident. Muttering, he rolled up his window and jammed the accelerator to the floor to get through the next intersection on the yellow light.

Trying to sound calm, Caroline said, "This isn't Indianapolis, Alex. Just get me home in one piece, will you? You don't have to break any speed records."

"Why not?" he asked, teeth clenched. "No date with Rupert tonight?"

"No, I'm not meeting him tonight. He's busy."

"So you *tried* to make a date with him?"

"For crying out loud, Alex, what's your problem? Rupert is our only lead! How will I gain his confidence if I'm not friendly?"

"Friendly doesn't mean fawning."

"I'm not an actress," she reminded him. "I'm doing the best I can."

"How come you can bat your eyes and play sexy games with Rupert and not with me?" Alex growled.

Caroline opened her mouth and closed it with a snap. She counted to ten. "Is that what this is all about?" she asked finally. "That was a ridiculous thing to say, Alex. I'm going to pretend you didn't say it at all. Let's start all over again, all right? Hello, Alex. Thanks so much for picking me up after work. Is this a new car?"

His hands loosened their white-knuckle grip on the steering wheel. He even slowed the car slightly and took the time to glance into the rearview mirror to see if he'd left any smashed vehicles in his wake. "All right," he said, taking off his glasses. "I lost my head."

"You nearly lost your life," she remarked. "That bus missed us by inches."

"I was mad," he said, tossing the glasses on top of the dashboard. "I had a rotten day. And seeing you with Pinkie was—"

Caroline cut him off gently. "What was so rotten about your day? What did you do?"

"I played detective. I found out some things, too."

"Great! Like what?"

"I met a man named Vinnie the Vulture."

"Alex, you're joking! I meant— Wait, you're not joking, are you?"

He shook his head and drove with more attention devoted to the road. "No, I'm not kidding. He's the sometime boss of the boy who came calling last night, though I had a feeling the kid was free-lancing last night. I took Vinnie to lunch today. I paid your sister's tab and got some information in return."

"You paid— Alex, you didn't have to do that. Let me reimburse you. I'll write you a check."

"Forget it," he said. "It's the least I could do."

"What do you mean?" Caroline objected. "You don't owe Jane or me any favors. At least not any worth a twenty-five-hundred-dollar debt. I can afford it—"

"Just shut up about that," Alex said brusquely. "I learned some other stuff."

"What stuff?"

"That Rupert owes a ton of money, and it's not all for gambling. Your boyfriend has a penchant for nose candy."

"Oh, heavens. Cocaine?" Caroline sighed. "I must be a total square. It's so sordid. It's awful."

"There's more," he said grimly. "You're not going to like it."

Caro looked at Alex's stony profile. "What is it?" Then, seeing his face, she knew. "Oh, Alex. Jane, too?"

He nodded. "She was in over her head in lots of ways, Caroline. Drugs, parties—"

"What kind of parties?"

"Don't ask," he said shortly. "Just believe me when I say they weren't your kind of scene at all."

Caroline put one hand to her mouth and was surprised to discover that she was trembling. She was ready to believe Jane had been in trouble. But she was just realizing she wasn't ready for the depth of that trouble.

Alex said, "You want me to stop the car?"

She shook her head, trying to steady her nerves. "No, I'm all right. Go on."

Alex sighed and took a different tack. "One of Vinnie's sidelines is fencing stolen goods. He didn't exactly say that, but he hinted. I had to promise that I wouldn't go to the police before he told me any of this. Vinnie is probably well-known to the cops, anyway. Information I might take to them won't be news. Anyway, he so much as admitted he accepts merchandise from anybody who's selling it. Judging by his close relationship with Rupert, I wouldn't be surprised if he fenced the coats and jewelry from St. Cloud's. Maybe he even pays in coke."

"Might he have accepted goods from Jane, do you think?"

"I doubt it. From the way Vinnie was talking, Jane wasn't selling anything except—well, she wasn't selling stolen goods."

"How—how bad was it, Alex? For Jane, I mean? Do you think she— Was she in bad trouble?"

Alex pulled the car into the alley behind Caroline's house. He slid the Volvo past the wrought-iron fence, but stopped just outside the garage. He put the engine in neutral, set the brake and half turned toward Caroline, one hand braced on the back of her seat. His voice was subdued. "She had fallen a long way, Caroline. She liked cocaine, she had a weakness for gambling, and she didn't mind moonlighting at Vinnie's parties—entertaining his friends to make a few hundred bucks a night. I don't know what else she was doing to make extra money for herself, but it might have included a conspiracy to steal from St. Cloud's."

Caroline was glad he had stopped the car. Suddenly she needed to breathe. She had to get out and inhale fresh air. She struggled with the door handle and finally wrenched it open. Stumbling, she got out of the car and leaned against the hood.

Alex shut off the engine and got out, too. He came around the hood and stopped, jingling the keys from one hand to the other. "There's more," he said.

Dully, Caroline thought she couldn't absorb any more. She had heard too much already.

Alex said, "I talked to the police today, too."

"You did? After promising Vinnie—"

"I wanted to hear their side of Jane's death. Did you get a report?"

She nodded. "Yes, we received an official report. My father talked with a Lieutenant Braggs, too."

Alex nodded. "I met him today. I said I was— I pretended to be a friend of Jane's. An acquaintance on the New York police force phoned to back up my story and lend some clout. I asked about the circumstances of her suicide—the way they found her, the blood tests, everything. But I wanted to hear it from the guys who found her, not their commanding officer."

"And?"

"And," Alex said steadily, "I'm not so sure it was suicide."

That was too much to bear. Caroline had to sit down. She tottered two steps, and Alex put his hand under her arm to help, but she plunked down on the stone steps and sat still. She looked straight ahead at the car. She had left the door open and knew she ought to go close it again, but she couldn't manage.

Her brain was suddenly occupied with irrelevant thoughts.

She said, "Jane used to be afraid to say her prayers at night."

"What?"

"You know. 'Now I lay me down to sleep.' She was afraid. Of the last part. 'If I should die before I wake.'"

Alex swore softly. He shoved his hands into his jeans pockets and turned his back to Caroline.

Caroline clasped her hands between her knees to stop their trembling. "She was afraid to die, Alex. She wouldn't have— I didn't think she'd have taken her own life. Despite the fact that she was always emotional about men. As a kid, she'd go off the deep end if a boy called to break a date. But even if she'd had a bad romance, I don't think—"

"Stop it," Alex said. "You're just rambling now."

She tilted her head and looked numbly up at him.

"I've got a headache," he said, squeezing the bridge of his nose. "Let's go inside."

Caroline didn't move. Looking up at him, she asked, "Did someone kill my sister, Alex?"

He dropped his hand and shook his head. "I don't know."

"Was it an overdose?"

"Yes," he said. "But she could have been helped. Cocaine and pills mixed with some booze—" He hesitated, then said it. "She might have been murdered."

"The police?"

He made an impatient gesture. "They're not interested. If she'd been a different kind of person, they might make the effort. But Jane was hooking and doing drugs, running around with a bad crowd. People like that die all the time and the police don't get involved. They figure people like Jane are going to die one way or the other and they— God, Caro, don't look at me like that!"

Shaking, Caroline cried out, "She was a nice person, Alex!"

"No," he snapped. "She wasn't, Caroline. She was messed up and in trouble!"

"She was my sister!"

"That doesn't make her a saint!"

Then they were shouting at each other. Caroline got to her feet, angry and half-hysterical. "Somebody did it to her!" she blurted out. "Somebody made her bad, Alex!"

"She changed out of her own free will, damn it. She made her own decisions!"

"She was a weak person. She wasn't smart. She— Jane was used!"

Alex seized her wrists. His face was dark and angry. "What are we supposed to do about that now? We can't save her. We can't change what happened to her."

"Find the person! We have to find the person who ruined my sister."

Alex shook her, trying to make his point by force. "*Who* ruined her, though? The first guy who paid her for sex? The person who sold her the first line of coke?

The last man she thought she was in love with? Who do we pin the blame on, Caroline?"

"There has to be someone—"

"How about you?" Alex demanded, his eyes blazing. "Where were you when your sister was getting into trouble? Aren't you responsible, too?"

Caroline slapped him. She hit him with all her strength and cried out even as the blow connected.

Alex's head snapped back, but he didn't let go. He held her tightly, and Caroline collapsed against him, crying. "Oh, Alex, I'm sorry. I'm *sorry*. I'm crazy. I never— I'm sorry, really. Please, I—"

She wasn't making sense. Not even to herself. Caroline only knew that the pain inside herself had grown unbearable. "Alex, I didn't mean it."

Gruffly, he said, "Come on. Into the house."

CHAPTER NINE

BY THE TIME they made it into the kitchen, Alex couldn't see straight anymore. The party in his head was going full swing, and he could hardly hear Caroline's voice over the commotion. He wanted to help her, to make her understand, but he couldn't even walk across the threshold without stumbling. The headache was swooping swiftly into his head, blinding him, dulling every sense. Soon the pain would come crashing into his brain.

"Are you all right?" Caroline asked. She didn't need his support anymore. *He* was the one who couldn't negotiate the floor without help. Caroline wrapped her arm around his waist. "Alex?"

"I've got to take some pills," he said, his voice coming out thickly as the pain in his head intensified. "My pocket."

She stripped off his jacket and found the vial of prescription capsules. Though her hands shook, she opened it rapidly. "How many?"

He held up two fingers, leaning against the refrigerator like a punch-drunk prizefighter. He pressed his forehead to the cool metal, but it didn't help. Nausea rose inside him.

"You should have said something earlier. Alex, what's—are you sick?"

She put the capsules into his hand when he couldn't take them from her palm. She even closed his fingers around them. He said, "It's a headache. I— It'll go in a little while."

He gulped the pills without benefit of water, but the act of knocking back his head set the party to jumping. With a full-fledged groan, he caught his balance on the counter. He'd let it get out of control again. Even his knees felt weak from the pain. A strobe light was flashing in his head, too, blinding him. Two headaches in two days. They were getting worse, coming more frequently—intensifying, too.

"Come on," said Caroline. "You'd better lie down."

He didn't remember how he got into the bedroom or stretched himself out on the bed. All he knew was that suddenly he was surrounded by pillows and sheets that smelled just like Caroline's delicate perfume. And she was flitting around the room like a soundless butterfly in a white dress, pulling the blinds and drawing the curtains. The darkness was sweet. Alex tried to relax, to let the pain evaporate into the dark.

Minutes passed, perhaps even an hour. Eventually Caroline was back and holding a cup to his lips. "Swallow," she murmured.

"It's all right," he muttered back. "It'll go away. Just takes a while."

"Why didn't you take your pills sooner?" Frustrated, she said, "You were breaking bad news to me instead, that's why. Alex, you should take better care of yourself.''

"Don't nag," he said, cracking one eye open far enough to look at her. She had brought a single candle into the room, and its glow was gently golden. That, and a soft light from the kitchen cast just enough illumination into the room so he could make out her silhouette. She was curled up on the bed and bending over him like Florence Nightingale. Her fair hair clung to the curves of her face, and Alex wished he had the strength to reach up and take a handful of it. Even in the half light, it seemed to give off a shine of its own.

She slipped her hand under the back of his neck and tilted his head so he could take a sip of water. She goofed, though, and half of it went down his chest. "Don't," he grumbled, closing both eyes again. "You'll drown me."

"I'd like to drown you," she whispered back. "You just scared me half to death."

"It's all right," he insisted.

"Sure. I bet you'll feel like going dancing soon."

"No, it's—that's what's in my head right now."

"What?"

"A big party," he said, for the first time in his life voicing what the headache felt like. "There's loud music and awful lights and—and somebody's throwing things."

Nervously, she said, "I think I'd better leave you alone."

He seized her wrist before she could slip away. "Stay," he said, but he couldn't quite get his hand to hold her.

But she didn't pull away. "You're sure?"

He subsided into the pillow. "It'll go. I did it to myself—not eating right, the bright lights, you. It's stress, mostly."

"We've had plenty of that lately."

"Talk to me," said Alex. "I'm— I feel bad about what I said—the way I told you."

Caroline sighed. She held his hand, tucking it unconsciously against her own cheek. "I'm sorry, too. I'm sorry I hit you. I was upset. It's not easy, Alex."

"I know," he mumbled. He was sorry for lots of things. For telling Caroline about her sister's terrible end. But more than anything, for his own part in what had happened to Jane Wexler.

It hadn't taken an interview with Vinnie the Vulture for Alex to understand that he, too, had figured in Jane's downfall. He'd known her. He'd known her well, in fact. His head thumped with the refrain. Had he been the final straw for Jane? Had Alex Varanov been the man to drive her over the edge of propriety? Had *he* sent her into a life of drugs and sex for money?

He swore softly at the thought.

"Hush," said Caroline. "It will pass."

He should tell her. Alex wanted to sit up and do it then and there. But the party was going strong and he knew he'd botch it. He was tired. Just then he wanted nothing more than to lie in Caroline's arms and breathe in the scent of her, feel her slender body next to his, listen to the strong beat of her gentle heart. He lay his head on her breast and heard the ceaseless rhythm of her breathing. It comforted him, relaxed his ache. She was good and sweet, and maybe if he lay still and held her tightly, he thought dreamily, he could draw some of her goodness into himself.

Caroline began to caress his temples. Her touch was feather-soft and somehow, the pain in his head responded. It started to fade. The pills had helped, but Alex knew it was mainly Caroline's angel-like massage that was smoothing heavenly relief throughout his head.

"Talk to me," he said again.

She touched her lips to his forehead. "You're sure? It won't make things worse?"

Hell, no. All he wanted to hear was her softness. It might blot the guilt, ease his pain. He wanted to get lost in her sweetness.

"When I was sick," she said softly, touching his cheek, "I used to hide in my room with all the windows open. Can you imagine it? I had an oak canopy bed with white eyelet covers, lace curtains in the windows, and the walls were painted yellow like daffodils."

Yes, Alex could imagine her in a room like that.

"The sunshine came in and kept me warm in my bed and chased the fever away. Jane taught me that. When I had the chicken pox, she'd climb the tree next to my room and bring me kittens. Our cat had litters every spring, and that year they were all black. Every one of them. We made braided ribbons to go around their necks. Even now, when I'm not feeling well, I think of those kittens and I always cheer up just a little. Jane used to be wonderful, Alex. I want you to believe that.''

''I know,'' he said.

''I loved her very much. We—we used to be a lot alike.''

''How?''

Caroline felt him relaxing, and she began to experience a calmness, too, as she brushed her fingertips—and occasionally her lips—over his temples. She liked holding Alex this way. It was pleasant there in the dark. Somehow, it seemed possible to tell him secrets, to talk about Jane without the ugly present crowding in to spoil her memories.

''You won't believe it,'' she said, ''but I used to be just like her. I wanted to be just like her! I looked up to her and tried to do everything she did.''

''Everything?''

''Everything.''

Alex opened his eyes, and tilted his head to look at her. Caroline smiled a little sheepishly down at him. He seemed safe lying there. It couldn't hurt to tell him. ''We were wild. You probably won't believe it, but I was considered a very fast young girl.''

''Fast?'' he repeated as if he didn't comprehend the word.

Caroline felt herself start to blush. ''Oversexed.''

Alex seemed to wake up very quickly. His blue eyes widened. *''You?''*

Smiling, Caro lay back and looked up at the ceiling. ''I was a hellion in my younger days, Alex. Be glad you didn't know me then. I've almost forgotten that time of my life. Most girls are boy crazy, but my sister and I—we could think of nothing else. I nearly flunked my junior year in high school because I was too concerned about boys.''

''I don't believe it,'' he said flatly.

''It's true. Those wild Wexler sisters. We were very anxious to grow up.''

''How wild were you?''

''We smoked cigarettes and sneaked out our bedroom windows at night to meet boys, drink beer and go skinny-dipping. I used to think that was very sophisticated.''

''What happened? I mean—''

''How'd I get so uptight? I saw the light eventually. That's another story.'' She smoothed his hair again, her fingers playing in the black strands. ''I was like her—wanting to be older than I was. But I learned. Something happened that made me realize I had better do something with my life. I was Betsy's age at the time. I straightened out, though. I found out that being grown up was more than partying and dates with older men.''

''Seems to me,'' he said with a trace of amused bitterness, ''you got a little *too* straight.''

Laughing suddenly, Caroline said, ''Believe me, if I'd met you ten years ago...''

She let her voice drift off. Her past had been successfully buried for nearly a decade. It seemed odd and a little embarrassing to be talking about it now, after the wages of sin had done their worst to Jane. Caro would have let the subject drop there, but Alex managed to get himself up on one elbow. He must have been feeling better, because he wasn't so white and his eyes almost glittered with curiosity. "What might have happened if I'd met you ten years ago?"

She smiled. With her fingertip, she traced a line down the buttons of his shirt, down his chest. "Things might have been different," she murmured. "You can be a skunk from time to time, Alex Varanov, but you're not bad to look at."

A distant cousin of his roguish grin started, curling his mouth, changing his face. Amused, he taunted, "I had a feeling you weren't all sweetness and light."

"You did?"

"There was a look in your eye the first time we met."

Laughing, Caroline asked, "What kind of look?"

"Like you'd read your Masters and Johnson and knew all about the Playboy Advisor. It was you who thought of sex games, remember?"

"How could I help it? You were slouching around looking like a Russian Heathcliff! The Prince of Darkness with a switchblade. What was I supposed to think?"

"Hmph," he said, disgruntled. "I was thinking of James Bond."

She laughed teasingly. He rolled onto his back and in the process managed to slide his arm underneath her head. Caroline turned with him, nestling against his frame. He looked long and powerful there in her white sheets, but vaguely vulnerable, too. His usual toughness was tempered. She'd seen him devastated by pain and had helped him through it. It was a role she rather liked. For once, he wasn't taking charge and bullying.

Softly, Caro said, "You're a sexy man, Alex. Why aren't you married?"

"I was," he said, surprising the dickens out of her.

Caroline sat up on her elbow, startled. "Really?"

He returned her look. "Yep. For eight years."

"What happened? No, wait, that's too personal. You don't have to answer that."

He chuckled. "I'm in your bed, Caro. What could be too personal? It's no big deal. I was married. We got divorced. Her name is Joyce and we lived on the Upper West Side. She's still got the apartment, in fact. We split last year." He hesitated. "The issue was kids."

"Children? You didn't want them?"

"I did," he said at once. "So did she. Just not with me."

"Alex! What in the world—"

"These headaches," he muttered, passing one hand across his forehead in exasperation. "They're heredi-tary—kind of like the Romanovs' hemophilia, I guess, but believe me, not as charming as the stories. My fa-ther has them and so does my brother. Joyce decided she didn't want her children to have them, too."

"Isn't there anything you can do? I mean, you were in such pain. I—"

He shook off that suggestion. "We're not sure what causes them, exactly. Stress, mostly. There's a doctor in New York who wants to try lasers, but I'm not ready for *Star Wars* in my head yet. What I've got is bad enough. Joyce just didn't think we ought to in-flict any kids with the problem. I had to agree."

So his wife had gone looking for someone else to
father a family for her, Caroline thought, even though
there were plenty of alternatives. What kind of woman
must she have been? How her abandonment must have
hurt a proud man like Alex! And every time his headache recurred, he was probably reminded of her leaving.

"Alex," Caro began.

"Don't," he said, his hands tightening on her arms.
"You don't have to say anything. I didn't tell you to
get sympathy."

"I wasn't going to talk," she murmured.

She kissed him instead.

Before Alex knew what was happening, she had
leaned over and pressed a soft, liquid kiss on his
mouth. She tasted sweet, smelled wonderful, and her
lithe body felt as if it was melting into his. He should
have stopped her, but it felt too good—as if the last
vestiges of his migraine were being washed away on the
gentle tide of her shy advance. Her hair caressed his
face and her lips were soft on his. Her supple legs were
unconsciously entwined with his own, and at once, a
seething spiral of desire flickered through Alex,
arousing every nerve and muscle in his body. He
tensed.

She felt the change and drew back, obviously not
having meant to arouse him. The kiss had been intended to comfort, it seemed. Caroline blinked in the
candlelight. Her eyes still glistened with emotion, but
turmoil was revealed in those green depths, too. She
had also felt a sexual stirring, Alex saw. He waited for

her to pull back completely, to stop the passion before it started.

But this time Caro hesitated. Perhaps she was as overwhelmed as he was by the heightened intimacy of the moment. Until then they had been adversaries, partners in deed, but not in spirit. Now suddenly the room seemed to echo with the sound of their matched heartbeats, the simultaneous catch in their breathing.

Rapt for a moment, Caroline touched his cheek with her fingers. Her eyes sparkled and her mouth tipped at the corners in a smile. Then her lashes fluttered down. She made a choice. Delving close once more, she resumed the kiss, making it count this time. Tremulous at first, she kissed him lightly. Then instinct took over and Caro sought a firmer coupling of mouth upon mouth. The sweetness of her tongue provoked a groan—his. His quick response and the catching of her body in his arms caused a moan—hers. She wrapped her arms around his neck and pressed close, reveling in the contact of knee to knee, thigh to thigh, her secret places nestling against his.

Alex's heart began to pound crazily. She was too good, too decent. A chaste little girl in a white dress. He didn't want to ruin her like he'd ruined Jane.

He seized her head, running his fingers deep into her hair and squeezing, forcing her to draw back. Caroline's eyes flashed open, surprised, hurt.

"Stop," he said.

"Alex, I—"

"I mean it," he said, grinding the words out so his anguish wouldn't show. "I'm not what you think, Caro. I'm not a fumbling teenager. With me, a little playful wrestling is going to lead somewhere you don't want to go."

Caro saw the darkness in his eyes. His grip on her head was fierce. Beneath hers, his body was rigid. She could feel the hardness of a man whose blood had been stirred, and he was right. His arousal didn't compare to the spindly, youthful erections she remembered from her past.

She sat up unsteadily, pushing her hair back. "I don't know what came over me. And you not feeling well! What an idiot I— I'm sorry. Talking about my misspent youth was a mistake, I guess."

"It's all right. My head's fine. It's not that." Trying to get himself under control again, Alex attempted conversation once more. "Why the change? How did the skinny-dipping teenager turn into such a—"

"Bitch?"

"I didn't say that."

"Thank you. I am sometimes, though." She smiled uncertainly. "I went to the other extreme. I was so leery of making the same mistake twice—"

He felt bad about having made her uncomfortable. He reached for her hand and linked their fingers to steady her. "What mistake? What do you mean?"

She tightened her hand in his, thankful for the support. Abruptly, she said, "I got pregnant when I was twenty."

That startled Alex into forgetting what he'd nearly let happen moments before. "You what?"

"Yes. My wild ways were soundly punished exactly the way my mother threatened they would be. I was in college at the time, but I went home on the weekends

to be with Mark—a high-school beau. We had a tor-
rid romance—as much as twenty-year-old kids can. I
wasn't very careful about protecting myself. When I
discovered I was going to have a baby, *that* was when
I finally read all the right books. I had to tell my parents, of course. What an uproar there was! You would
have thought I was the original sinner. Mark and I had
to get married.''

Of course. That was what good girls did, and Caro
was a very good girl. Not thinking, Alex brushed his
lips across the back of her hand. ''Not the abortion
type, hmm?''

''Heavens, no. My parents insisted we marry. His
parents weren't so keen on the idea, and Mark definitely dragged his feet, but—''

''What about you?''

''I had mixed feelings,'' Caroline admitted. ''I liked
Mark. At times I thought I was in love with him. And
I was bored with college. But we seemed to spend most
of our time together watching television and drinking
beer.'' Her smile was rueful. ''He had this joke book.
One Thousand Beer Jokes. I think I can still remember all of them. We had fun together, but after the
wedding, I realized I was headed for a life of *The Price
is Right* and knock-knock-who's-there. It came as a
shock.''

''So you have a child?'' Alex asked. He'd never
heard about her offspring before, hadn't imagined
Caroline as a mother.

She shook her head. ''No. At the time, I'd have
been a terrible parent, and Mark was just as irrespon-
sible. I— For better or for worse, I lost the baby. I

went into a terrible depression afterward. I felt as if I had somehow killed the child just by thinking how unhappy I was in the marriage."

"Caro," Alex began, determined to stop her if the memories got too painful.

"It's all right. I saw a shrink. I had developed a terrible fear of the dark, and I needed professional help. She said it was— Well, I got over thinking I'd killed the baby. It was a bad time for me."

Alex smoothed a lock of her hair from her face. He'd seen her surround herself with light. Though she thought she was cured of her fear of the dark, he could see she still harbored a nervousness. Even as they spoke, her safety candle burned by her side.

She smiled gratefully at the gentleness of his touch. She said, "I'm better now. Six months later Mark Conover and I were divorced. I felt as if I'd been given a second chance. I finished college in record time and went straight to law school. I wanted a life *much* different than the one I'd nearly landed for myself."

"In a way, you're still worried you might end up there, aren't you?"

"Yes. I learned that having fun could get me into permanent trouble."

"Having fun?" he repeated.

"Well—making love, I guess. Sex is nothing but trouble."

"You really believe that? Even now?"

She nodded. "Of course."

"But you've had lovers since then, though. Right?"

"One," she said. "In law school. But I was too— I was very careful about birth control. The pill had side effects so I had to—well, I wanted backup protection at all times. It—it drove him crazy."

"He was the only one?"

She nodded again, matter-of-factly.

Amazed, Alex asked, "How long ago was that?"

"Four years ago—no, five."

"Five— And you never— A smart woman who looks the way you do— Nobody's ever tempted you?"

"Sure I've been tempted, but the consequences—"

"You'll make *yourself* crazy!"

"Frustrated hormones, you mean?" She laughed. "Come on, Alex, do you really believe in that stuff?"

"Look," he said seriously. "After I got divorced, I played the monk for months. I wanted no part of anyone. But after a while, I—I started seeing women and it—well, it was a cleansing kind of experience. It was healthy. I needed to get out and prove something to myself, I suppose, but it felt good. In my head as much as anywhere else. You have to let out some of that energy just to keep on an even keel."

"You think my keel needs adjusting?"

"You've got a beautiful keel," he countered, allowing a grin, "but you're—well, you can be one uptight lady, all right."

"What's wrong with that?"

Alex found himself regarding her. She was easy on the eyes, certainly, and sweet-tempered most of the time. But he'd seen her react in frustration, try to bottle things up inside herself. She hadn't been able to cry about her sister, he suspected, until he had pushed her past the limits of human endurance. Caro was too tight inside, too controlled. The effort of restraining herself had begun to wear on her. She seemed brittle—easy to rile and hard to settle. But there was more to it than that. She didn't need sex just to ease her tension.

Honestly, he said, "I think you have a lot to give, Caroline. And that's what intimacy is about."

"I've given before," she said. "And it's not what it's cracked up to be."

"I don't mean the kind of sex that's like giving blood to the Red Cross. You might find that things have changed in the years you've been abstinent. I'm not advocating an occasional quick tumble with somebody you've met in a bar. The right guy could change your life for the better."

"Alex, you sound like an ad for a dating service." Amused, she started to get off the bed.

"I mean it," he said, stopping her with a hand laid across her arm. "You can't shut yourself up in a law office like it's a tower of purity. A woman like you deserves a richer life."

Cautiously, she said, "I like things the way they are now."

He withdrew his hand. "Nice and safe, right?"

"Yes, exactly. In this day and age, single people have to be more careful than ever—"

"But aren't you afraid," Alex interrupted, "that while you're fighting off the bad stuff, something good might just slip by?"

Caroline smiled. She even reached across and tweaked his earlobe. "Are we talking about you, Alex?"

He grinned. It probably did sound like a single's-bar line. Catching her fingers, he brought them to his lips and kissed them lightly. "I'll tell you one thing, Miss Caro. Fate has provided you with just the right man to experiment with."

"What do you mean?"

He gathered her into his arms. It was easy. She was relaxed, and he knew he wasn't forcing anything she didn't enjoy. "I am the proud owner," he said distinctly, brushing his nose across hers, "of a guaranteed, foolproof, Park Avenue surgeon's vasectomy."

"Alex!"

She objected to his bluntness, but she was laughing. It was a sexy, knowing laugh, too. The sound sent tingles sizzling all through Alex's system. The tingles ended up gathered in one particular area, however, as the idea of making love to her warmed into a physical response.

"What do you say?" he asked. "Want to see what improvements have been invented since you were last seduced?"

CHAPTER TEN

HIS SMILE WAS SO BEGUILING. Rough, temperamental Alex, Alex the cossack, Alex the wicked, had a glimmer of light in his eyes that promised a night to remember, a night of joyous abandon, of fun. A week of pleasure, no strings, fantasy lovemaking—that was what he had described. It had sounded exciting when he'd first suggested it...forbidden, but tantalizing. And now, with the sweet, unhurried taste of the kiss they'd just shared lingering on Caroline's lips, she was tempted to accept the deal. Sorely tempted.

"No lie," he said. "You can't get pregnant with me. You can only find out what you've been missing."

"What if I find out I haven't missed a thing?"

He kissed her. At the same time, he caressed her breasts softly, and then brushed his hands across the fabric of her dress until they came to rest on the exposed flesh of her inner thigh. It was an expert caress, calculated to melt an ice maiden into quivering jelly. Alex drew a pattern there and dropped more languorous kisses down her throat. "You think that could be true?" he murmured against her skin.

The caress did everything it was intended to do. Caroline recognized quivering jelly when her bones were transformed into it.

"I'm not a boy, and I'm no harried law student," he said. "I've got lots to show you, plenty to give."

"Alex—" she started, then stopped.

"I love your voice when it gets husky that way. It sounds like we've already made love and you're begging for more."

"Oh, Lord." Shakily, Caro said. "You're scaring the daylights out of me!"

He obeyed when she pushed out of his embrace and didn't pursue her when she got up from the bed and stood over him. He sat up and swung his legs over the edge of the bed, still smiling that sure, unhurried smile of his in the light of the flickering candle. "You can't get into trouble—not the way you're most worried about. What are you afraid of? Me?"

"No."

"Of what we might find together?"

"Maybe that," Caroline admitted. "I don't know you, Alex. We're still strangers sometimes. This is too soon."

"You know more about me than most people. Some of the things I've told you tonight are secrets I haven't even acknowledged to myself. And you've shared things with me—"

"Yes," she began. "But—"

She couldn't say it—couldn't explain what she was most afraid of. But Caroline knew that if she allowed herself a physical intimacy with Alex, the next step was sure to follow. Sooner or later she'd begin to fall in love with him. It wouldn't be hard. Already he seemed to occupy most of her waking thoughts. Certainly all of her *sleeping* thoughts were consumed by his presence! She couldn't be in love with a man she'd only met days ago, she knew. But it might happen in time.

If she told him her fears, she thought, he was sure to laugh. And at that moment, Caro did not want to be laughed at. She felt uncertain as it was, off balance and jumbled up inside.

"I can't think," she said.

"Then don't. Feel instead."

"Alex, can I trust you?" Caro put her hands out to him beseechingly.

He reached for her hands. "Don't expect me to think straight, either. I know what I want. I'll take it if you let me. I want you. I can make it good."

He drew Caroline to him so that she was standing between his spread knees—close enough so that her belly made contact with the hard expanse of his chest. He clasped her bottom with his hands, then eased them up the back of her dress, reaching for the buttons and watching her eyes.

"Stop me," he said.

Suddenly drunk with courage and shivering with anxiety, she said, "Don't stop, just hurry—before I change my mind."

"You're sure?"

"Yes, yes. Take me now while I'm feeling impulsive."

He laughed and spun her around so he could manage the buttons better. He didn't hurry, but unfastened them one by one, waiting for her to snatch back her decision. "I don't do any taking," he said in her ear. "Only giving."

In another moment he was peeling her dress off her shoulders and Caro still didn't speak. With her heart hammering, she kicked off her shoes and turned around again, dressed only in a silky pink teddy with ruffled garters that held up transparent stockings.

"Wow," Alex breathed, startled by her choice in underwear. "I didn't think you were the type."

"I'm not." She lifted her chin. "Not most of the time, anyway. This morning, though..."

"Yes?" he said, grinning. "Were you thinking of me, Miss Caroline?"

Caroline smiled, too, no longer scared. "Take off your clothes, Mr. Varanov. You'll see what I was thinking of."

He kicked off his shoes first, then practically tore his shirt getting it out of the way. His chest was broad, and a thick, curly triangle of hair disappeared down into his jeans. Caroline drew her fingers across his chest and then plunged inside his belt with both hands.

Alex groaned and fumbled with the buckle, rushing to get out of the jeans. "Hold it," he said.

"I will," Caro promised. "Just get the pants off first, will you?"

He was laughing, and so was she, and they tumbled backward onto the bed to wrestle with his jeans, then his shorts, then his socks. In seconds, Alex was gloriously naked and unashamedly ready. He ripped the bedcovers wide open. Kneeling, they pressed to each other, mouths meeting in headlong collision, breast to chest, belly to belly. And the most bold evidence of his excitement dove eagerly between her ready thighs. They fit perfectly, like fated lovers, irresistible magnets—like cosmic partners who had been held apart until nature allowed the union. They laughed together at the perfection.

They forgot the problems, let go of reality. Jane and the stolen coats and the smallest inconveniences vanished from time and space. There was only heat and pounding hearts, sweet kisses and the terrible ache inside that demanded fusion and relief. It was wild. It was right.

"Now," Caroline whispered. "Let's not wait."

"You poor innocent!" Alex laughed. "You think I'll be satisfied with that? Darling, this may take all night."

"Touch me, then."

He did. He found the place where her pulse throbbed. With his fingers, he pushed aside the delicate fabric of her teddy and plunged deeply into Caroline's darkest wish. She arched, stifling a cry.

"No fair. No holding back, Caro. Yell if you want."

She opened her lips and let a moan escape, but Alex was there to smother it. He had found her tenderest spot with his hand, and she wanted him to fill it, warm it. She wanted many things. She clutched his shoulders, half afraid of losing him too soon.

"Don't panic," he soothed, drawing down the silky straps of her teddy.

"Just don't stop."

Then, his blood pounding, Alex dragged her to the edge of the bed, kneeled on the floor and stripped each of her legs bare. The stockings slithered around her knees. She shimmied out of the teddy, and the first sight of her delicate body made Alex's throat catch.

He kissed her breasts, her belly, and downward. With his mouth, he proceeded to explore every sinew from her ankles upward. Caroline writhed. It might have been hours or moments, Caro didn't know. She only felt the terrible, wonderful fire in her veins, pulsing inside her like millions of shooting stars. She ran her hands into his hair, guiding him unconsciously until he made her shudder uncontrollably. Never had she felt such abandoned pleasure. Half frightened, she cried out, exultant at the intense effect of culminated desire.

When Alex looked up at her, his eyes were suffused with delight, desire and something even more carnal. Caroline drank in his expression, wanting to carve his face in her memory forever. Everything that was Alex was reflected in his expression at that moment—triumph, laughter and cocksure arrogance—but more, also. Longing. And need.

Caroline landed on the floor with him, and together they rolled onto the heap of bedclothes he'd thrown there.

"Darling," she said. "Let me have you."

She explored him, then, and found his tenderest spots, his ticklish places and the pleasure centers he most liked. Tossing as if on uncharted waves at sea, they tumbled in each other's arms, tousling the sheets, tangling their limbs, panting and laughing. Alex swore and laughed. He begged one minute, goaded the next.

In that golden candlelight, they alternately grappled and learned, fought and surrendered, moaned and laughed until at last he pinned her to the floor. Alex had only to open her thighs and kiss her once before Caroline breathlessly cried out yet a second time. While her body quaked out of control, he pressed inside her and thrust so deeply into the sweetest spot that Caro felt the explosion start all over again.

"Wait!" she panted. "I can't! Give me some time."

He linked his hands with hers, smiled into her eyes and gave her strength. He felt raw and wonderful inside her.

"Alex," she said and smiled back.

"You're beautiful," he said. "Caro, darling Caro. Sweet, but so sensual."

She lay beneath him looking so beautifully ecstatic that Alex wondered how they had avoided that moment for so long. She had loved everything, had treated each nuance as if it was new. It probably was. Sweet, virginal Caro knew nothing about grown-up lovemaking—but her ignorance excited him, heightened his pleasure. All along he'd seen how her natural innocence mingled with the sophistication she had learned. But the sophistication was an act, something she used like armor to shield her tenderhearted nature from the real world.

He had wanted her from the time they had met, and yet he hadn't imagined how glorious it would feel to be with her, how freeing, how purifying. Her body was like a marvelous pool, washing his soul, cleansing his spirit. He kissed her mouth, her face, her throat.

Then Alex caught Caroline in his arms, and carried her to the bed. He wanted her there on the pillows. He wanted to be tender with her. Once nestled in comfort, Caro reached her arms for him and drew him down, down into her honey-warm softness once again. Her mouth curved, and he covered it with his own, making her his, establishing his place, obliterating anyone who'd gone before him. He found his way inside her, uniting himself with her goodness. The tempo was perfect—slow at first, and he savored every thrust. So good. So good. He could lose himself in her sweetness. Slowly, slowly, they tumbled over the edge of a blissfully dark abyss. Caroline's voice mingled with his own hoarser cry.

"My love," he said.

As she gave in to exhaustion and drifted close to sleep with the scent of passion fragrant in her head, Caroline thought she heard Alex speak. He said the words too softly, though. But she knew it was a kind of benediction. She felt they didn't need to talk. The night surrounded them, pulled them close.

On the table, her candle guttered out and left them in darkness. But Caro wasn't afraid. They slept curled together, man and woman safely entwined.

AT DAWN, Alex lay for a long time in thought, holding her, wishing she might awake and begin the dream again. But daylight intruded. Common sense returned.

Alex rolled out of bed and stood looking down at lovely Caroline. The blinds and curtains didn't allow much sunlight to penetrate, but there was enough to see. She slept like an angel with her sunny hair streaming across the pillow they'd shared, her nose tucked against her creamy shoulder. He couldn't see her mouth, but he could remember the taste of her lips, the teasing nip of her teeth. She made love sweetly—with imagination and passion and occasionally with wildness, but always gently.

She was a gentle lady. And he was a rat.

"I had a one-night stand with your sister," Alex murmured to her sleeping form. "What would you do if I told you, Caroline?"

He went into the bathroom without waking her and turned on the harsh light. He looked at his reflection in the mirror. His face looked hard. His eyes were cold. Alex shook his head. He was a bastard, all right. The kind of a man who slept with a woman once and let things go at that. He had rejected Jane Wexler by going back to New York without even returning her phone call. For him, she had been recreation—a fun, post-divorce evening that he hadn't meant to go any further. They had had a good time together. She had nursed him out of the worst depression of his life and he'd never thanked her for it. He hadn't known she'd been depressed, too, and riding a dangerous, plunging roller coaster that would eventually come to a brutal halt the night she overdosed.

"Maybe I did know," he said to his reflection. "I just didn't want to get involved."

He'd had his own share of problems at the time, but that shouldn't have mattered. He could have done something for her—given her the simple courtesy of a returned call, at the very least. That's what Caroline would say, he was sure. But he'd been in a rush to get back to New York—back to his family, to show them his spirit could be healed. He'd been selfish. Alex

Varanov was a self-centered bastard. He had contributed to Jane's downfall.

And if she ever found out, Caroline would never forgive him.

Now what had he done? He had started with Caro in the same way he'd ruined her sister.

He splashed cold water on his face and dried it off with one of her pretty pink towels. He knew what he had to do. Leave her before she got hurt. She was strong enough. She'd survive a one-night stand.

There could never be more between them. Once Caro learned about his short-lived liaison with Jane, she'd terminate things. And Alex was sure he couldn't keep it a secret forever. It weighed too heavily on his mind. It was better to end the relationship now—before either of them laid their hearts on the line. He would allow things to die before they went beyond the physical.

Alex realized he'd been standing there with his face in the towel. His throat was tight, and the aura of last night's headache was a dull light in the back of his eyes. He remembered how poignantly she'd cried out the first time. She had never climaxed before, and he knew it. Remembering how he had wanted to give her that, Alex wasn't so sure their lovemaking had been purely physical. But he collected himself and put the towel back on its ring. He had to leave her, to make her understand their night together had been a mistake. He'd been weak again. Now he'd have to be strong.

He would be in Chicago only a few more days. On Friday, he could go home and start getting her out of his system. Until then, Alex knew he had to drive a wedge between himself and Caroline Conover. He had to make sure she thoroughly disliked him before the week's end.

He heard the telephone ring in the other room. He let the rude sound wake her. Opening the bathroom door a crack, he heard Caro rouse herself and answer the call. Her voice was husky and made something in his chest move. Maybe it was his heart turning over.

"Yes?" she murmured. "Oh, Rupert... That's all right. My alarm should have gone off by now. I— Yes." She listened for a moment and said with more brightness, "Of course. I'll be there in thirty minutes. No, better make that an hour."

She said goodbye, then cradled the phone and called for him in tones so full of light that Alex nearly cringed. "Alex! Where are you?"

He steeled himself for a performance. Turning off the light, he went back to the bedroom.

She had started out of the bed, but smiled radiantly when she saw him and lay back. "Hi."

How a woman could pack so much into one syllable, he didn't know. But in a rush, the memory of their night of love flooded Alex's head so that he could barely restrain himself from diving into the mussed bed with her. In fact, the one part of his body he couldn't control began to respond to the sexy undercurrent in her voice. She looked beautiful lying there with her perfect breasts peeping out from under the covers, her lush pink mouth still raw from the kisses he'd given her, and the sheets tangled tantalizingly around her slim legs.

Alex reached for his jeans before he gave himself away. "Hi, yourself."

"Sleep well?"

"Sure. You don't steal the covers. You've got a date with Rupert already, huh?"

"Yes, I'm meeting him at the store. I'd much rather spend this morning with you, though. I'm so *tired*. But it's a nice tired." When he said nothing and made no move to join her on the deliciously rumpled bed, Caroline sat up and pulled the sheet up to her breasts. "Alex?"

He finished with his jeans and went looking for his shirt. It had to be around the room somewhere. "I have a thing about cover stealing," he said, searching methodically. "Drives me nuts when women want them all and expect me not to mind the cold."

"Oh."

"Yeah. You see my shirt anywhere?"

She had it under her pillow. Without a word, Caroline pulled it out by its sleeve and dangled it in her fingers.

"Thanks," he said, taking the shirt.

She watched him put it on and start buttoning before she spoke. "Alex, is something wrong?"

"Wrong? Baby, everything was *right*. More right than I've had it in a long time. You getting up?" With a grin, he abandoned his shirt. "Or do you want me to climb back in there with you? Didn't get enough last night, is that it?"

She allowed him to climb back onto the bed and didn't even protest when he tore the sheet aside and pushed her bare body down across the pillow. Trustingly, she let him take charge, but her voice warned gently, "Alex."

He didn't kiss her. Instead, he trapped Caro beneath him. Her green eyes widened as he used his knee to thrust her thighs apart. He pinned her arms against the headboard. At once, she arched her back to escape.

"That's it," he murmured when she twisted under him. "Let's have it rough this time. Quick and rough."

"Alex, wait!"

"What's the matter?" He loosened his grip, but let his weight ride against her body. He nibbled her earlobe so he wouldn't have to look her in the eye. "Aren't you in the mood?"

"No," she said stiffly. "I'm not. Let me go, will you?"

"How come? I'm just getting you ready for your buddy Rupert." For good measure, Alex ground his hips against her. "I'll get you all hot, and then you'll really be able to put the moves on him."

She shoved him away with surprising strength and scrambled off the other side of the bed. Spinning around, Caroline stared at him as if she didn't know who he was. Alex rolled over and relaxed, linking his hands behind his head. "What's up?" he inquired, and joked, "besides me?"

Which was a lie. Alex was glad he'd put his jeans on, because he no longer felt the least bit sexy. He felt sick.

With her green eyes wide and confused, Caroline said, "You're— This is—" She stopped herself and said, "I'm sorry. I'm not a person who wakes up well in the morning."

"We'll change that," Alex promised with a leer. "Unless you wake up with Rupert tomorrow."

That did it. Caroline proceeded to snatch clothes out of a drawer and off hangers. With a final, fiery look at him, she exited into the bathroom and closed the door. Hard.

Alex dragged himself off the bed—the place where he'd felt the happiest in a long, long time. It didn't hold any appeal at the moment, however. He finished getting dressed and slowly took himself to the door that separated them. For an instant, he leaned against it, his forehead pressed to the cool, unrelenting wood. He longed to go in and take her in his arms. He wanted to hold her and kiss her, make her understand. But he knew what he had to do.

So he knocked sharply and raised his voice to a rude bellow. "Hey, honey, I gotta run. I'll try calling you later, huh? If you're home."

She didn't answer, but Alex knew she had heard. Grabbing his jacket, he let himself out of the house and into the morning air. He put on his sunglasses, and chose a street at random. He didn't care where it was going to take him. He began to walk.

CHAPTER ELEVEN

CAROLINE SAT on the edge of the bathtub and pressed a towel against her face. She didn't want Alex to hear the awful sob that was sure to escape at any moment. He thumped on the door and shouted to her, but she didn't answer. Squeezing her eyes tightly shut, Caro willed herself not to cry.

What had happened? How could she have let herself make such a mistake? What combination of factors had driven the prim Caroline Conover into the arms of such a man?

He'd seemed so vulnerable, that was part of it. For the first time, Alex had been open with her last night. He had shared thoughts and feelings Caro hadn't dreamed he was capable of. They'd been intimate, and not just in the sexual sense. Alex had given her a glimpse into his soul, and she had liked what she'd seen. This morning, Caroline didn't recognize the wolfish oaf who had pounded on her bathroom door and shouted his goodbye. A stranger had crudely pushed her down onto the bed and forced her legs apart. Surely he wasn't the same man who had coaxed her so gently to the heights of lovemaking, who had cried out with such abandon in the night.

She heard his footsteps recede and listened for the closing of a distant door. It was shut softly, but it sounded final—as if it had closed on a part of her life.

Caro crushed the towel in her hands and cast her head back to glare through teary eyes at the ceiling. "Why am I so *stupid*?" she raged, shivering with anger.

Abruptly, she got up and turned on the shower full blast. Clouds of steam erupted all around her, but she cranked the faucet marked hot as high as it would go. "I should have kept my mind on what I was supposed to be doing!"

But in the shower with the hot water streaming down her bare body, Caroline slumped against the wall. "Oh, Alex!"

If he had come back just then, she thought, she would have made love to him in the water. With the spray to warm them, and the darkness to envelop them once more, she would have done anything to seduce him—to bring back the man who had been her perfect lover. Caroline surprised herself with the ideas that came to mind. How quickly she had discarded her carefully self-taught attitudes where men were concerned!

"Stop it," she lectured herself. "You can go on the way you did before. Just because you slept with him once doesn't mean you have to again."

She pulled herself together in time. Dressing in a high-collared sweater and a long, full skirt, Caro prepared to meet Rupert Watkins at the store. She even took a cab to make the trip more expedient.

Bob greeted Caroline as soon as she entered the store, stepping forward to match her steps.

"Good morning, Miss Conover."

"Hi, Bob. What's with you this morning?"

He looked unusually down in the dumps. His uniform was starched and pressed, but his face was long. He couldn't even look her in the eye. "I'm sorry," he said. "But I gotta take you up to the executive offices."

"What for?"

He shook his head dolefully. "I can't say. This way."

Caroline obeyed and headed toward the elevator located behind the security booth. "Okay," she said. "But you don't have to come along. I can find my way."

He sighed. "My orders are to take you myself." He closed the elevator and pressed the button. "Course, I ought to be down at the vault, if you ask me. Today's a big day."

"What do you mean?"

"The sale," he said, as if that explained everything. At Caroline's blankly inquiring expression, he went on, "Well, there's a heck of a pile of money in that vault today. I told my boss we ought to send for an early armored truck, but he said, 'No, Bob, I trust you to keep an eye on things.' I ask you! How am I supposed to keep an eye on the vault when Mr. Watkins also wants me looking after you?"

Caroline smiled. "I'm sure it's temporary, Bob."

He shook his head some more and stole an uncertain glance at her. "I don't know, Miss Conover. I don't know."

He delivered her to the fourth-floor offices where the store executives did their daily work. Apologetically, he held the door open so she could enter the conference room. Caroline stepped inside, expecting to find Rupert waiting, but instead, she got a shock. Sitting around the large, polished table were several store officials. Rupert was there, but so was Mrs. St. Cloud, the owner of the store, a man Caro recognized as the head of the security team, and the director of personnel. Sitting in a chair in a far corner was Betsy. The girl was huddled up and refused to look up from the table. Seeing them all gathered there, Caroline stopped short.

"Good morning, Caroline," Rupert said. "Come in. Sit down, please."

Sitting at the table, Betsy felt worse than she had the time she'd been sent to the principal's office with half the cheerleading squad because somebody had stolen a necklace out of Miss Hanniford's desk drawer. Her stomach felt terrible, just the way it had that day so long ago. Betsy *had* taken the necklace. She'd only wanted to try it on, and she'd planned on putting it back, but Miss Hanniford had returned from the teacher's lounge too early and had started a big ruckus. Betsy had ditched the necklace in a trash bin, but had had to endure two hours of excruciating cross-examination by the principal. In the end, Betsy's good friend Darlene had taken the blame and was kicked off the cheerleading squad. Betsy had been too scared to admit she'd taken the necklace. She'd have lost too many friends that way. So she had kept quiet. And just like the other girls, she had snubbed Darlene for months after the episode. Betsy's reason for steering clear of Darlene was different from the other girls', though. In the back of her mind she had always suspected that Darlene knew the truth.

Looking at Miss Conover gave Betsy the same sick feeling she'd had so long before. Betsy knew Miss Conover was innocent. But there was no way to help her without getting into deep trouble herself.

So Betsy kept quiet.

Caroline was looking around the table, blinking. "What is this? What's wrong?"

"A great deal is wrong, young lady," growled the head of security, a paunchy, balding man with a military bearing even as he was sitting at the table. He scared Betsy to death, half because he had a deep, rumbling voice just like the school principal back in Chesterville. He said, "Three more coats were stolen last night, and your passkey was used to get into the store."

"My—" She started to object, but the big man interrupted her rudely.

"And yet here you are," he went on, "bold as brass, walking in the morning after you stole valuable merchandise. We'd like an explanation!"

"I didn't steal anything," Caroline said at once. "I was supposed to have dinner with you, Rupert, remember? How—"

"But we didn't," Rupert Watkins said gently, smoothly. Betsy was willing to bet *he* wasn't feeling guilty. "I had other business to attend to," he said. "But surely you have an alibi?"

Caroline went blank. "What?"

"You said you were going to spend the evening alone, but surely you saw *someone*? You can prove you weren't really here, can't you?"

Caroline hesitated before speaking. She had an alibi, all right. Alex. But explaining her relationship with him wasn't anything she wanted to do in the room full of people. And asking Alex to come forward on her behalf wasn't a scenario Caroline found the least bit appealing. Alex wanted his presence in the store to be a secret, anyway. He was under orders from Mrs. St. Cloud herself. Until the thief was caught, Alex had to remain undercover. Caroline was on her own.

"Listen," she began, stalking forward to lean her hands on the table, "I didn't come to the store last night."

"The computer tells us otherwise! You sneaked in when my men weren't looking. This girl Betsy says you spent yesterday afternoon going through the coats and picking out the ones you wanted."

"I wasn't going though them. I was cleaning up in the vault. Bob can tell you that! He helped. And last night I was at home. *All night*."

"Can you prove it?" Rupert asked.

"I—"

The security chief banged his fist on the table. "I say we get a search warrant and go to her apartment. Call the cops. It's about time they got involved in this—"

"Not yet," said Mrs. St. Cloud, speaking for the first time. She was a petite, elegant, graying-blond woman who chain-smoked. She stubbed her cigarette out in a crystal ashtray that was already overflowing with butts and ashes. When she had the attention of everyone in the room, she said, "Let's hold out another day, if we can. The insurance company is killing me at the moment, and I'd like to deprive them of this final spear. I'm sure Miss Conover wouldn't mind if we visited her apartment. Would you, my dear?"

"I have nothing to hide," Caroline said firmly.

"Excellent. Then why don't you take these gentlemen and—"

"I'd prefer to go without her," the bullish security chief interrupted. "Leave her here, and keep her away from the phone. We'll have a look around her place and find the goods."

"As you wish," said Mrs. St. Cloud, and the man rose from his chair, eager to get started.

"Honestly," Caroline began, "this is a waste of time. Rupert, you must know that I—"

"I think you'd better keep quiet, Caroline," Rupert advised. "Unless you'd like to call a lawyer?"

She stared at him. "No," she said, adding wryly, "there's no need for that."

At the suggestion of a lawyer, Betsy made a small, distressed sound and crumpled deeper into her chair. Mrs. St. Cloud and the director of personnel stood up and after exchanging glances of concern, left the room together. Rupert remained.

"Caroline," he said. "I think you'd better confess if you've got something to say."

"Rupert, you know I'm an honest employee."

He looked pained. "All I know is that you told me you were broke. I hope you haven't found a way to supplement your income."

"Rupert! I'd never—"

He patted her shoulder. "All right, stay calm. I'll go with the boys to your house. May I have a key?"

Caroline dug into her handbag and found her keys. "Here. Not that you'll need it. There must be a million ways of getting inside that barn."

He accepted the key. "I prefer to do things legally. Stay in this room, if you please?"

"What if I don't please?"

He smiled humorlessly. "Bob will be here."

Poor Bob, Caroline thought. His precious vault would have to stand alone.

Rupert turned to Betsy. "Come on," he said to her, no trace of courtesy in his voice. "You can get to work."

Obediently, Betsy slid out of her chair and slunk from the room, feeling worse and worse with every step. She hated to think she was getting Miss Conover in trouble. Rupert had told her his plan, and Betsy hadn't liked the sound of it at all. She liked the execution of the plan even less. Making somebody else take the blame was rotten. Hesitating in the doorway, she began miserably, "Miss Conover, I—"

"Get going," Rupert said to her. "You don't want to get fired, do you?"

No, she didn't want to get fired. And the other alternatives Rupert had promised were even worse. She was in pretty deep, she thought. Too deep to try climbing out now. Betsy bowed her head and left the room. Saying nothing, Rupert followed her.

Caroline sighed. A moment later, Bob came in and closed the door behind him.

"Jeez," he said. "Nobody's lookin' very happy around here this morning. Not even Miss Nofsinger, and she's always so pretty and nice."

"Bob," said Caroline, rubbing her forehead. "I'm in a hell of a mess."

"Yes, ma'am," he said respectfully, forgetting all about Betsy Nofsinger. "I know all about it. Do you have an alibi, Miss Conover?"

Caroline considered her position. The last thing she wanted to do was ask a favor of Alex Varanov. "I do have an alibi," she said slowly, "but not one I want to make official just yet."

"Miss Conover," said Bob, "I think you'd better give it soon or you're going to end up spending tonight in jail."

She made up her mind. She had to *discuss* the situation with Alex, at least. "I need to use the telephone."

"Sorry," Bob said, shaking his head woefully. "I can't let you out of this room until they come back from searching your house."

"Then you call," Caroline said swiftly. "Will you, Bob? I'd be more grateful than you can imagine. Please? One phone call."

He smiled. "Sure. Anything for you, Miss Conover. Just promise me you won't leave this room."

She raised her hand. "Scout's honor."

"Okay. Who do I call?"

Caroline wrote down Alex's name and hotel. "Just ask him to call me this afternoon," she told Bob. "Or have him come to the store as soon as possible. Tell him it's urgent."

Bob took the paper as if it contained the secret to ending nuclear armament. "Right," he said. "It's *very* urgent."

ALEX SPENT THE MORNING walking. Finally, the party in his head began to demonstrate signs of starting up again, so he took his capsules and headed for the quiet of his hotel room to think some more. He wanted to cut and run for New York. Not much was stopping him—until he arrived at the Hilton and found the message light on his telephone going berserk.

"Three messages," said the hotel operator, "all requesting you return their calls. One Tommy Hollingsworth in Philadelphia, one Isobel Varanov from New York City, and one Caroline Conover, who asks that you call her at the St. Cloud's department store. That message is marked urgent, sir."

"Thanks," said Alex.

He intended to ignore the message from Caroline. He knew what she might consider urgent on a morning after a night like they'd spent last night. But he wasn't ready for that. He'd let her cool off, forget a little. Alex pulled the blinds and lay down on his bed in the resulting darkness. He called Tommy first.

"Hey, Alex!" Tommy cried delightedly when the call went through. "How are you doing in the windy city?"

"Terrible," Alex snapped. "And thanks for not asking why."

"Why?" Tommy asked. Then he laughed. "Let me guess. Is she blonde? With great legs? And—"

"She's got nothing to do with it."

"Convince me," Tommy challenged, chuckling. "You haven't forgotten our bet, have you, Alex? You said you'd have her in the sack before—"

"I said nothing of the sort. What do you want, Tommy? I'm returning your call."

"Oh, well, nothing much. Just checking up on you, pal. I wanted to see if you'd started any bedroom sports since I talked to you last."

"I've been working," Alex lied.

"Oh, that. Yeah, how's it going? You find your thief yet?"

"Maybe. It's tough, though. Unless we get the police involved, I don't know what else I can do except catch him red-handed."

"Stealing coats, you mean?"

"I'd be happy," said Alex glumly, "if I could catch him stealing a pack of gum."

"Hmm," Tommy said. "I know what you mean. We had a situation like that two years ago last Christmas—an employee walking off with thousands of dollars worth of goods."

"How'd you catch him?"

"Her. It was tricky, as a matter of fact. She was stealing little things from all over the store. You know—a dress here, a necklace there, a radio, even a portable TV. Random merchandise, it seemed, but it got expensive after a while. We beefed up security on her, just in time for her girlfriend to steal eight diamond rings out from under our noses. Ninety grand's worth."

Alex whistled. "So the first woman was a decoy? Trying to divert your attention from the big heist?"

"Right. Like you, we didn't want the insurance company to get wind of the smaller losses, so we kept quiet and didn't contact the police. It paid off. The girl who stole the diamonds slipped on the ice as she went out the door—frozen ice, not diamonds. The Salvation Army had a couple of guys ringing a bell on the corner—Christmas, you know—and she saw the uniforms and thought they were cops. She surrendered to the Salvation Army."

Alex laughed. It felt odd to be amused just then, but he laughed anyway. "How like you, Tommy, to be saved in spite of yourself."

"Yeah," Tommy agreed. "How I wish the Salvation Army had shown up at my wedding."

"Second thoughts already? I thought there was a baby involved?"

"There is." Tommy sighed. "No second thoughts. Not really, anyway. I was just thinking about Caroline after you and I talked last week. She's a class act, Alex. But sexy as hell, too. That's quite a package. Sometimes I wonder if I didn't make—"

"Tommy," Alex warned. "Stick with the one you've got. The classy Miss Conover might not be everything you think she is."

"What's that supposed to mean?"

"Nothing," Alex said. "Just—nothing."

"Getting under your skin, is she?"

The expression was apt, Alex thought. Yes, Caro had gotten under his skin, all right. She'd found a shortcut to his heart, in fact. He could almost see her beautiful, laughing face as he made love to her, feel her slim but exciting body next to his, hear her quick retorts and tender words at odd moments. Yes, she had worked her way into his system but good.

"Alex?"

"I'm here," he said.

"What's the matter?"

"Nothing. She's— It wouldn't work, Tommy. Caroline and I don't get along. I'm not—she's nothing but trouble."

"Caroline's in trouble?" Tommy asked, misunderstanding. "Should I get in touch with her?"

"No, no, I just meant—I was giving her a hard time, that's all. It backfired. But she can handle it," Alex said shortly. "You don't have to play godfather, Tommy."

"Hmm," said Tommy, unconvinced. "I told you to take it easy on her."

Alex laughed. "You told me nothing of the kind, old buddy. You gave me a week to get the woman into a haystack."

"Am I going to win the bet?"

"*Goodbye*, Tommy. Unless you've got something else on your small mind?"

"Nothing else," Tommy replied. "Just good luck. With your investigation, I mean."

"Thanks. And thanks for the information, too. Your story about diamond thieves has given me something to think about."

And helped to take his mind off Caroline. Alex was glad to end the phone call, for he wanted to stir a few clues around in his head for a while. Tommy said goodbye and hung up. For a while, Alex lay in the darkness and wondered. Caro used as a decoy? To draw attention from a larger theft? What were the possibilities?

He was tempted to call her. But that would be a mistake until he had something definite to say. Alex wanted their personal relationship terminated. It would be strictly business from now on. He dialed another number instead and waited for the familiar voice. After three rings, he heard it.

"Mom?"

"Alex! Darling, where are you?"

"In Chicago still. What's going on?"

Isobel Varanov's voice still contained a twinge of the Russian accent she'd brought to America when she'd emigrated at the age of nine. "Oh, Alex, I'm so relieved. Mrs. St. Cloud called this morning to say they've found their criminal! You can come home now, yes?"

"They've caught somebody?" Surprised, Alex said, "Who?"

"I don't know, darling. She just said they found the person. When can you come?"

"Mother," he began, "I haven't talked to Mrs. St. Cloud yet. I can't—"

"She would not lie to me! Please, Alex, your father has been asking for you. You haven't called him in days."

"I'm sorry," Alex said, meaning it. "He's still in the hospital?"

"Yes, and—oh, Alex, when can you come? The doctors are talking about operations again, and you know he's so frightened of that!"

"So am I," Alex retorted. "How am I supposed to help?"

Instantly, he was sorry for the bitter tone he'd used. His mother cried, "Oh, darling, just by being here! We miss you. You've been so distant lately, and we— I don't want your father's last hours to be filled with the anger between you two...."

"Mother," Alex said patiently, "he's not dying. It's just the same old complaint getting gradually worse— *very* gradually. I'll come home as soon as I can. Dad and I have plenty of time to forge a peace agreement. For the first time in his life, he's asked me to do something. I'd like to do a good job."

"I understand, I understand," she said hurriedly. "When this trip is over, you will be friends, yes? I want you to reconcile with your father, Alex."

"So do I," Alex said, and suddenly he knew he meant the words. He and his father had been oil and water for many years, but more and more Alex was feeling the need to get back to his family, to reestablish some ties to the stable life he'd once known.

His mother said, "I'm so happy to hear you say that, darling. Hurry home, will you?"

Alex sighed. "Yes, Mom. I'll call Mrs. St. Cloud right away."

"Thank you, darling. I love you."

"I love you, too."

Alex didn't cradle the receiver, but just held his thumb on the button while he looked up the St. Cloud's number in the Chicago yellow pages. He punched the buttons quickly.

"Mrs. St. Cloud," he said to the woman who answered. A full minute later, the line clicked and the refined voice of Agnes St. Cloud came on. "Good afternoon," Alex said. "This is Alex Varanov, Mrs. St. Cloud."

"Yes, Mr. Varanov. I'm glad you called." Mrs. St. Cloud's voice was smooth as always, but excited, too. "I think you'd better come to the store as soon as possible. We've found our crook."

"You have? Who is it?"

"A young woman who works in the fur salon. Her name is Caroline Conover."

Alex sighed in frustration and rubbed his head. "Forgive me, Mrs. St. Cloud, but I can assure you that Caroline Conover is the last person who would steal from your store. I'd bet my entire fortune on that."

"I wouldn't be too quick to give up your financial security," said Mrs. St. Cloud. "My employees just found three fur coats hidden in her house."

Alex sat very still, unable to move.

"Mr. Varanov? Are you coming?"

"Yes," he said. "I'll be right there."

CHAPTER TWELVE

"THAT'S IMPOSSIBLE," said Caroline. "I never saw those coats before."

The cast of characters glowered at her from around the conference table. Even Mrs. St. Cloud looked angry and betrayed as she smoked her fourth cigarette. The harried director of personnel removed a roll of antacid tablets from his coat pocket and proceeded to eat three.

"I say we call the cops," declared the burly chief of security, red-faced and pointing a stubby, quivering finger at Caroline. "Arrest her. Send her to jail. To the state penitentiary!"

"Harold," said Mrs. St. Cloud. "Be quiet, please. This matter is more complicated than that. Rupert?"

Rupert sat up alertly as if he'd been waiting to be called on. "Yes, ma'am. It's very complicated indeed. If we send Ms Conover to the police, we'll have the insurance company in this store by noon tomorrow."

Mrs. St. Cloud nodded grimly. "And our insurance rates will have doubled by the end of the week. I don't look forward to that, Rupert. Even if we promise that Miss Conover will go to jail, the insurance people will claim we will always have a problem with employee theft. I'd rather take the loss on the merchandise that's already gone than face a million-dollar hike in my premiums."

"Perhaps we won't have to take a loss," Rupert said.

Mrs. St. Cloud raised her eyebrows. She sat forward and crushed out her cigarette. "What do you mean?"

Conveying solemn sincerity, Rupert folded his hands on the tabletop. "Let me talk to Miss Conover. Perhaps I can—well, perhaps we can recover some of the things she's already stolen."

"I haven't stolen anything," said Caroline through gritted teeth.

"Let her come with me." Rupert went on as if she hadn't spoken. "Perhaps I can talk some sense into her."

Mrs. St. Cloud looked at Caroline for a full minute. Caroline knew she was a savvy woman who had amassed a large personal fortune in addition to establishing one of the nation's finest luxury department stores. Not many details escaped Mrs. St. Cloud's eye. Though the store owner obviously wasn't sure why, she wasn't quite ready to condemn Caro yet. "All right," she said finally. "I don't seem to be coming up with any alternatives. Do your best, Rupert. I have confidence that you'll do everything you can."

"Thank you, Mrs. St. Cloud. I appreciate your trust."

The owner of St. Cloud's made a signal that caused all the men in the room to rise to their feet. They trooped out of the room, leaving Rupert and Caroline alone.

"Rupert," Caro said when the door had closed behind the rest of the meeting's participants, "those coats were planted at my house. I didn't steal them, and you know it."

"Shut up," he said, and went quickly to the door. He poked his head out into the hall and said, "Betsy? Come in here, please."

Caroline hadn't expected Betsy to be waiting in the hall. She knew Bob stood out there like a faithful guard dog, but apparently Betsy, too, had been waiting for admittance. The girl slipped into the room and reached automatically for the shelter of Rupert's arms. Her glasses practically trembled on her nose. She looked terribly frightened.

"Oh, honey," she said, a little lost girl dressed like a grown woman.

"Stop it," he ordered, holding her off sharply. "What did you find out?"

"I talked to Vinnie," she replied, scooting a nervous glance at Caroline. "Just like you told me."

"And?"

Shoulders hunched under his grasp, Betsy faced Rupert again. "I don't like him very much, Rupert. He—he touched me."

"What's that got to do with anything? What did he say?"

"He said you'd better hurry up."

"What?"

"He said somebody had been sniffing around. That's what he told me, at least. A man had been around asking questions because one of his messengers made a mistake and—"

"One of his henchmen, you mean. What else did he say?"

"He said if you're going to get the money, you'd better do it tonight."

Rupert released her and turned away. He muttered a single expletive and began to pace.

"What money?" Caroline asked. "What's going on, Rupert?"

He didn't answer, and Betsy seemed not to have heard Caroline, either. She had eyes and ears only for Rupert Watkins.

More frightened than she'd ever been in her life, Betsy said, "Rupert, I don't know if this is right. It's going farther than I thought it would. I didn't like that man. You said he'd help us, but—I think he's only worried about himself."

"Shut up," said Rupert. "Let me think."

But Betsy knew she had to be brave. "He isn't nice, Rupert," she insisted, still unnerved by her audience with Vinnie the Vulture. The man was scarier than anybody in the movies. "He thinks we're amateurs," she said, gulping. "If we mess up, he won't help us. He's a mean man. He wanted me to take off my clothes. He said he wanted to see what I looked like in case—"

"Shut *up*, will you?"

Betsy clutched his arm, half in fear, half in need of comfort. "That man *touched* me, Rupert!"

Quick as a striking snake, Rupert slapped her. The pain exploded across her cheekbone. The blow knocked her glasses off, and they clattered on the table. Betsy stifled a cry and fell into a chair, holding her cheek and staring at Rupert. She saw Miss Conover move uncontrollably in her direction, like a mother protecting her child.

"Stop complaining," Rupert ordered, and then he turned on Caroline with a furious face. "Sit down," he said, trying to intercept her by stepping into her path. "It's your fault this is happening too soon."

Furious, Caroline disobeyed, moving around him and kneeling beside Betsy's chair. She put her arm around the quietly crying woman and glared up at Rupert. "That was completely uncalled for, Rupert. Will you please tell me what's going on?"

He glared back at her, his eyes angry. A sweat had begun to pop out on his tanned face, though the conference room was quite cool. He pulled a white handkerchief from his pocket and wiped the perspiration away. "You're the one who wanted some extra income," he said with a thin smile. "I was working on getting it for you."

A tide of excitement welled up in Caroline. Almost breathless, she asked, "How?"

"We had intended to find some cash at the end of the week. But we'll have to move early now, thanks to—" He punched a fist into his palm, frustrated. "Damn! This means a lot less money."

"Rupert—"

"What?" he demanded, angry once again. "Do you want in, or not? Say so now, Caroline, or the whole thing is over."

"I want in," she said at once, prepared to play her charade until the last possible moment. "I definitely want in."

"Good," he said, mollified by her determination. "First we have to get you out of the store."

Betsy lifted her head. Her voice was small. "What about me?"

"You, too," he said shortly. "Let's go. That dumb kid from security is hanging around outside the door. Don't say a word to him, either of you, understand? We don't want to tip anyone off. Got that, Betsy? No more stupid mistakes."

Caroline tightened her arm around Betsy and helped the shaken woman stand up. Together, they moved toward the door. Rupert held it open for them. Betsy pulled herself together and walked into the hallway unassisted. Caroline followed.

"Miss Conover!"

Bob, the security man, walked hastily toward them from the open door of the office across the hall. He glanced worriedly at Betsy, then remembered his mission and snapped his attention back to Caroline. "There's a call for you."

Caroline's heart leaped. Finally! Alex was telephoning, she was sure. And just in time. He hadn't returned her call all day, and she had started to worry. But she glanced toward Rupert, silently asking for his permission to take the telephone call.

Rupert hesitated, no doubt expecting a trap.

Bob said, "It's some guy from Philadelphia. Hollinghead's his name, I think."

"Holling— Oh," said Caroline, recognizing the bastardized version of Hollingsworth. "It's Tommy. Rupert, I—this is something quick, I'm sure. It'll just take a minute."

Caroline could see the exasperation building inside him. But to order Caro to ignore an innocent telephone call might have aroused Bob's suspicions, she knew, and Rupert reluctantly nodded. "Make it quick," he said.

Caroline went into the open office. She didn't close the door so as to demonstrate to Rupert that she wasn't going to pull any tricks. She picked up the receiver. "Hello?"

"Caro!" Tommy Hollingsworth's relieved voice crackled on the line. "I was afraid something had gone wrong."

"Tommy," Caroline said, loud enough for Rupert and the others to hear. "How nice to hear from you."

Caroline didn't especially care for Tommy Hollingsworth. She thought he was shallow and noisy most of the time, but she knew he was respected in his business. She had asked him for help, and she felt she owed him a polite phone conversation, at least.

He said, "I just talked to Alex Varanov. Did he explain to you that we're old friends?"

"Yes," she said carefully.

"Then you know he's on the up and up. I should have called earlier, but I thought—well, you said you didn't want any interference." Tommy hesitated. "I thought maybe it was time to check in, though. Things all right between you two?"

"Couldn't be better," Caro said, mustering some cheerfulness in her voice.

Tommy laughed. "That's great. Couldn't be better, huh? Does that mean what I think it means?"

Caroline smiled grimly. "Don't be coy, Tommy. You know I like things straightforward whenever possible. Say what you mean, please."

"Straightforward?" He laughed again. "Yeah, all right. Then Alex told you about the bet, I guess?"

"The bet," Caroline repeated blankly.

"Yeah, you know. About bedding down in a week or less. I said he couldn't do it. I lose, is that it? Or maybe we all win this way. I get the satisfaction of knowing my good buddy is back in circulation again. I underestimated him. Course, he used to be hot stuff in college, but—"

"Tommy," Caro began uncertainly, "what's—"

"Yeah," said Tommy, clearly pleased with the situation, "I ought to start a consulting business on the side. Hollingsworth Matchmaking. What do you think?"

"We're not a match," Caroline snapped, beginning to understand. "We hardly know each other."

"Oh, right. Well, then, Hollingsworth Sex Partners. Easier than sitting in a bar getting to know a bunch of losers while you're looking for Mr. Right, don't you think? And you won't need to worry about catching something contagious. Alex is probably as clean as they come. I'll vouch for that."

"You bet Alex he couldn't do it in a week, hmm?" Caroline asked, seething inside. She barely prevented herself from slamming the phone to pieces. So that's

what Alex had been up to! All those sweet words and
candlelight had been part of a ruse, that was all. He
had wanted her in bed so he could prove his juvenile,
womanizing friend was wrong!

"Yeah, that was it," Tommy confirmed. "He told
you about it, right?"

"Oh, you know Alex," Caro said bitterly. "He
doesn't tell anything unless he has to."

"Uh, right," said Tommy. "Listen, are you okay?
You sound—"

"I'm fine," she said shortly. "You just caught me
on my way out. Can I call you back sometime,
Tommy?"

"Yeah, sure," he said. "Whatever you like."

"Good. I'll call you. And Tommy?"

"Yeah?"

"Thanks. You just saved me from making a big
mistake."

"Oh," he said. "Well, anytime."

Caroline slammed down the phone. Of all the adolescent foolery! What a line of crap Alex had fed her!
All along, he had never taken her mission seriously.
He had been playing sex games from the beginning,
only she hadn't been able to prove it! Caroline stalked
out of the office.

"Well?" Rupert asked.

"Let's go," she snapped.

"Miss Conover," Bob bleated. "What about—
Should I . . . ?"

"You've been a big help, Bob," Caro said briskly.
"Thanks. But I can handle things on my own from
now on."

He got the message and backed up a step. "Oh. Okay. See you around, then. Tomorrow, right? I'll be here if you need me."

"Right," said Caro, already following Rupert to the elevator. She didn't need any help—not from Bob and certainly not from Alex. She should have stuck with her vow to find out about Jane alone. Outside help had only distracted her from her purpose. Now she had a chance to find things out from Rupert once and for all. She got onto the elevator with him.

"You're sure about this?" Rupert asked.

"Absolutely," said Caro.

The doors closed and the elevator started downward.

ALEX PUSHED through the revolving door of St. Cloud's and rushed across the main floor against the traffic of sale customers heading home after a long day of shopping. He vaulted up the escalator two steps at a time. Just as the polite ring of the store's closing bell began to sound, he arrived at the executive suite. In the hallway, he stopped a young kid in a security uniform.

"Hey," he said. "I'm looking for Caroline Conover. She around?"

The kid shook his head. "Nope. Just left."

"She *left*? You mean she was arrested?"

"I dunno," said the kid. "They don't tell me any more than what I have to know to do my job. She went out of here with Mr. Watkins, is all I know. I don't know where they were going. I could do my job a heck

of a lot better if people *did* tell me what was going on,
I can tell you that!"

Alex felt like punching a wall. Damn Caroline. She
could have waited. "Is there a phone I can use? My
name's Varanov. I'm helping Mrs. St. Cloud with a
store matter."

The kid glanced at Alex's jacket. He shook his head
slightly, indicating that anyone helping Mrs. St. Cloud
ought to dress the part. But he said, "Yeah, sure. In
there."

Alex entered the empty office the kid had gestured
at. There was a phone on the desk, and the receiver
was still warm from somebody's hand. Alex picked it
up and called information for Caroline's number. In
another minute, he got through to her answering machine. Her recorded voice went through the usual
speech, and then the tone sounded.

Alex hesitated. He had a lot to say to her, but nothing he wanted to deliver on an impersonal recording.
He hung up without speaking.

In the hallway again, he caught the uniformed kid
as he was leaving. "Is Mrs. St. Cloud here?"

"Sure." The young man pointed. "In the last office. Personnel. See the sign on the door? Right in
there."

"Thanks," Alex muttered and headed for the office.

He had an idea.

CHAPTER THIRTEEN

BETSY FOLLOWED Rupert Watkins and Miss Conover downstairs and across the street to the parking garage. She wished she hadn't gotten mixed up in this whole mess. She wished it more than anything else in the world. Her mother would never forgive her for stealing fur coats with Rupert. And her father! He probably wouldn't speak to her ever again. If she ended up in jail, he'd probably be delighted. Betsy wished she could erase the last two weeks completely.

Her only hope was that Miss Conover looked like she knew what she was doing. Maybe Rupert would decide to use her for his assistant and Betsy could just melt out of sight. Betsy didn't want to help Rupert anymore. She didn't care if he thought she was a baby. She just wanted out!

The parking garage had emptied quickly after St. Cloud's had closed for the day. Rupert led the way to his car, his brown Mercedes parked all by itself on the third deck. He stopped and opened the trunk with his keys.

Miss Conover had gone briskly past him and stood beside the passenger door. Betsy went there, too, and stood waiting for Rupert to unlock the car. But he was busy in the trunk, and soon lifted out a set of jumper cables.

"What're those for?" Betsy asked, spotting the coil of red cable in his hand. "You have car trouble, Rupert?"

"No," he said. Slamming the trunk lid, he tossed the car keys to Caroline. "Unlock it, will you?"

She caught the keys and bent to do his bidding, inserting the key and turning it.

"What are they for?" Betsy repeated when Rupert joined them. She had a bad feeling all of a sudden. The look on his face was scary.

"Shut up," he said nastily. Then, in a smoother voice, "Caroline, the lock on the other door doesn't work very well. Lean across and open it, will you?"

She did exactly as he told her—she opened the passenger door and leaned in. With one hand braced on the seat to balance her weight, she reached clumsily for the handle of the opposite door.

Rupert pushed past Betsy. She staggered, caught by his momentum as he went past her. Roughly, he shoved Caroline down onto the car seat. She landed on her stomach and sprawled. The lever of the parking break gouged into her ribs. In a strangled voice she cried, "Rupert!"

"Be quiet." He drove his knee into her lower back, pinning her to the seat. Roughly, he grabbed her left arm and pulled it behind her back. "Just be quiet, and we won't get into any trouble."

Betsy screamed, really scared now.

Caroline struggled to get up, but Rupert wrapped two quick coils of the cable around her left wrist and then reached for her other arm. Caroline kicked viciously to escape. She still had the keys in her hand. Clumsily, she tried to scratch him. *"Rupert!"*

Her position was too awkward, though. She couldn't swing a good blow at him. He swiftly bound her right hand against her left, imprisoning her in the biting grip of stiff, plastic-coated wire. Her wits about her now, she started to shout. "Damn you, Rupert, let me up! Let *go*! Betsy, help me!"

Betsy darted to him and grabbed his arm. "What are you doing? Stop it!"

"Cut it out," he growled at her, throwing her off as if she were an irritating insect.

Betsy lost her balance on her high-heeled shoes and landed hard on the pavement. It hurt, but mostly Betsy was scared. She began to cry.

Then Caroline started to scream. The car's plush interior muffled most of the sound, but she let loose anyway, and her voice echoed in the parking garage. Rupert swore and dug his knee deeper into her back. When he bent closer, panting, she saw his handkerchief in his hand. She twisted her head, but he stuffed the hankie into her mouth. She spit it out and tried to bite him, but he grabbed a handful of her hair and succeeded in jamming the balled-up fabric back in her mouth, nearly to her throat.

Betsy clambered to her feet. "Rupert, you've got to stop. This is crazy."

"Shut up," he said again, not even bothering to look at her as he spoke. He tightened the cable on Miss Conover's arms. "You're in this, too, kid, up to your neck. You'll end up in jail faster than any of us."

"I'd *rather* go to jail than get—"

"Oh, yeah?" Rupert swung on her. His face was red and distorted. He grabbed her arm. "You didn't like the way Vinnie treated you today? Well, that was nothing compared to what will happen to a sweet thing like you in the county jail. And in prison—honey, you'll wish you were dead!"

He let go, and Betsy fell back, clutching her arm where he'd twisted it.

"Just keep your mouth shut," he told her. "Do what I tell you, and you'll be out of this mess in a few hours."

That sounded good. Betsy nodded fearfully.

Rupert bent over Caroline again. "Settle down," he said to her, going back to tightening the cables. "You'll strangle yourself if you struggle. We're not going to hurt you, Caroline. This is just a precaution."

She thrashed harder, and managed to kick him squarely between his legs.

Rupert cried out and flung himself out of the car. Caroline struggled to roll over onto her back. Her eyes frantically sought Betsy's. Betsy clapped both hands over her mouth. She hadn't meant to get into this much trouble. She hadn't thought anyone could get hurt. But Miss Conover looked really scared. Betsy felt her own tears starting again.

"Oh, Rupert," she began.

"Shut up, shut up," Rupert snapped at her. "Can't you do something useful for once? Give me your scarf!"

Obedient and stunned, Betsy unraveled the scarf from around her neck. Rupert snatched it out of her grasp.

Caroline guessed what was coming. She flailed her legs, but succeeded only in hitting her head on the steering wheel. Her hips slipped off the seat, and she sprawled helplessly on the floor in front of the passenger seat. Rupert quickly tied her legs with the length of polyester scarf. He untied his tie, then climbed onto the seat and used it to anchor the handkerchief in her mouth. In less than a minute, Miss Conover was securely hog-tied and tightly gagged.

When he finished, she was making a scared but angry animal-like sound behind the gag, and he was giggling breathlessly. Betsy couldn't believe it, but she thought he was enjoying what he had just done. He turned to Betsy.

"Help me get her into the trunk. We'll take her to Vinnie."

"I FIND THIS very hard to believe," said Mrs. St. Cloud. She lit another cigarette and blew the smoke across the desk at Alex. "You think Mr. Watkins is stealing from his own store?"

"Yes," said Alex. "I can't prove it yet, but I've got an idea that might take care of that."

"Which is?"

"A stakeout. I think we ought to station some people in the vault without telling Mr. Watkins."

"What people? And when?"

"Myself," Alex said at once. "And probably somebody to spell me. If more coats disappeared last night, we should start immediately."

"You might be sitting in the vault for weeks, you know."

"I don't see any other way," Alex replied. "We could turn the matter over to the police for a proper investigation and be assured that everything is done properly so that the evidence stands up in court, or we could try to catch the thief red-handed ourselves."

Mrs. St. Cloud twirled the tip of her smoldering cigarette against the side of her ashtray and watched the procedure while she considered the matter. She frowned and glanced up at Alex. "And you truly think it's Mr. Watkins?"

"Yes."

"Not Miss Conover?"

Alex sighed. "It's not my place to explain what Miss Conover is doing, ma'am. She will tell you herself when she's ready. But I know she's not stealing anything."

"You believe her story?"

"It's not a story. It's the truth."

Mrs. St. Cloud looked skeptical. "Mr. Varanov, it sounds as if you've had your head turned by our pretty Miss Conover."

Alex didn't smile or respond to the remark. "I've got a job to do," he said. "I think a stakeout would prove Watkins is your man."

The elegant woman across the desk sucked on her cigarette and shook her head as she expelled the smoke. "All right," she said. "But I have no desire to embarrass a valued employee. You must conduct this operation of yours in complete secrecy. I'll assign you one of our men, and the two of you alone will know the story. Understood?"

"Understood."

She pressed a button on her telephone, and the voice of a secretary crackled in the air. "Put me through to Harold," the store owner commanded, and a moment later when a gruff male voice responded, she said, "Harold, I need a security man—someone who can keep his mouth shut and do a job for me."

"I'll do it myself," Harold said.

"No." Mrs. St. Cloud glanced speculatively at Alex. "I think we need someone who's willing to take orders. Is there anyone available at the moment?"

"I think so," said Harold, and he paused, disconnecting the line for a few seconds before returning. "Yes, I've got Bob down here. He's on his way home, but he's willing to put in another shift."

"Send him up," said Mrs. St. Cloud. "We need him."

CAROLINE CHOKED on the gag and then screamed behind it in the blackness. She drummed her tightly tied and now shoeless feet ineffectually against the inside of the trunk lid. But Rupert turned up the volume on his car stereo as they passed through the attendant's booth at the parking-garage exit. Her own pathetic sounds couldn't have been heard, she thought frantically. Rupert laughed loudly, and she could hear him talking. They were not detained at the booth; Caro felt the car thud going out of the garage and then pick up speed.

She hadn't expected the momentum of the car to affect her so violently. Within seconds, Caro was hurled against the jagged rear wall of the trunk. She thunked her head so hard that a shower of stars exploded behind her eyes. At once, she stopped struggling against her bonds and concentrated on not fracturing her skull. Something soft lay on the bottom of the trunk. Caroline guessed at once it was a fur coat. She put her face into the fur to protect herself and pray. And to think. She had to keep her wits about her.

Rupert knew something was wrong; that was obvious. Judging by what he'd said to Betsy in the conference room, she surmised that Vinnie the Vulture had guessed someone was tracing the stolen fur coats as a result of Alex's visit. He had warned Rupert, and Rupert had responded by making Caro some sort of prisoner. A part of Caroline rejoiced. She and Alex had been right! Rupert *was* behind the thefts. The coat in the trunk of his car was proof of that, too.

But at what price had she learned the truth? The car swerved around a turn, throwing Caroline painfully against the other side of the trunk. She cried out behind the gag, and felt tears on her face. Her arms and legs began to blaze with the pain of contorted muscles. Helplessly, she rolled around the confines of the cramped trunk, bruising her legs, whacking her head.

She'd let the detective game get out of hand. That litany played in her head over and over. She should have admitted who she was when confronted this af-

ternoon. She should have forgotten her foolish charade and produced Alex as her alibi for not stealing the
coats that disappeared last night. Mrs. St. Cloud
would have believed him.

Alex. That bastard. He hadn't answered her call for
help, and then she'd learned about his stupid bet with
Tommy. He was truly a skunk—an arrogant, conniv-
ing son of a bitch. It was ridiculous to be angry with
him at a time like this, but Caroline raged against him
as she squeezed her eyes shut and tensed her body for
the treacherous swings of the car. She wanted to
scream at him, berate him, pound her fists against his
chest. But soon she was screaming *for* him—inside and
soundlessly, perhaps, but she needed Alex. Oh, she
needed him. More than anything.

The car stopped at last. Caroline thought she was
dead for an instant. The darkness was absolute, the
sudden silence complete. But her heart slammed uncontrollably and her body ached everywhere. Then
someone banged a car door shut, and a key scratched
in the lock by her ear.

A moment later, dazzling light poured down upon
her. Caroline winced. They were inside a large building, she guessed—a garage again, or a warehouse with
powerful overhead lights. No traffic sounds reached
her ears. She figured they were still in the city, but in
a place big enough to be private. She twisted in the
trunk, trying to get a look at her captors as they stood
above her.

"I'll be damned," said a raspy male voice. Caroline craned to look at him, but she couldn't get her
head around far enough. Angrily, she kicked and

struggled. She tried to shout, but the noise came out as a strangled, choking sound. Her only hope was Betsy. Surely the young woman could find a way to escape, to call the police—anything! Caro tried to twist around so she could see Betsy and convey a message. It was no use.

"It's her," Rupert said. "The one I told you about."

"She's something, all right," the raspy voice replied. The man reached down and touched Caroline's chin, forcing her face farther into the fur coat. He ran his thumb down her jawline—not gently—and said, "But you banged up her face."

"It's all right—no big deal."

"Whaddaya mean no big deal? Marks are hard to explain! You don't get a banged-up face from an overdose. Marks on the body start people asking questions." He released Caroline's chin and stepped back—completely out of her limited line of vision. "We don't want any questions asked this time, Rupe."

"It's all right, Vinnie, it's all right, I'll wrap her head up in the coat better before I take her back."

"Just see she don't smother. You going alone?"

"With Betsy."

The other man laughed. "The little girl? Aw, leave her here, why don't you? I'll look after her. Just one gander at this sweetheart all trussed up makes me want—"

"I need Betsy. She's part of the plan."

"Yeah, right." Sounding disgruntled, he said, "Well, the rest of this plan ain't going so hot."

"What d'you mean?" Rupert protested anxiously. "This whole thing would have gone like clockwork if it hadn't been for that idiot who collects for you. He should have known Jane Wexler was dead."

"Yeah, well, he's an impulsive boy. He's anxious to make good and thought he was doin' me a favor collecting old debts. I talked to him about it. He won't make any more mistakes like that. Just see you don't screw up, either."

"I won't. I've got it all figured out down to the last detail."

The raspy-voiced man clapped his hands together and rubbed them happily. "Okay, Rupe, things are looking good. Go ahead with it."

"You think it'll work out, Vinnie?"

Vinnie laughed. "If it don't it's no skin off my nose! You're the boss on this one, Rupe. I'll take my cut, but it's your baby."

"And you'll help me later? Getting rid of this one?"

"Sure. Tonight when you're done at the store. My boys'll plant the rest of the evidence to make it look like she did all the stealing before. Then we'll give her the stuff."

"You don't think the cops will wonder where the money is?"

"So what if they do? They won't be able to trace it to us, right?"

"Right. We won't get caught," Rupert promised. "I've seen to everything. The store will be empty. The guards will be busy elsewhere in the store. I've got Betsy if I need any help, and she looks like she just got out of choir practice. Nobody will suspect her. Honest, Vinnie, I got all the details taken care of."

Vinnie the Vulture laughed. He slapped Caroline's buttock so hard it stung. "If all your details look as good as this one, Rupe, you're in good shape."

Somebody bundled Caroline's face into the fur coat. For a second, she thought they were going to smother her, and she fought hard. She heard Betsy weeping and Rupert breathing hard. But she forced herself to remain still, hoping they meant to protect her face with the fur. They fumbled some more with the coat, and a hand fondled her briefly.

Then somebody slammed the trunk lid.

CHAPTER FOURTEEN

ALEX WAS IN no mood to explain himself when the young kid from security turned up for his assignment. Mrs. St. Cloud had told him to go along with Alex, and he was willing to do that. He addressed Alex as "sir." His name was Bob and he wore a spotless uniform with all kinds of gear snapped to various loops and epaulets. A flashlight, keys, a holstered gun, a nightstick and a dog's leash all swung from various points on his body. After one look at his dimpled baby face, however, Alex was willing to bet his friends called him Bobby.

"Let's go," he said gruffly.

He took the youngster up to the fur salon and locked the door from inside. Alex opened the refrigerated fur vault, and Bob turned on his flashlight to get a look around.

"Shut that thing off," Alex snapped. The last thing he needed on a night like this was one of his headaches.

"Yes, sir."

"Listen, kid," Alex began when the light was out, "the important thing is not to let anyone know we're up here."

"Not anyone?"

"Right. Not a soul."

"What about tonight's security team? There are two extra guys patrolling the store. And there's Stu in the security booth downstairs. He probably saw us come up on his video screens."

"I didn't mean that one. Mrs. St. Cloud is going to silence the man in the security booth for us." That had been her promise, at least.

Alex glanced around the empty salon, trying to decide on the best places to hide and the way the operation ought to be conducted. "We just have to stay out of sight of the other two guys. If they catch us, that's that. We can use their help. It's just that the fewer the number of people who know what we're doing, the better off we'll be."

"Right! Uh, sir?"

Alex grunted.

"This is a real stakeout?"

The eagerness on Bob's face made Alex think of a beagle, dying to get hunting. "Yeah, kid," he said. "But look, it's going to take a while. Probably all night. You want some coffee or sandwiches? I suggest you go get them now."

"There's a vending machine in the basement, sir."

"Well, get going."

"Oh, no," Bob said hastily. "I'm rarin' to go, sir. I can wait."

Alex acknowledged that with a nod. He had a dedicated one on his hands, at least.

CAROLINE GOT HUNGRY. It seemed silly to be plagued by such an ordinary complaint when she was bound and gagged in the trunk of a car and headed for probable execution, but when the car stopped and didn't move for nearly an hour, the hunger pangs began to growl in her stomach. She thanked her stars her bladder was empty. Her head hurt, too. And the cables that bound her had begun to create agonizing cramps in her arms.

But she could still think.

Caroline figured Rupert had driven back to the St. Cloud's parking garage. He and Betsy had left the car alone, and Caroline kicked and pounded and made as much noise as she could, but to no avail. He must have parked far away from any other cars, she thought despondently.

Alone in the unmoving car, she began to work at her bonds. Eventually, she managed to loosen the cable on her wrists. Her arms ached, and the flesh on her wrists burned terribly, but she felt good about making progress. Every minute loosening of the cable was a tiny victory that spurred her on.

But then she heard voices. Rupert and Betsy had returned to the car. Betsy was crying.

Rupert rapped on the trunk lid. "You okay in there, Caroline?"

She didn't move and didn't speak, thinking for one crazy minute that she could spring out of her bonds if Rupert opened the trunk.

But he didn't. He laughed. "I know you're all right in there, Caroline. I can hear you breathing. You're trying to trick me."

She held her breath and kicked the inside of the hood as hard as she could, wishing fervently it was Rupert's smiling face.

Rupert laughed at the sound. He knocked again and said, "Well, take it easy, honey. We'll be back in half an hour, then we'll go to your place and get you untied. That sound better?"

"Rupert," Betsy began.

"Don't start," he said. "Just shut up and come on. You're going to sit in the security booth and warn me if anybody comes in the store. It's not difficult. Just sit and keep your eyes open."

"Rupert, I didn't know things were going to go like this. Miss Conover was nice to me."

"Shut up," said Rupert, his voice fading as they walked away from the car.

Betsy, Caroline thought, was an even more abused victim than she was. At least Caro still had her self-esteem. Betsy sounded thoroughly beaten, completely dominated. The poor kid had been brainwashed. Just like Jane, Betsy was the dupe of immoral men.

Enraged, Caroline doubled her efforts to free herself. There was more at stake than just Jane's reputation. Jane was dead, and Betsy was alive.

Caroline wrestled with the cables like a woman possessed. If she could get loose, she could get rid of the gag. If she got rid of the gag, she could scream. Surely someone would hear. Frantically, she jerked and pulled at the cable. Then she cried out joyfully. It had moved. She was going to make it.

"I THINK I'LL GO for coffee," Bob said to Alex at ten o'clock. "And stop in the men's room. Can I pick up a sandwich for you, sir? It's just vending-machine food, but it's better than nothing."

"Sure," Alex grunted. He had learned his lesson about not eating well, and vending-machine food was better than nothing. To hell with dieting. He dug into his jeans pocket for some change.

"No, no," said Bob hurriedly, smiling in a friendly way. "My treat, sir."

"Do me a favor, kid," Alex said, eyeing the boy. "Call me Alex?"

The kid's smile broadened with pleasure. "Yes, sir! I mean, Alex. I'll get the sandwiches and be right back."

"Okay, Bob." Alex accompanied him to the salon door to let him out. "Just be careful to avoid the security patrol."

"Oh, I know their routine, sir—Alex. I'll just go down the stairwell when they split up on the fourth floor. They go in opposite directions and don't patrol the stairwell for at least twenty minutes—more if they stop to shoot the breeze in the furniture department. Sometimes they sit on the display sofas for a smoke."

"You really know the routine," Alex observed. "How long have you been working in this store?"

"Eleven months. But this is my first stakeout."

"Hmm," said Alex, noting the gleam of excitement in the boy's face. "What's your assignment most of the time?"

"I'm specialized in canine security. I like animals. I train retrievers in my spare time. Mostly, though, I just stay down in the basement with one of the store dogs and we guard the vault."

"The vault?"

"Yep. The money vault, not the fur vault."

"I see."

"We stand by the vault all day. I'd go nuts if I didn't have a dog with me, at least. It's pretty boring. Except the day the armored truck comes." Bob flashed a shy grin of modest pride at Alex. "This is a big change for me."

Alex smiled wryly. "This will be pretty boring, too, I imagine."

"Oh, no, sir. Standing by a vault is *really* boring. Even knowing there are hundreds of thousands of dollars in it, I get real tired. Well, I'll see you in a few minutes. You want coffee, too?"

"Decaf, if they have it." Alex let Bob out of the salon and relocked the door behind him.

Then Alex strolled back into the salon, the place where Caro had worked for so many weeks in search of an ending to her sister's story. Just being in the salon caused Alex to start thinking about her, and the resulting ache in his chest was real. He wished things had been a hell of a lot different. If he'd been honest with Caroline in the beginning, he might have had a chance to reconcile with her. But now—Alex shook his head. The only thing worse than having known Caroline's sister was having to keep that relationship a secret from Caroline.

Caro had strong feelings where her sister was concerned—stronger than Alex could compete with. Even if the mystery did get solved, Alex doubted she would ever forgive him for his part in the early stages.

Catching Rupert stealing coats would be satisfying, though. Alex was looking forward to it. If only he knew exactly when Rupert would strike next....

He paced and began to play the ideas and scenarios around in his mind. Tommy's suggestions came back to him, and Alex paused in midstride. Could Tommy have been right? Might Rupert have stolen jewelry and coats just to shake up the security team? Could he be headed for more valuable merchandise now? If so, what might it be? Alex filed through the possibilities. Surely furniture was too bulky to smuggle out of the store. The same for appliances. What could possibly be worth more than fur coats and diamonds?

"Cash," Alex said aloud.

In seconds, he had the salon keys out of his pocket. He headed for the door. To himself, he said, "The vault."

Alex longed to leave the salon immediately and go in search of Bob. The kid knew more than he realized!

But Alex knew he had to wait. He was liable to get stopped by the security guards and get himself arrested. It was better to sit tight and wait for Bob to get back. He would be able to guide Alex through the store without anyone noticing. Together, they could go inspect the vault and decide what came next. There was no sense rushing. Alex had been playing detective for days now, and nothing had happened. A few more minutes wasn't going to matter.

"Patience," he told himself.

BETSY DIDN'T WANT to go into the store with Rupert. But he grabbed her arm and pinned it inside his own so they looked like they were real friendly.

"Stu," he said to the man who stood guard in the security booth. "I'm here now."

"Oh," said Stu. "Hello, sir."

"I've got a present for you," said Rupert, once they had been admitted into the store. He pulled an envelope from his pocket and handed it directly to the night watchman. "Here. A token of my appreciation. For your cooperation."

Stu smiled. "Sure thing, sir. What screen do you want me to shut off tonight?"

Rupert went into the security booth and studied the bank of video screens. "Number four," he said. "And two, just for good measure."

"You got it." Stu did as he was commanded, turning two screens black. He said, "There's some activity in the store tonight, sir. Mrs. St. Cloud says there's a couple of guys hiding up in the fur salon."

"Are they?" Rupert asked, surprised. "Lying in wait, is that it?"

"Yes, sir."

"Well, they're in the wrong place tonight," said Rupert. "Let them wait as long as they like."

"Should I try and stop 'em if they come downstairs?"

"Yes," said Rupert. "But I won't be long. Fifteen minutes at the most. Ready, Betsy?"

"I'm going to be sick," she said.

It was the truth, too. The queasy feeling in her stomach had turned into something a lot worse. Betsy figured she looked pretty bad, because Rupert believed her.

"Not now!" he objected. "You stupid—"

"I can't help it!" she wailed, all attempts at sophistication forgotten. "I gotta go to the bathroom!"

He shoved her out of the security booth, and Betsy ran for the employee locker room, sure she was going to throw up at any second.

She did, too. Betsy upchucked and just sat on the ceramic floor afterward, wondering how things could possibly get worse.

She knew, of course. Things would get a lot worse when Vinnie and Rupert killed Miss Conover. That's what they were planning. After Rupert took the money, he was going to murder Miss Conover. Well, *he* wasn't going to do it exactly. Rupert wasn't that kind of guy. But Vinnie was another story. Betsy shivered at the thought of Vinnie the Vulture and how he'd touched her earlier. He'd treated Miss Conover as if she were a side of beef, too. He'd have no qualms about seeing her dead. And there was nothing anybody could do to stop him.

Betsy got unsteadily to her feet. She washed her hands and face and didn't look at herself in the mirror. As she tore a paper towel out of the dispenser, though, she caught a glimpse of her reflection in the metal. She looked sick, all right, but something else struck her. Betsy recoiled at the sight. She looked young. Like a kid.

Though she'd been brave as a child, Betsy remembered. She'd been a tomboy—tough and brave and spunky.

She could be the same person tonight, if she wanted to, she realized slowly. She could save Miss Conover if she just had the guts to try.

Betsy left the bathroom. Rupert had already gone. Probably he'd gone down to the vault and was unlocking it according to the code he'd stolen. The security guard, Stu, was sitting in the booth watching the video screens. He glanced up when Betsy appeared.

"I'm gonna wait in the car," she said.

He nodded, clearly not willing to share his cozy booth with someone who might vomit at a moment's notice. Betsy pushed the security door open and went across the street. In the parking garage, she ran up three flights of steps and found the Mercedes.

IN THE TRUNK of the car, Caro won her first triumph in the hard-fought battle. Delighted, she threw off the last of the cable. With her hands finally freed, she tore off the gag and sucked in the first deep breath of air in many hours. Thank God. The trunk was hot, the air thin. For a while, she'd thought she was going to smother. She breathed gratefully for a few seconds, then began to shout for help. She pounded on the trunk lid with her numbed fists and screamed.

Within minutes, the scratch of a key sounded in the lock. Caroline was hoarse already, and she gave a croaking kind of sob. Help had arrived.

Betsy's voice said, "Oh, please, don't scream, Miss Conover."

"Betsy? Betsy!"

The shaken woman managed to unlock the trunk, and the lid popped up at once. "Please, Miss Conover—'' At the sight of Caro she clamped her hands over her mouth, her eyes huge behind her glasses.

Caroline didn't waste any time worrying about her appearance. Half afraid she was going to end up tied in the trunk again, she frantically tore at the scarf on her legs and freed herself. ''Thank you, Betsy. Thank you. You're a doll. You're very brave.''

Betsy mustered the strength to help Caroline clamber out of the trunk. Caro rescued her shoes next and slipped them on. ''What's happening?'' she demanded, leaning against the car for support. Her legs were cramped and weak, and she flexed them purposefully. ''What's going on?''

''What do you mean?''

''You *know* what I mean. Where's Rupert?''

''He— In the—''

Caroline seized the girl's quaking shoulders. ''He went into the store?''

Betsy nodded in jerks.

''To do what? Steal more coats?''

''N-no. Money. From the vault in the basement.''

''Betsy,'' Caroline began fiercely, ''do you know what you're doing now? You're willing to help stop him?''

Again, the girl managed to nod. She couldn't speak.

''Good girl.'' Caroline took her hand and began to pull her across the concrete floor. ''Let's see what we can do.''

Betsy whimpered, but she obeyed Caroline, following her down the steps to the street level. Caroline checked her watch. Ten-thirty. A few cars moved in the street. The two women ducked between them and hurried across the road to the employee entrance. Caroline pounded on the door.

"Hey!" she shouted hoarsely. "Let us in!"

The security guard in the booth looked more than a little startled by their appearance at his door. He swiveled his chair away from the video screens and slid over to the window. "What do you want?"

"I'm an employee," Caroline shouted through the safety glass. "Will you let us in, please! It's important!"

The guard was not going to admit Caroline, she could see. It was the same man who had been on duty the night she'd broken into the store with Alex. Perhaps she looked worse than she realized, she thought. The guard didn't seem to recognize her. But he did recognize Betsy. With a nod at her, he came around the booth and out into the lobby to let them into the building.

"What's going on?" he asked, addressing the question to Betsy.

"I think there's a burglary going on," Caroline said at once. "Are you the only man on duty?"

"What's it to you, lady?" he challenged, glowering at her. He kept one hand on the gun that was buckled on his hip. He shot a belligerent look at Betsy, who sidled closer to Caroline for safety.

"It's important," Caroline insisted. "The store's being robbed. You should stop it."

"Who are you?"

"My name's Caroline Conover. I've been working—"

"You?" he said suddenly, and peered closely at her face. "We're supposed to keep an eye out for you, young lady."

"I *know* that. But I'm—look, why don't you call for help? Search the building."

"And while I'm gone, you can run upstairs and steal something!"

"Of course not! I am not— All right, look, if you call the other guards, I promise not to move. I'll sit right here and twiddle my thumbs until they get here. Just call for help!"

The guard's look said nothing doing. He shook his head. "Forget it, lady. You're not in charge around here. The store manager is in the building right now. I'll just call him and—"

"No! You can't do that. It's—"

The guard reached the end of his patience. He pulled his gun out.

Caroline had never so much as seen a handgun up close in her life. The experience of having one aimed at her had a surprisingly shocking effect. She was silenced and could not breathe.

"Come in here," the guard said, and he gestured with the snub nose of his weapon toward the open door of the security booth. "Sit down and shut up," he ordered. "I'm gonna call my backup."

Caroline did exactly as she was told. Betsy edged behind her, unconsciously using Caroline's body as a kind of shield. Like a dance team, they slid into side-by-side folding chairs and didn't move. Both clutched the seats of the chairs as if they might fall off.

"Stay," the guard said, speaking to them as if they were dogs. Still aiming the gun at them, he picked up a large walkie-talkie from the desk and flicked a button on the side of it. "Hey, Andy."

Static crackled, and then another male voice answered. "Yeah, Stu?"

"Where are you?"

"Third floor looking at girls' undies. Why?"

"Get down here," said Stu, in no mood for jokes. "We got visitors."

"Roger," said Andy.

The guard put down his walkie-talkie and they waited. Caroline and Betsy looked at Stu, and Stu looked back. Nobody spoke. Andy arrived, breathless, in about two minutes. He held one of the Doberman guard dogs on a short leash. The dog growled. When Andy saw the two women sitting quietly in their chairs, he looked disappointed that they weren't escaped convicts trying to blast their way into the store.

"Watch this one," Stu commanded, indicating Caroline with his gun. "I'll take the other one with me. We're going to find Mr. Watkins."

"Okay," said Andy, and he wound one more coil of the dog's leash around his meaty hand.

Stu left, dragging Betsy by her arm. She sent Caroline a terrified look over her shoulder.

Caroline was left with the dog and Andy. The dog did not take its eyes off Caroline, and she was careful not to look directly at it. The last thing she wanted to do was anger the dog. Andy was big enough to be a football player. He was young, but unlike Bob, he did not have a friendly face. He and the dog made a good pair. Caroline decided it was time for the police.

"Look," Caroline began cautiously, "I came in here because I wanted to call the police." She showed him the bruises on her arms. "See? I was attacked. I want to report it."

"Sure," said Andy. "When Stu gets back."

"But what happened to me has nothing to do with Stu," Caroline argued. "Won't you call the police for me?"

He shook his head. The dog growled softly in the back of its throat.

Caroline looked into Andy's immobile face and decided to give up that line of attack. She let her gaze scan past him and rest on the flickering video screens. Nothing seemed to be moving in the store. Then she saw one of the cameras had picked up Stu and Betsy as they moved quickly across the main floor of the store. Even Andy turned to watch their progress on the screen.

Then Caroline noticed another movement. Her eyes widened.

"Alex!"

"What?"

Sure enough, there was Alex. He had come out of the fur salon and was standing still, fiddling with the key and looking impatient.

"Who's that?" Andy said, pointing at Alex's image on the screen.

Pretending ignorance, Caroline said, "Where? I don't see anybody."

Suddenly, though, all the screens seemed to get busy. Another guard and dog were patrolling an upstairs floor. And, bless his heart, there went Bob, strolling down a hallway past some vending machines, whistling.

"Look right there," Andy insisted, still surprised at Alex's appearance. "That guy doesn't belong here!"

"Maybe he's the thief," Caroline suggested. "Maybe he's stealing something."

"Yeah," said Andy, reaching for the walkie-talkie. "Maybe."

He started to communicate with another man in the store, his eyes glued to the video screens. Caroline looked at the dog, and the dog looked back at her. She figured that moment was the best chance she was going to get. Caroline got up and slipped out the door.

"Hey!" said Andy.

If he had turned the dog loose, Caroline would have been a goner. As it was, Andy hesitated, his left hand clamped on the leash, his other hand busy fumbling with the walkie-talkie. It gave Caro just enough of a head start. She bolted for the stairs. The dog went crazy barking.

Her first thought was for Alex. She ran past the cosmetics counter and headed for the escalator. At the bottom she saw the fire alarm, plain as day.

Firemen were almost as good as cops, she decided instantly. Caroline crouched and broke the alarm mechanism with the heel of her hand. At once, emergency lights all over the store flashed on. And a steady bell began to peal. Caroline knew an alarm like that would also be triggered directly at the nearest fire station. She prayed it would, at least. She raced up the escalator, shouting.

"Alex! *Alex!*" Caro charged up one flight of escalators and started up the next.

Behind her, she heard dogs. Andy must have turned his loose, and it was on its way. On the third floor, Caro threw a rack of coats across the top of the escalator, hoping to slow the animal down a bit, at least. A second dog was in the store somewhere, too, though. The fire bells rang. The emergency lights blazed. Caroline ran.

"Alex!"

CHAPTER FIFTEEN

SOME IDIOT HAD SET off the emergency lights, and they were blindingly bright. Alex started down the escalator toward Caroline's voice, but one of the excruciating lights caught him square in the eyes. At once, he felt the beginnings of a headache, the band tuning up. He tried to push it aside. There wasn't time to cope with a headache.

Caroline rounded the corner at the bottom of the escalator and, still running, saw him above her.

"Alex!"

The joy in her face hit him like a fist in the stomach. Her eyes were bright, glistening, glowing. She ran to him, arms outstretched.

He caught her and hugged her tightly. "Caro! What the hell are you doing here? Your face—what happened?"

She looked like hell, actually. Bruised and dirty, with blood drying on the bridge of her nose, she looked like she'd been in a brawl. Even her clothes were wrinkled and smeared with something black—grease, perhaps. But she shook her head. "Quick," she gasped. "Please, there's a dog coming."

She wasn't kidding. Before he even had time to absorb the warmth of her body, touch her bruised cheek or wipe away the trickle of blood, Alex heard and saw the dog.

It was a sleek Doberman, and it moved like a launched missile up the escalator. Like a rocket with teeth, it came at him. Alex pulled Caroline behind him just in time and braced himself for the impact. The dog leaped, snarling, and clamped his jaws around Alex's left arm.

"Alex!"

Alex felt the dog's teeth connect through the leather of his jacket, and the force of the animal's momentum threw him backward against a rack of clothes. They crashed through the display rack and hit the floor in a welter of clothes. Caroline screamed. Alex's head reeled. The dog clawed his chest, growling as if possessed. With his free hand Alex groped and grabbed for anything he could use as a weapon. The only thing within reach was a piece of clothing—a man's sweater on a hanger. With his right hand he used it to cover the dog's face, to blind him.

The dog jumped back, snarling and barking, then flew in for a second attack, teeth slashing. It gave him enough time, though, to think. This time Alex wedged the sweater in the animal's jaws. He whipped his arm around its head and trapped it with all his strength. It was like wrestling an enraged bull.

"Get a fire extinguisher!" he shouted, grappling with the beast.

There wasn't one in sight. Caro spotted something else, though. She ran out of Alex's line of vision and returned in moments, hauling a fire hose out of its wall cabinet.

She turned it on. The hose filled and became a writhing snake. Water blasted from the nozzle, but Caroline wasn't strong enough to hold it steady. The force of the water flung her back against a wall, and there she braced herself and trained the gushing water on the dog.

It worked. Alex released the dog, and they separated. He staggered to his feet, clutching for balance. The dog snapped and barked at the stream of water, backing off all the while.

Soaked to the skin, Alex lurched to the wall and caught himself. "You don't do anything halfway," he gasped, "do you?"

"Alex," she choked. "Alex—"

"I'm okay."

Caro was still spraying the dog, holding him at bay, and the job required nearly all her concentration. But she said. "Your arm. It's bad?"

He didn't want to think about it. He didn't even look. "Not bad," he said.

His head, though, had started to pound, and there was no ignoring it. The party would be in full swing in less than a minute. Alex fumbled in his pocket for the vial of pills. "What happened to you?"

"It's a long story," she said breathlessly, fighting with the hose. "But there's a happy ending—I think. Alex, Rupert's here. In the basement—"

"Stealing money from the vault."

She looked at him, her green eyes wide. But she bobbled the hose and had to train herself on the task of holding the dog at bay. "How did you—" She glanced at him again. Then her gaze dropped to his hands where he was trying to shake a couple of pills into his palm. Her face went pale. "Oh, Alex."

"Not very convenient, I know." He popped the pills without water. "It'll pass in a few minutes."

"We haven't *got* a few minutes! The fire alarm will have scared him. He'll run."

"So let him run. We'll—"

"Alex, he may have Betsy, too. We've got to stop him! He'll hurt her."

Alex clutched his forehead, trying to think, to press the pain out of his skull. There was too much to do, too much to think about. He cursed his luck.

"Oh, God," Caro began, her voice quavering.

She felt more scared than she ever had in her life. The dog, the hose, Betsy in danger, Rupert prowling, and now Alex hurt and near to fainting from one of his headaches all added up to a much more frightening scenario than she'd imagined when she'd been locked in the car all alone. Now there were other people in trouble. For an instant, Caro was almost paralyzed.

But Alex shouldered her out of his way and took the hose from her hands. "Let me," he said, his voice thick.

"You can't," she objected. "If you let the water slip, the dog will—"

"I can do this better than I can run downstairs to stop Rupert," he snapped, clearly fighting the pain in his head with all his strength. He took over the hose and trained it on the dog, blasting the animal backward another ten feet. Water gushed all over the floor, all over the displays, and ran in a bubbling stream down the escalator. Alex said, "You'll have to stop him yourself, Caroline."

"But—"

"Listen," he commanded. "There's an emergency stairwell somewhere. You know where?"

"Yes, but—"

"Use it. You might even find a kid along the way named Bob. Go down to the vault and hold Rupert there as long as you can. The fire department ought to be here in a few more minutes. Is Rupert armed?"

"What?"

"Does he have a gun?"

"No, but the other man does—a security guard that Rupert pays off."

"Are they together?"

"I don't— I'm not sure. But I'll do what I can," Caro said, making up her mind. She grasped Alex's good arm. "Darling—"

"It's okay," he said with a ghost of a grin as he glanced down at her. "I'll catch up with you. Ready now? I'll distract Lassie while you run. Go!"

She ran.

BETSY TRIED TO HANG like a dead weight in Stu's grip, but he doubled her arm behind her back and it hurt! She straightened up quickly and shuffled ahead of him as they descended a wide flight of stairs and arrived in the basement hallway.

"Stay on your feet," Stu said to her, then called, "Mr. Watkins!"

The darkened hallway was lined with small glass-doored offices used by lesser executives of the store.

Each office contained a desk lamp that was left on overnight so that the hallway was lit only by the glowing lights that shone through frosted-glass doors. Halfway along the hall stood a bank of illuminated vending machines, which also cast light into the hall. Betsy knew that the store's vault stood in an alcove at the opposite end of the hallway, but because of the lights on the vending machines, she couldn't see that far. Rupert wasn't in sight, but he could have been there in the shadows. Betsy squinted, trying to peer into the alcove.

"Mr. Watkins!" Stu called again, obviously also unable to see anything.

There was no answer. Just before they reached the vending machines, Stu stopped walking. Betsy stumbled, but he jerked her arm painfully, and she straightened up. Together, they stood still and listened. No sound could be heard.

Suddenly, though, the place was exploding with noise. A horrendous bell began to clang. Betsy cried out.

"Fire!" Stu said, dumbfounded. "That's the fire alarm!"

He spun around, dragging Betsy with him.

But suddenly there was another person with them. A young man jumped out from behind the candy machine, grabbed Stu around his neck and pressed a gun to his cheek. Sounding dead serious, he said, "Drop the girl."

Stu felt the gun and certainly saw it next to his right eye. Instinctively, he released Betsy. She slipped out of his grasp and tried to run. Her legs didn't seem to be working, though. Progress was slow.

"Aw, hell," Stu said, catching sight of his attacker. "Bob, what in tarnation do you think you're doing?"

Betsy turned in midflight and realized that her savior was none other than Bob, the security guard who had been assigned to Miss Conover. He looked very serious as he pressed the muzzle of his gun to Stu's perspiring cheek.

Above the noise of the fire alarm, he said calmly, "Just don't make any sudden moves, Stu."

"*What?* Bob, have you gone *crazy*? What's happening? There's a fire somewhere and you're playing games with—"

"This isn't a game, Stu. Be quiet."

He wasn't as tall as Stu, but he looked like he was in lots better shape, Betsy observed admiringly. His arm was locked expertly around Stu's neck. Betsy had never really noticed Bob before; she had thought he was just a kid and not worth her attention. But when he glanced at her and said sternly, "You okay?" she felt light-years younger than he was.

She nodded weakly. "Yeah," she said. "I'm okay. But Rupert—he's still around here."

"I know," said Bob. "He went up the emergency stairs."

CAROLINE LEFT ALEX and clattered down the steps. She clutched the railing and hurried, anxious to get to Rupert before he did something terrible to Betsy. That was all that mattered. Caro knew she could take care of herself. But Betsy needed her help.

She knew she was confused just then, rattled by the day's events and the noise of the fire alarm, but Caro felt somehow that rescuing Betsy could square what had happened between herself and Jane—that she could make up for not having helped her sister by taking care of Betsy now.

She ran headlong down the steps, and almost nothing could have stopped her. But Caro heard something and slowed. Footsteps. Someone was coming up the stairs toward her.

She halted, hanging on to the rail. She sensed it was a man, and he was in a rush. Before he rounded the landing below her, she knew it was Rupert. He looked frazzled, and scared. His normally suave good looks were marred by the panic in his eyes.

He stopped dead and stared up at her. "My God!"

"I'm not a ghost," Caroline said over the clanging fire alarm. "I'm still alive, Rupert."

"WAIT," said Bob. "You can't go up there."

Betsy pushed past him as he held Stu captive, and she headed for the emergency stairs at the end of the hallway. If anyone was going to stop Rupert Watkins from escaping, she wanted to be the one—or be on the scene to help, at least. He wasn't going to hurt anyone anymore—not if she could prevent it.

"*Wait,*" Bob cried.

"I can't," Betsy said, panting. "I've got to stop him."

ALEX FIGURED he might as well make a break for it. His headache was improving with each passing heartbeat, but his arm was getting worse. It wasn't just water that had soaked his sleeve and was dripping on the floor—water wasn't red. Dragging the fire hose to the limit of its length, he headed for the emergency door through which Caro had disappeared. The dog followed, still barking, still trying to get at him.

And judging by the flashlight beams that waved from the direction of the escalator, there were more dogs on the way. Alex dropped the fire hose and ran.

He made it through the crash door with seconds to spare. The dog hurled itself at the door, barking and snarling, but Alex was safe on the other side. With relief, he turned and started down the stairs after Caroline. He heard her voice and called to her. "Caro!"

"Down here," she said.

He hustled down the steps and came upon the tableau—Caro still looking like a deer surprised in a thicket, and Rupert Watkins several steps below looking stupid with shock. He gaped up at Alex and made a connection.

"You!" he said. "You're Varanov!"

Alex stopped on the stair, certain of what was going to happen next. He could do nothing to stop it now. Rupert knew him. He'd avoided the store manager until now, but the time had come. For the next full minute, everything seemed to happen in slow motion. It was like watching a film of a terrible car accident. Alex couldn't stop it, and he could do nothing to change it.

Shaken, Rupert Watkins blurted, "You were Jane Wexler's friend!"

Caroline turned. Slowly, she turned around and looked up at Alex, totally baffled and partially paralyzed. "What?"

The fire alarm continued to blast, but Alex was sure his heartbeat was the louder sound. His arm still hurt and his head hurt, too, but the pain in his chest felt like an expanding bellows about to explode.

Caroline said, "You knew Jane, Alex?"

Her green eyes filled with doubt. He could see the play of emotions as clearly as if she'd spelled them out. Doubt first, then mistrust. She even looked back at Watkins and said, "What did you say?"

Rupert pointed a trembling forefinger up at Alex. "That's Jane Wexler's boyfriend. He was here before—when we bought furs from his family."

Caroline went on staring at Alex with the most terrifying expression on her face. Alex thought he was pretty tough when it came to summoning courage, but the look Caroline wore scared him.

Watkins was no fool. He saw he had a chance for escape and took it. While Caroline stared at Alex, the store manager turned and bolted back down the stairs.

Caroline said, "It's not true, is it?"

"Yes." There was no sense denying it anymore. Alex nodded grimly. "I knew Jane, Caro. I met her in the spring."

"In the spring," she repeated dully.

"I didn't lie," said Alex. "I just let you believe something that wasn't true."

"Why?" she said. The word was barely audible, but Alex knew that was her question.

"Because I fell in love with you."

He could see in her face that what he felt didn't matter. Caroline's heart had closed to him, and no words could have won her back. Not then, anyway, and perhaps never, he thought with a sinking heart. Alex didn't speak. He didn't answer her question.

Below them, Betsy screamed.

Caroline was too stunned to move. Alex reacted more quickly. When he heard the cry, he pushed past Caro and went immediately down the steps toward her voice.

But Betsy had come charging up the steps like the cavalry, and Rupert had her and was trying to use her body as a shield. He didn't have a gun, though, and neither did Alex. Betsy blinked at Alex, surprised to see him but game for anything resembling a rescue attempt. Using the heel of her shoe, she stamped on Rupert's instep just as he got a stranglehold around her neck. He yelped and dropped her, and Alex went in for a tackle.

But he connected badly, and Rupert twisted to get away. Gravity prevailed. Together they plunged down the stairs, legs tangled, bodies tensed. Betsy shrieked.

On they tumbled, finally crashing and breaking bones, Alex was sure—plenty of them.

The next thing he knew, Bob was standing over them with the yawning maw of his gun pointed at Alex's knee. Or maybe it was Rupert's head. Alex wasn't sure. His head had started to thump, and he couldn't see straight. The party was starting all over again.

In a pretty fair imitation of Clint Eastwood, Bob said, "Everybody freeze!"

No problem, Alex thought. No problem at all. He was pretty cold already. He even closed his eyes.

"Why did you have to tackle him?" someone asked near his ear. It might have been Caroline, but Alex couldn't quite see her. She kept breaking up into pieces and drifting away. Her voice said, "You could have used your knife."

"I never thought of it," Alex replied, muzzy inside. He didn't hurt anymore. He just felt queerly disembodied. "I'm just an amateur at this."

"Like hell," said somebody else.

CHAPTER SIXTEEN

ALEX WOKE UP in a hospital bed. He had a recollection of an ambulance ride and lots of fire trucks and a couple of policemen, but he didn't remember seeing Caroline anywhere in that nightmarish jumble of memories. That figured. He just lay there for a while and thought about what might have been and ended up getting depressed.

Judging by the slant of light through the one window in the room, it was late afternoon. An attractive nurse who stopped in confirmed that.

"You've slept all day," she reported, tilting up the bed so that he could sit and tucking the sheet around his legs more securely. "I heard the paramedics brought you in last night, and you've been asleep since then. I'll let the doctor know you're awake."

Alex said, "I have to get out of here."

She patted his arm. Or rather, she patted the bandages that were wrapped around his arm. "Honey, you aren't going anywhere for a while. Not even the bathroom."

When she left, Alex investigated under the sheet. She was right. He wouldn't be going anywhere until somebody unhooked him.

A doctor came next—a very young, towheaded and bespectacled intern who chewed gum and wore headphones around his neck along with a stethoscope. He pulled up a chair and propped his Hush Puppies on the edge of Alex's bed, looking a little like a poster for *Andy Hardy Goes to Medical School*. "You've had quite an adventure, haven't you?" he asked, reading notes from a clipboard. "Dog bites, a broken wrist—"

"When can I get out?" Alex interrupted, not interested in hearing the list of his injuries. There was nothing more depressing than a hospital. Unless it was Caroline Conover exiting from his life. "When can I leave?"

The intern was taken aback by the question. "Why—you don't want to go yet."

"Yes, I do," Alex said, looking the kid straight in the eye with as much force as he could muster. "Where are my clothes?"

"See here," said the intern, scrambling out of his chair as if afraid for his life. "I think you'd better talk to Doctor Redmond first."

"Okay, send him in."

Doctor Redmond turned out to be a woman. She was in her fifties, and Alex would have bet she played professional tennis or ran marathons in her spare time. Her body looked tight as a gazelle's, and her face was long and sharp-featured. Her hair was blond, flecked with gray and swept back into a no-nonsense ponytail. Her eyes were brown and commanding, and her hands were long and strong. Surprisingly, she wore many rings—one on every finger. Most of them were silver, set with a variety of colorful stones, and looked as though they'd been made by hand. She was dressed in running shoes and a white lab coat over stretchy exercise pants. The tight fit looked good on her.

She examined the bandages on Alex's arm while she talked. "I hear you're not happy with us," she said neutrally.

"It's not that you haven't been nice," Alex said. "I just don't like hospitals."

"Oh? You want to tell me about that?"

Alex eyed her. "Are you a shrink?"

She smiled and let go of his arm. "In my leisure hours only. I'm the headache lady."

"The what?"

"I specialize in headaches. I hear you get some whoppers."

"Who told you that?"

She smiled some more and put her hands into the pockets of her lab coat, apparently ready for a long chat. "A little bird. It's true, then?"

Grouchy, Alex said, "Yes."

"Had them checked out?"

"In New York, yes."

"Surgery?"

"No," said Alex. "I'm trying to avoid that."

"You're being foolish," she replied calmly. "It's not as bad as you think. We quit using Black and Decker equipment years ago."

Alex put up one hand to stop the sales pitch that was sure to follow. "I've heard all the propaganda about lasers."

"Then you know it's a safe procedure."

"Relatively speaking."

She nodded, amused. "All right, I won't make any promises. But the odds are good we could eliminate your headaches. I saw the X rays they took last night. I'd like to do some other tests, but I think I know what the trouble is already. Your condition is unusual, but I've been studying other patients with the same kind of problem. I think I could fix yours. You might still get a twinge once in a while, but it wouldn't be nearly so bad as what you're suffering now. Why hesitate?"

"I'm *scared*," Alex said, exasperated that such a commonsensical woman couldn't see the obvious.

She smiled. "You're honest, at least—not the typical macho rooster putting the blame on doctors. What's so scary? Afraid you won't wake up?"

"There's that," he admitted.

"You don't strike me as a Woody Allen type, nervous about dying, Mr. Varanov." Doctor Redmond looked at him for a while and finally said, "Are you afraid of living?"

"What? For Pete's— No. That's nonsense."

She shrugged. "Maybe so. But I see that a lot. You'd be surprised. Some of my patients use their handicap as a way to avoid living. Some people have their lives organized in nice, safe ways and they worry that if their headaches go away they'll have to go out into the world and face things they'd rather avoid."

"What kind of things?"

Doctor Redmond looked directly at him. "All kinds of stressful situations. Their work. Other people. The opposite sex. Are you married, Mr. Varanov?"

"Divorced."

She raised one eyebrow.

"It's not what you think," Alex began. "I wanted to stay married. That was unrelated. Sort of."

She let that pass. "How's your job?"

He let out an explosive sigh. "Not good, either," he admitted. "I took a leave of absence."

"When was that?"

He considered lying, but decided it was probably unwise. "Eighteen months ago."

"I see," she said. "Have a girlfriend?"

Alex frowned. "I'm not sure."

"Well," the doctor said brightly, "it certainly sounds like you've got your life in tip-top order."

"I've had girlfriends," Alex said quickly. "I don't have any trouble in bed, if that's what you mean."

"Good for you," she replied smoothly. "Now if you could just get everything else in order, you could run for president."

He looked at her. "I never liked a sarcastic woman. It's unfeminine."

"I save my female hormones for more important matters," she said, taking no offense. "Now, how about that surgery? I'll hold your hand until you wake up, if you like."

Alex didn't answer for a moment. There were a great many issues involved in the matter of his headaches, but he didn't talk about them. Not to anyone. But Doctor Redmond was unusual. She looked tough and smart, and she had a sense of humor. And she wasn't going to bully him the way other, more omnipotent physicians had tried to.

Finally Alex said, "I had an uncle who died."

"On the table?"

"Yes. His doctors said they could fix his headaches, too. But he died, and there was nobody to— He
was alone. We're all alone when we die, I suppose, but
he was *really* alone." Alex glanced up at the doctor.
"You know what I mean? His wife had left him and
he didn't have children and even my father and he had
quarreled. He—he didn't have anybody who was sorry
when he died." Alex caught himself. "That sounds
stupid—"

"No, it doesn't."

"He was a mean old bastard, and—hell, some of us
were almost glad he wasn't in the neighborhood to yell
at us anymore. But when I got older I realized that he
was—well, he was alone."

"I see," said Doctor Redmond.

"I don't want to die like that," Alex said at length.

"I would think not," said the doctor.

"I'm not close with my family anymore."

"You could be," she said. "They've been calling—
a whole bunch of brothers and sisters. And look at all
these flowers!" She waved a hand to indicate the win-
dowsill and nightstand, both of which were covered
with florists' masterpieces. "The big one's from a Mrs.
St. Cloud, who's apparently very grateful. And your
mother sent candy. She says she'll fly out here tomorrow."

That caught Alex off guard. "She shouldn't. My
father's not in great shape at the moment."

"Maybe you ought to let her come."

Alex shook his head. "No. I'll be okay. I'm all
right, aren't I? I feel okay. Sore in the arm, but—"

The doctor nodded. "You're healthy. The wrist will heal, your ribs are just bruised and the dogs had their rabies shots so you don't have to worry about that. Your body will take care of itself. The laser surgery, though, could do your head a lot of good. Like I said, I'll be glad to hold your hand if you need a friend."

Alex smiled a little. "Thanks, Doc. But . . ."

She grinned. "Oh, I get it. There's someone else, isn't there? Go ahead. Let me down gently. You've got a girlfriend after all, haven't you?"

She was a good sport. Alex liked her more and more. "Yes," he said, "there's someone else. But she's not— I can't have her sitting by my bedside."

"Why not?"

"Because she—we—"

"You're afraid to ask her?"

"The lady probably isn't speaking to me these days."

Briskly, the doctor pulled up a chair and sat down. She reached for the nightstand and plucked up a box of chocolates, which she unwrapped and proceeded to examine carefully as she spoke. "Look, Mr. Varanov, you're a grown man, and not bad looking. Unless you've got a secret vice you're not telling me about, I think you'd be the sort of fellow any woman would be happy to settle down with. You've got a complex! Pull yourself together before you turn into an emotional cripple. Forget this headache thing. We'll operate and put it behind you. You can live happily ever after just like everyone else—have a dozen kids with this girlfriend of yours. Have a chocolate?"

Smiling, Alex took a caramel and popped it into his mouth. "Obviously, you didn't give me a complete physical. I had a vasectomy."

The doctor laughed and shook her head with pretended regret. "Why aren't you twenty years older? I'd marry you myself." She patted his cheek, in an almost motherly way, and stood up. "Talk to your lady. I'll bet she throws herself into your arms. You've been hailed as a hero, you know. She won't be able to resist you. And I'll expect you in my office in a few days, all right?"

"You're springing me from this place?"

"Why not? You'll only terrify the interns if I make you stay."

Alex caught her hand, preventing Doctor Redmond from taking her leave. "Doc," he said, "you're all right. I like you."

"Prove it," she said. "Let me have the chocolates."

CAROLINE WAS PACKING when the doorbell rang. She considered not answering it, because she was in a hurry. Her open suitcases were scattered all over the bed, clothes spilling out of them. But she could hear the rain drumming against the windows, and she took pity on the poor soul standing out in the storm.

She ran through the house and pulled the door open. Bob and Betsy Nofsinger stood under the portico, both holding umbrellas and looking blissfully happy.

"Can we come in, Miss Conover?" Betsy asked.

Startled by their appearance on her doorstep, Caroline hesitated only a split second before opening the door wide. "Sure. Come in out of the rain."

"We don't want to stay long," Bob said. "We just came to say goodbye. We heard Mrs. St. Cloud say you were going back to Philadelphia."

"Soon," Caroline said. She led them into her meagerly furnished living room. "I'm anxious to get back to my family."

Betsy sat on the sofa, but Bob stood with his hands clasped. "Then you—you're satisfied with everything? With the way things turned out?"

"Yes," she said. "And no. Nothing will bring my sister back. But I feel much better now that I've learned the circumstances of her death."

"And the crooks are behind bars," Bob added. "Rupert and Vinnie the Vulture, I mean."

"Yes."

"You'll come back for the trial, I hope?" he asked. "I mean, if Betsy's going to get off she'll need you—"

"I'll come back," Caroline assured them both. "I know your heart wasn't really in what you did, Betsy."

The woman smiled uncertainly. "Thanks, Miss Conover. For putting up the bail money, too. That was really nice of you. Thanks loads."

Caroline smiled, too. "There are some things a girl shouldn't have to ask her parents for."

"We just came from the hospital," Bob volunteered suddenly. "Mr. Varanov wasn't awake yet."

"I know. I— I've been calling."

"You went to see him, though, didn't you?" Betsy asked.

"Yes," Caro replied, suddenly feeling very tired. She'd been awake for two days, and the strain was beginning to tell. She said, "I spent the night and this morning in his room. But I—well, I came back to get some rest. I couldn't seem to sleep, though. I ended up packing instead..."

When her voice trailed off, Betsy said anxiously, "You won't leave without saying goodbye to him, will you? He was so wonderful to help me. I used to be scared of him—when he was Mr. Smith, remember? But everything he did was so brave. And he's so—so handsome, too." Longingly, Betsy pleaded, "You won't leave yet, will you, Miss Conover?"

Caro could see that a happy ending seemed the only answer for the young and starry-eyed store clerk.

"There's lots of other stuff going on, too," Bob added. "The insurance investigation and everything with the police. They'll probably need your help—especially since it was your sister who was murdered during the whole thing and you stepping into a job at the store to find out what happened. You probably know more about this case than—"

"The police know where they can reach me," Caroline said gently. "I have my own life to pick up again. My family needs me."

"*We* need you," Betsy protested.

"I think," said Caro, "that you two will have each other for that."

Betsy and Bob blushed in unison. It was a cute picture, Caroline thought. The two of them were the same age, came from the same kind of small-town background and suited each other very well indeed. A matchmaker couldn't have paired them up any better.

"Well," said Bob, avoiding the impulse to glance in Betsy's direction.

"Um," said Betsy, also casting down her eyes demurely.

"Just look after each other for a little while, okay?" Caro said, amused at their sudden shyness. "Bob, Betsy's going to need some help finding a new job. I don't think Mrs. St. Cloud is open-minded enough to take her back. Maybe you can lend a hand."

"I'm thinking about going home," Betsy volunteered. "To Chesterville. I could go to junior college for a while and—and see what happens."

Seriously, Bob said, "I'm thinking about furthering my education, too."

Caroline nodded. "Good idea. A little extra schooling never hurt anyone."

Gushing again, Betsy said, "I want to be a lawyer. Just like you!"

Caro laughed at the woman's unbridled enthusiasm. "Then go for it," she said. "Don't let anything stop you from getting what you want."

"You, too, Miss Conover," Bob said when she ushered them to her door. "I hope you get what you want, too."

She closed the door behind them and thought for a moment, standing there in the darkening foyer. What *did* she want now? What was left to go after? Once she had learned about Jane and the circumstances of her death, the momentum—the feeling of driving toward a goal—should have died down in Caro's heart. But something still burned inside her. There was unfinished business that needed attention.

"Alex," Caro said to the empty house.

Slowly, she walked into the spare living room, the empty room that he had filled with firelight and so much more. She could almost picture the picnic they had shared before the hearth. The taste of vodka and the sharp aromas of Russian delicacies, the glow of warm embers and the savory taste of sweet honey, and Alex's equally sweet and melting kisses were all memories so vivid that Caroline could close her eyes and experience them all in her mind.

She opened her eyes, though, and stared at the cold fireplace. "Alex," she said softly, "why did you have to lie to me?"

From the kitchen doorway, he said, "Because I fell in love with you, Caro."

CHAPTER SEVENTEEN

CAROLINE NEARLY CRIED OUT. She spun toward the sound of his voice, but suddenly couldn't move. The unresolved conflict between them lay like a barrier and prevented Caro from running into his arms.

"Damn you, Alex," she said, managing to speak coolly in spite of the way her heart had begun to slam. "You can't just—just break in here like some kind of cat burglar."

"I'm sorry," he said, making a gesture to indicate the guests who had just departed. "I waited until Bob and Betsy left. I didn't feel up to talking to anyone else."

In truth, Alex wasn't feeling up to much of anything but climbing into bed and going to sleep for another day. His arm hurt, and he'd had a devil of a time getting the bulky bandages through the sleeve of his black jacket. He felt sick and woozy, but hungry inside, too, as well as tired.

But Alex figured he wasn't going to sleep soundly ever again until he knew where he stood with Caroline. The look on her face as she kept her distance in the half-lit room was not promising. She looked angry. A little scared, too, but that would pass, he knew. Her anger might remain much longer. A lifetime, perhaps.

"Please," he said before she spoke again. "I'll go if you like, but I've got to talk first."

"What are you doing walking around like this?" she demanded, staying rooted to her spot. "You're supposed to be in the hospital."

"I was given a special dispensation."

"For what?" she asked suspiciously.

There would be no joking around. Alex could see he had a long battle ahead of him. Caroline wasn't going to give an inch. Her posture was stiff, her expression cold. Even her clothing seemed impenetrable. She was dressed in a starched buttoned-up shirt and a pair of wool slacks. For once, she looked severe and unyielding. Her hair was pulled tightly back from her face in a taut ponytail; it didn't flow around her features in silky profusion. Her green eyes were as hard as emeralds as she stared at him.

Suddenly Alex wasn't sure he was capable of convincing her, of making Caroline understand how much he needed and wanted her. He couldn't even force himself to walk across the bare floor to stand beside her. He told himself it was because he was sick, that maybe the medicine still floating around inside him was causing him momentary weakness, but Alex knew the true cause was something else entirely. He was afraid.

"Why did you come?" she asked.

"I had to see you," he said, mustering the strength to explain. "I was— I thought you might try leaving Chicago before—before we saw each other again. Judging by the suitcases in the other room, I was right."

"I want to go home," she said stiffly.

He nodded, and came forward a few uncertain steps until they were standing within the same circle of gray light that slanted through the bare-faced window. "I understand that. You did what you came here to do."

"I found out about Jane, yes."

When he moved toward her, Caro backed up. With just that step, Alex could see she had no intention of letting him get close.

She put her hands into the pockets of her trousers. "I learned more than I wanted to learn, of course, but it— I'll have some information to give my parents, at least. I think we'll be able to rest easier now that— well, now that we know."

Alex studied her. She looked controlled and cool, but he knew that was a charade. Caro had warmth inside her, a gentleness that couldn't have been so completely obliterated by the events of the past several days. She couldn't mean the words she so flatly pronounced, he knew. Coming to terms with the circumstances of her sister's murder was going to be a task more difficult than anything Alex could imagine.

Softly, he asked, "It won't be harder?"

"Harder?"

"Wouldn't it have been easier," he said, "to go on believing that Jane had taken a simple overdose?"

Caroline shook her head. "The truth," she said, "is very important to me."

He knew that, of course. But hearing her say the words so bluntly was like a blow. She was talking about more than Jane's death now. Alex turned away and sat down on the quilted sofa. He braced his elbows on his knees, not sure what he should say next.

"Caro," he began, when he felt ready to try explaining himself, "I'm sorry."

"Being sorry won't bring Jane back," she interrupted. "But thank you for the sentiment."

Alex sensed she wasn't ready to discuss his involvement in the whole mess yet. It seemed to him that she'd deliberately misinterpreted his apology.

Her voice was colorless as she went on. "My sister was a weak person," she said. "I knew that, and my parents knew it, too. We should have done something to help her, but we didn't. She became the victim of a lot of people, but ultimately she belonged to *us*. We should have taken better care of her. My family and I are going to have to live with that. It's time we faced it."

"She belonged to herself," Alex said sharply, staring at Caroline. "She wasn't your responsibility."

"She was everyone's responsibility," she replied. Looking at him finally, she added archly, "Don't you think so?"

Anger stirred inside him. "You want to know my part in your sister's downfall?" he asked. "Are you ready now?"

Caroline nodded. "Yes."

"You don't intend to make it easy on me, do you?"

"I want to know the truth, Alex. All of it."

He stood up and began to pace, infuriated by her manner, but determined to make her see his point of view. Wisely, Alex kept his distance from her. He suspected that if he moved too close Caro would step smoothly out of his way.

He began. "I knew Jane," he said. "I met her when I came to Chicago last spring with my father. It was family business and I— I wanted to patch up a quarrel I'd had with my father, so I came to help him when he traveled out here. I met Jane in the store that day and we had dinner together the same evening—"

Caro interrupted, going straight to the heart of the matter. "Did you sleep with her, Alex? Tell me the truth."

"I *will*, damn it," he snapped. "Just let me do it my way."

She folded her arms, ready to listen.

"We had dinner," he said, resuming the story through gritted teeth. "And we talked. I liked her. I liked her a lot, Caroline. You have some of the same qualities, in fact. She was a good listener and she— There was a fun side of her that appealed to me. And she seemed to understand. I was having some problems at the time, but I couldn't really talk about them. If you think I'm a skunk these days, you should have met me then! But Jane didn't mind. She didn't— She let me have a good time. I hadn't been able to laugh in a long while and she—she *helped* me. And yes," he said finally, "I slept with her."

Caroline didn't move a muscle. "Why?"

"Why?" he repeated, laughing bitterly. "Why not? She was attractive, she was nice and we hit it off. It was natural. She was the first woman I'd made love to since my divorce. And it was *fun*. She made it good again."

"But—"

"But it was short-term," Alex said. "We both knew it. At least, I thought she understood that. I had to get back to New York, and she—she made it sound as if her life was full of nice people and good parties and all

of that. I thought she was *happy*, for crying out loud.
I didn't know about the drugs and everything else. I
wasn't in very good shape myself. I couldn't see past
the front she put up."

"Was she in love with you, Alex?"

"We knew each other for twenty-four hours, Caro!
Maybe thirty-six, I forget. Falling in love wasn't possible." He stopped pacing and looked at her—just an
arm's length away. "At least, I didn't think it was
possible."

Caroline turned abruptly from him. "Alex—"

He stepped into her path. "I meant what I said
when I came in."

She put her hands over her ears. "Alex, stop."

"Caroline, I know it's a lot to ask— I'm afraid to
ask, in fact! I just— I want to erase what's happened
in the last week. I want to start all over again."

"That's not possible."

"It could be."

She wheeled around and faced him. "Alex," she
began, so angry suddenly that every bone of her body
was vibrating. "You *knew* how important my sister
was to me. How could you lie the way you did?"

"I didn't care," he said. "Not at first. I had a job
to do, Caro. I wanted to prove my worth to my father, to show him I could still be a part of the family.
That part doesn't matter now. I was ready to do anything to get the information I needed. I had a mystery
to solve, and you were my only clue."

"You used me."

"Just the way you used me," he said. He caught her
by one wrist and held on, determined that she
shouldn't escape from him. "We were a couple of

strangers who had missions to accomplish. We got something else along the way, though—something good we didn't expect amid the sordid stuff.''

"No," she began, resisting his grasp, but not energetically enough. She was weakening.

"Yes," he argued, holding her fast. "We got each other. If we'd met under different circumstances, we might have started differently, but we would have started nevertheless. We're a match, Caro. You felt it that first night—in the vault at the store. Tell me you didn't."

"That night," she said steadily, "was a jumble. A string of mistakes that—"

"No," he said. "When I kissed you—"

"That was an act! You said so yourself. It was a ruse to make the police car go away."

"Not that kiss," he said, drawing her closer until he could feel the contours of her body. "That was a preliminary to whet my appetite, that's all. And yours, too. Admit it. That kiss turned you on. It made you want to know more."

"What I learned," she said, "I didn't like. You were a skunk, Alex."

He smiled. "Part of you likes skunks, Caro. Inside that proper-lady shell of yours, there's a real woman who appreciates—"

"Alex!" She started to struggle.

He was relentless, though, holding her tightly, drawing her closer. "She appreciates the impulsive, the unexpected, the sensual."

He kissed her then. It happened too fast, but Alex couldn't stop himself. He was keyed up and desperate. And excited. Holding Caroline once more had sent a torrent of adrenaline through his veins. He felt alive and strong. She met his lips stiffly, but didn't pull away. In a split second, she even parted her mouth, softening, surrendering. It lasted only a moment, but suddenly Alex knew he had a chance. All was not lost. Not yet, at least.

She remembered herself and pushed out of his embrace, breathing raggedly. "Stop it, Alex."

He released her—all but her hand. To that, Alex held on as if it was a lifeline. "I'm sorry I was such a bastard before. The morning after we made love I felt guilty and figured I had better get out of your life before I ruined it. I know better now. We belong together, no matter what." He rushed on. "Why go on punishing yourself, Caro? That's what you're doing, I think. You want to punish yourself for not being Florence Nightingale for your sister."

"Don't make it sound silly," she warned, flashing a look at him.

"It *is* silly," he shot back. "Jane's life is over. Do you want yours to be finished, too?"

"I never—"

"We could have something good, Caro. Don't turn away from me because of someone who's gone."

"You *lied*, Alex!"

"I saw no reason to tell you everything," he said. "And when I realized I'd let things go too far, I knew that I could hurt you. I didn't want that to happen, Caro. I thought there would be more time—a better time to tell you about my relationship with Jane."

"There would have never been a good time," she said bitterly.

"True," he said. "I can't change what's already happened, Caroline. I can only ask you to forgive me."

She caught her breath. Struggling with something inside herself, she couldn't speak.

"Please," he said softly. "We can't let this tear us apart."

"What makes you so sure," she said finally, "that we'd be so terrific for each other? From the moment we met and you flashed that—that damn knife of yours at me, I—I..."

"Yes?"

"I don't know," she said stubbornly. "It just isn't right."

"What do you know about right?" Alex asked, smiling down at her. "You married a teenager because it seemed like the right thing to do at the time. You wouldn't know love if it bit you."

"Would you?"

"I know how good it feels to be with you," Alex said, serious again. "The night we spent together was—"

"You were an oaf, Alex. You—"

"I already told you—the morning after was an act," he countered quickly. "I made love to you like you'd never had it before. Come on, Caroline. Tell me it wasn't good. Tell me you didn't feel changed after we made love."

"Did you?" she challenged.

"Yes," he said, and was rewarded by seeing surprise reflected in her beautiful eyes. His honesty had startled her, thrown her off balance. He touched her face lightly, tilting her closer. "I felt changed. I felt as if I'd started my life over again. I felt as if I'd been given a second chance. Didn't you?''

''N-no.''

''You're lying,'' he said softly, stroking her throat with the backs of his fingertips. ''I can feel it in your pulse. Here.''

Caroline trembled under his caress. He was gentle and coaxing, and though she knew she ought to go on denying the truth, her body could not. She longed to throw her arms around his neck, to forgive him entirely and give herself over to the passion that was bubbling deep inside her.

''We've got a chance to pick up the pieces,'' Alex murmured. ''We could start fresh.''

He was right. All she had to do was forgive him, to say what had already passed didn't matter.

And it didn't. Not really. Caroline knew that.

''I'll do whatever it takes,'' Alex said. And he stopped the caress. He stepped back, in fact, and might have dropped her hand, too, if Caroline hadn't tightened her own grip. He said, ''I want to make everything right this time. We can start from the beginning.''

''What do you mean?''

''Forget what we've already done,'' he said earnestly. ''Forget we've argued and fought.''

''Forget about the bet you made with Tommy?''

''You know about that?'' he asked, surprised. With an impatient gesture, he said, ''Forget any stupid suggestions Tommy made. I never took him seriously anyway. Forget it all.''

''Forget we made love?'' she asked, her throat catching at the thought.

"Yes. We'll start over. Go home, if you have to. I'll call and we'll have dinner and be civilized. I can act like a gentleman if I have to. I want everything to be right this time, Caro."

It could be right, Caroline thought, but not if she had to wait for a stupid telephone call. Waiting would be agony. She didn't want to be parted from Alex for more than ten minutes. If he went back to New York— It would be torture.

"I'll be good," he was promising. "I don't want to cause you any pain. If you need some time, I'll wait."

"No," said Caro.

"Darling," he said, "I'm in love with you. What can I say to convince you?"

"Don't say anything," Caro replied, fully determined to shut him up before he vowed to stay away for a year. She touched his arm and slid her palm up the soft leather to the broad plane of his chest. Looking directly into Alex's pained blue eyes, she whispered, "Don't make any more promises. Just kiss me."

Alex's expression faltered for an instant, then suddenly he was full of fire. "Caro—"

"No more talk about making me wait for the phone to ring. Alex, I care about you, too. I love you—at least I think I do."

He laughed. "I haven't given you much time to decide, have I?"

"I don't need time."

She wound her arms around his neck and felt a soft flush of color begin to bloom on her cheeks. Standing on tiptoe, she tilted her face up and kissed him, touching her lips gently to his. Alex gathered her tightly against him, pressing her back against the steely band of his arm so her breasts nestled provocatively against his chest. With his other hand, he tore at the ribbon that held back her ponytail, freeing her hair and filling his fingers with it. His mouth melted warmly with hers. Their tongues clashed, teased, then rejoiced.

At last, Alex broke the kiss and held her still, looking deeply and questioningly into her eyes.

"I do," she said quietly, smiling despite the trembling that wracked her. "I do love you, Alex. I want to stay with you and be a part of your life."

He smiled, too, though a shade unhappily. "It's a mess at the moment."

"So's mine," she admitted cheerfully. "But we have a chance to start a second time. Together."

Alex hugged her, pressing her tightly against him.

Caro laughed at the sensation. It felt so secure—but with a kindling of something more exciting at the same time. "My love," she whispered.

"I know," said Alex. "I want you, too. I want you so much!"

"Now," she said.

"But your bed's all covered with suitcases."

"That shouldn't stop us. The floor was fine before."

She led him by the hand, and once in her bedroom, Caro began to help him out of his jacket.

The job proved to be very complicated. More than once Alex gasped.

Caro finally protested. "Darling, you're hurt. Maybe we shouldn't."

"It'll hurt more if we don't," he said lightly. "Just take care of me."

Caro smiled, touching the lightest of kisses to his cheek, his throat, then his mouth. "I think I can do that. I was planning to, you know."

He stopped in the midst of trying to unbutton her blouse with his good hand. "What do you mean?"

"I have a bottle of vodka in the freezer. I was going to bring it to you tonight."

"Tonight?"

"To the hospital. I wouldn't have left town without seeing you again, Alex. I couldn't have. I planned to smuggle the bottle in and spend the night getting you drunk, if that's what it took to convince you."

Smiling, he asked, "What were you trying to convince me of, lady?"

"I'm not sure," she admitted. "I just knew I couldn't leave things the way they were. Maybe I intended to say exactly what you said this evening—that I loved you and the past didn't matter."

"Skip the bottle," Alex advised, catching her face in his hands and cupping her cheeks tenderly. "We won't need it."

EPILOGUE

DOCTOR REDMOND TUCKED her clipboard under her arm and reached for the handle on the door. "Take him out of here," she said to Caroline. "The man's a menace to the entire hospital staff."

Alex protested. "I behaved myself! Ask one nurse if I lost my temper."

"It's not your temper that bothers them," replied the doctor tartly. "Even with Miss Conover sitting by your bedside every waking moment, you're still the focus of far too much attention from the nursing staff. Please, Miss Conover, get him out of my hospital."

"You're sure?" Caroline asked. "It's not too soon?"

"Not a moment too soon. He's as healthy as they come."

"And the headaches?"

Doctor Redmond addressed her answer to Alex, who was already dressed and sitting on the edge of his hospital bed looking ready to tackle a good, square meal. She said, "I will make no promises. Not yet, at least. I'd like to see you in my office in two weeks, and again at the end of a month. That's a lot of trips to Chicago, I know—"

"That's okay," said Alex. "We're thinking about settling down here."

The doctor looked to Caroline for confirmation, and she nodded. "It's true. I was offered a job here, and Alex seems to think he can run his business from Chicago as easily as New York. With his health improved he should be able to make it work this time."

"And," said Alex, "if my entire family is going to come out here and let you poke around inside their heads, it might be a good idea to have a base of operations. We're looking for a house."

"A small house," Caroline added. "One that won't need a full-time renovation crew."

Doctor Redmond looked amused. "You two can certainly move mountains when you work together, can't you? Or should I thank you, Miss Conover, for convincing this stubborn Russian to come in for surgery?"

"He decided himself," Caroline replied honestly. "In fact he didn't even tell me about the possibilities until he'd made the arrangements with you. I'm just here in the hand-holding department."

That's the way Alex had wanted it. Of course, Caroline had been ready to support him in anything. He had certainly stuck by her side during the trials and convictions of both Vinnie the Vulture and Rupert Watkins. Without Alex's help, Caroline wasn't sure she could have made it through those emotional days. When it was over, he had taken her on a trip—driving her down to visit Betsy Nofsinger and Bob in their shared apartment near the junior college Betsy had started to attend. Caroline believed that relaxed trip had started her own healing process. She could think about Jane now without getting weepy, thanks to

Alex. She was prepared to see him through any crisis now.

"See?" The doctor fondly tapped Alex's cheek with her knuckle. "You couldn't have picked a better mate. Good luck, Mr. Varanov."

"I won't need it," he said, giving her a wink. "I've got you on my side."

Doctor Redmond departed, and Caroline finished zipping up Alex's suitcase. There was only one vase of flowers left, since Caro had already distributed the other arrangements to the nurses and to other patients in the hospital who hadn't been so well-loved as Alex. But Caroline had kept the one vase intentionally. She handed it to Alex to carry.

"What's this?" he asked. "Can't we leave it for the kids' ward or something?"

"No," she said. "That particular arrangement means too much to me, Alex."

"Means too— What's going on? Who's it from?"

Caroline reached into the flowers and turned the card over so Alex could read the name. The gift had come from Tommy Hollingsworth.

"Oh," said Alex, looking sheepish.

"I will leave it behind," she said, "if you promise never to make a bet with Tommy again."

"That's an easy promise," he said.

Caroline turned and slipped into his arms, smiling. She was happy to see him looking so fit. The stay in the hospital had been frustrating for him, but Caroline had devoted herself to keeping his mind off the surgery. Feeding him apples and sweets, making plans, teasing and joking had been fun for her as well as for him. It had been a time to get to know him better. And the more time Caroline spent with him, the more she came to enjoy his company. They had a bright future together, she was sure. It wouldn't be a traditional marriage with two kids, a dog and a station wagon, but that was okay. They were unusual people with an extraordinary love and that required a life-style that didn't always follow the rules of tradition. And Alex had started to make friends with his father once more. That was a step in the right direction.

Like Caroline, Alex had responded well to their enforced time together, and now looked dangerous as ever. Wild horses and a team of burly orderlies couldn't have kept him in that bed much longer. It was time to get on with their life together.

"Let's go," he said.

"We have to wait for the nurse."

"Wait for her? I want to be alone with you. I've missed you!"

"I've been here every minute," Caroline argued, amused by his eagerness to be gone.

"It's not the same if we have to worry about a nurse popping in every four minutes." Alex kissed her mouth swiftly, coaxing. "Come on. Let's go."

"We have to *wait*, Alex. It's hospital policy. You have to ride in a wheelchair."

"I'm not riding in any silly wheelchair," he retorted, climbing to his feet. Holding her hand in his, he reached for his suitcase with the other one and pulled Caroline toward the door. "Let's get out of here."

"Wait!"

From the nightstand, Caro picked up the pocket-knife they had used to slice apples. It was the same blade Alex used to keep in his jacket pocket, and she handed it to him. "Don't forget this."

"Right. Let's go."

In the hospital corridor, they nearly ran into the nurse who was pushing an empty wheelchair. "Sir," she said, "you'll have to ride in this."

"Forget it," said Alex.

"Sir," she began hotly. "It's hospital—"

But she caught sight of the knife in Alex's hand and closed her mouth abruptly.

"Alex," said Caro. "She'll think you're a thug."

Alex sighed. "Oh, hell."

He handed the knife to Caroline and obediently sat down in the wheelchair. Then he folded his hands behind his head and grinned. "Actually," he said, looking every inch like a visiting Russian prince, "I like the attention."

"I'll remember that," said Caro. "Let's go."

PAMELA BROWNING

...is fireworks on the green at the Fourth of July and prayers said around the Thanksgiving table. It is the dream of freedom realized in thousands of small towns across this great nation.

But mostly, the Heartland is its people. People who care about and help one another. People who cherish traditional values and give to their children the greatest gift, the gift of love.

American Romance presents HEARTLAND, an emotional trilogy about people whose memories, hopes and dreams are bound up in the acres they farm.

HEARTLAND...the story of America.

Don't miss these heartfelt stories: American Romance #237 SIMPLE GIFTS (March), #241 FLY AWAY (April), and #245 HARVEST HOME (May).

HRT-1

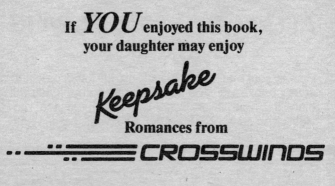